Liam stopped mid-stride as the realization hit him. Turning on his heel, he charged back into the room. Hannah looked up at him as he strode into the room. His face had gone pale and she hastily shooed everyone from the room. Closing the door behind them, she slowly turned toward Liam. In a shaky voice, Liam looked down at Hannah. "Is it her?" Hannah hesitated and swallowed a lump in her throat. Looking up at him, her eyes glistening with unshed tears, she whispered to him. "Aye. The lass has returned to us." Liam made his way over to a cushioned chair by the large fireplace and collapsed into it. "Why?" he wondered aloud. "Do ye think she's returned to claim her place? She would be alpha after all." Liam looked at Hannah for answers. Taking a deep breath, she looked into his face and was reminded of when he was a child. "I think she's come for help. Nothing more. We will know soon if she possesses the gift." Hannah's calmness took away some of the sting of his discovery, but Liam still remained unsure. "I smelt it on her," he confessed, and Hannah's lips formed a grim line.

I0598345

Praise for Kate James

"This was a fantastic book! Kate James does a great job of setting the scene for each part of the book. Love the characters and I cannot wait for her next book!"

~*Brandi*

"Could not put down! MUST READ!"

~*Tessie*

"Not your typical shifter story...I'm a sucker for werewolf romance novels, but I still thought it would just be another werewolf romance story. Desiring The Alpha is a unique story and a breath of fresh air. I liked the pacing of the story and the story itself. It's new and exciting."

~*Kaylin Meier*

Desiring the Alpha

by

Kate James

This is a work of fiction. Names, characters, places, and incidents are either the product of the author's imagination or are used fictitiously, and any resemblance to actual persons living or dead, business establishments, events, or locales, is entirely coincidental.

Desiring the Alpha

COPYRIGHT © 2021 by Melinda Morris

All rights reserved. No part of this book may be used or reproduced in any manner whatsoever without written permission of the author or The Wild Rose Press, Inc. except in the case of brief quotations embodied in critical articles or reviews.
Contact Information: info@thewildrosepress.com

Cover Art by *Jennifer Greeff*

The Wild Rose Press, Inc.
PO Box 708
Adams Basin, NY 14410-0708
Visit us at www.thewildrosepress.com

Publishing History
First Edition, 2021
Trade Paperback ISBN 978-1-5092-3738-8
Digital ISBN 978-1-5092-3739-5

Published in the United States of America

Dedication

To Jimmy, my husband, my best friend and my soulmate—thank you for your love and support and patience.

To my kids, never stop chasing your dreams!

To my friends and family, especially to Heidi and Melissa, thank you for being my biggest cheerleaders and for pushing me to keep writing and realizing my own dream.

Chapter One

Kenna ran as fast as her legs allowed, the exertion burning her lungs. She heard the men gaining on her as she tried to push herself even faster. The woods were just ahead of her and if she reached the tree line, she could shift.

"Four legs are faster than two," she thought to herself as she clawed through the freshly fallen snow, leaving a trail of blood for them to follow. Her wounds made it next to impossible to keep moving. Bleeding heavily, she was getting weaker by the second.

Silas had outdone himself this time. She had used her hands to block most of the attack causing several deep cuts along her palms. Her right eye was swollen from where he hit her, using the leg broken off a chair when his hands weren't enough.

Blood was streaming down her cheek, and she reached up to feel the source. The large gash on her head must have come from being thrown against the stone wall. Her shoulder had become dislocated from the monster shaking her, and she was sure more than one rib was broken.

Only a little farther, she told herself, and she'd be in the cover of the woods. Her vision started to blur as she blinked away the blood, dirt, and snow beginning to cake around her eyes. She felt her body shaking and trembling. She needed to reach the tree line quickly.

She had only shifted a few times but knew she didn't have long before the wolf took over. Her body wanted to heal itself and as usual, it did so more quickly in wolf form.

She prayed no bones were too badly broken this time. If she healed before the bones were set, she would have to have them rebroken. Silas usually took care of that during one of his rages, but she wouldn't allow him the opportunity this time. She was free and swore to die before allowing herself to be taken back to him.

She made it just inside the dense line of trees before she turned to look back at the men advancing on her. The distance between them was closing, but she knew they dared not risk entering the woods. As she backed deeper into the dark forest, the last thing she saw was Sampson, their leader, pull his mount up short when the blood curdling howl escaped her lips and her vision went black.

****

She lay on her side in the snow, becoming increasingly aware of the bitter cold. Slowly, she tried to open her eyes and take in her surroundings, but her right eye refused to open, the swelling too severe. She saw only a sliver of what surrounded her, and even it was blurred. She was unsure of how long she had stayed in her wolf form. Still just inside the trees, and with wounds far from healed, she imagined it hadn't been very long.

What remained of her scant clothing was scattered throughout the trees. Too weak to gather the pieces, she reached for what was near, feeling through the snow for anything to cover her freezing body. Her thin shift was closest. The last garment to come off. It was typically torn to shreds. This one had managed to stay mostly together, with only a few tears in the fabric. She must be getting better at this.

Doing her best to get the garment on her weakened body, she knew she had to get out of there before she caught frostbite. Willing her arms under her, she mustered what little strength she had and managed to get onto her knees. Breathing heavily from the effort it had taken, she closed her eyes and waited for the spinning to stop. After a few moments, she opened her willing eye to take in her surroundings.

A sense of familiarity crept over her. She had a distant memory of playing in these woods as a child and knew she was only a couple of miles from her father's castle—or what may be left of it. If anyone was there, they had no choice but to help her. She would make sure of it.

As she started to stand, a sudden onslaught of pain caused her to scream out. She noticed the puddles of blood had started to thicken in the snow around her. Wounds that had started to heal with her shifting had reopened with her movements. Assessing her injuries, she felt a wave of nausea and a blackness began to creep into the edges of her vision, the metallic taste of blood on her tongue.

Dragging herself under some brush, she thought she heard men approaching. Too weak to fight any longer, she resigned herself to the fact this was her end. Her face hit the cold snow once again, and her last thoughts were of her mother. The sorrow and guilt she felt for leaving her behind were forgotten as she succumbed to the blackness.

****

The howling was close! Too close! Sampson knew the stories of the Cameron wolves. It was lethal to encounter one, or the pack it was sure to be with. These wolves were hunting Kenna. He was sure of it. She had been beaten to the brink of death. How she had escaped surprised them all, but she would be dead soon, regardless, either bleeding to death or claimed by the wolves.

Sampson made the decision and signaled the others to make camp where they stood, waiting until they were certain she was dead, then retrieving her remains to return to Silas. Crossing the wood line was dangerous in itself, as it was Cameron territory, but Silas needed proof.

He would be furious with him, of course, for not bringing her back alive, but Sampson rather the girl be eaten by the wolves than suffer more of Silas' brutality.

As the men began to prepare food and build small fires to ward off the cold, mumblings of the old stories started to travel through the group. No one knew where the stories had begun, but the legends had been passed down for centuries. He knew them by heart, having heard them over and over as a child. Warnings of playing near the woods. He always considered them folklore to scare the young kids from wandering too near Cameron land—men who transformed into large, vicious, and bloodthirsty wolves and attacked any McLindon without warning.

While not a single one of the men with him had actually seen one of the wolves, they had seen the tracks, usually when they were poaching on Cameron territory. The tracks were bigger than a man's hand and twice as deep as a man's footprint, but the tracks had never been seen outside of the woods.

The fact there were wolves on the land was not in question. After all, he had seen the proof. He did not, however, believe men possessed the ability to shift into a beast, although the superstition ran deep in the men surrounding him. They believed the Cameron clan were not the only ones to possess the trait, and he listened as questions started to arise. What other clans held this secret? Were wolves the only beast a man could shift into? He shook his head at the speculation and whispers. Right now, they only needed to focus on the Camerons and retrieving Kenna.

The group waited until dark, when they were hidden under the cloak of night, should any of the Camerons be lurking in the woods. Braving the territory line, the men silently made their way into the trees, following the trail of blood Kenna had left like breadcrumbs. The scene they came upon only validated their superstitions. Dark red stained the fresh white snow and human footprints mixed with massive wolf tracks covered the area. Kenna's blood-soaked clothes had been torn to shreds and were scattered around. Her body, however, was nowhere to be found.

"The wolf dragged her off," one of the men sneered, confident in his assumption, using his boot to point to several smears of blood in the snow.

"Probably hiding it from the others," another nodded in agreement.

He listened to them ramble, but the scene made him wonder if the stories may be true. Only one set of tracks mixed with footprints, and wolves hunted in packs. And where was her body? Or at least body parts? Was he the only one who saw the signs? She was a

Cameron by blood after all. Ordering the men to gather what was left of her clothes, he turned his mount out of the woods and back in the direction of their keep.

The ride back was not a long one, but the snow had started falling again, creating a soft, fresh layer. Trudging through this, with only the moon to guide them, caused them to move at a slower pace than normal. He didn't mind the ride, however. It offered him a chance to think about Silas' reaction to the news his future bride was dead. He didn't expect sadness. The man had no feelings for Kenna. It was anger he expected, at him and the men instead. After all, she was only property to Silas. He sighed to himself.

He had joined the McLindon clan as a lad, brought to be a companion for Silas. In exchange, he learned battle skills and how to lead an army. He and Silas had not become friends, as Silas never allowed anyone close to him, but they were always together. Silas' father had hoped he would be an older brother figure and his calming personality may rub off on Silas. It didn't.

He had seen Silas mature into manhood, from a gangly youth to a large and fierce fighter. He had trained hard, learning the necessary skills to defend his keep from any enemy. Unfortunately, Silas did not hold his fighting men to the same standard. They had no loyalty to the man after witnessing his barbaric nature. Silas had not only grown physically, but his thirst for power had grown as well.

He was sure there was no line Silas feared to cross to gain power, and Kenna had become one of those lines. He thought back to when Kenna was just a girl and she, her mother, and uncle had come to live with the clan. Silas became possessive of the girl, separating her from her mother and was cruel, never kind toward her.

He made sure Kenna knew he was doing her family a favor by allowing them to live with the clan, and the favor needed to be repaid. By her. Wherever the child went, there were whispers. Rumors of her father, Laird Cameron, being poisoned by her mother surrounded her. Whispers of their banishment and fear they may be linked to the terrifying wolves kept people at bay.

Through all of this, both Kenna and her mother remained kind and gentle. He didn't believe the rumors. He didn't think Lady Cameron was capable of killing her husband. Silas had seen an opportunity though. He planned to wed the mysterious young lass when she was of age, using her blood line to reclaim the Cameron lands. Then, Silas' power would have no equal.

Until that time came, Silas made cruel remarks and kept her busy doing demeaning chores around the keep. Over time, Kenna grew into a beautiful young woman, and Sampson had watched Silas' treatment of her change. There was a fear in Silas, and he suspected fear drove the abuse Silas dealt her. She had quit cowering from him, and the abuse had gotten more and more extreme.

Her cheeks were always swollen with fresh bruises and cuts and more than once bore the insignia of Silas's rings. With each attack, she had grown stronger and seemed to recover quickly from the wounds. Emotionally, Silas tried to break her as well. Keeping her isolated from her mother, Silas allowed only brief visits during mealtimes, and he was always within earshot. If the conversation turned to Kenna or her mother's well-being, Silas always declared it time for them to retire.

When they were young, he and Silas used to talk about the wolves in the woods. Silas was more than obsessed with the stories and spent all of his free time studying them. He was convinced the Camerons were the fabled werewolves. He just laughed at him, but after meeting Kenna, he wasn't so sure Silas wasn't right.

Watching Kenna's reaction toward Silas after one particularly harsh beating had given him his first inkling of suspicion. He had been there when Silas had finished beating the girl and turned his back on her. A low growl escaped her lips and sent chills down his spine. He was certain if she had shifted then, she may have torn Silas' throat out.

If Kenna was a wolf, he wished to see the day when she discovered her powers. He had a soft spot for the girl, who had always been kind toward everyone, even when she realized she was more captive than clansman.

His loyalty, out of duty, was to Silas, but letting her get "eaten by wolves" was a kinder fate than bringing her back to let Silas finish the job. He knew Silas would see through the lie when they delivered the news. After all, her change had been what Silas was waiting on all along.

He led the parade of horses and men through the gates of the keep. The air felt thick with tension. It was midday but instead of the hustle and bustle they usually encountered, no one seemed to be found. No one was on the parapets, no one manning the gate.

The keep had been basically left wide open for anyone to enter, although no one ventured to the

McLindon keep of their own accord. Stories of Silas' cruelty spread wide and far. He sensed this cruelty had been shown to quite a few of the servants recently, and everyone was keeping a low profile, staying out of harm's way. He dismounted, giving his horse to one of the young stable boys who came forward.

"Is it true?" Cam's dark brown eyes were wide with curiosity. "Did you really see her get torn apart by the wolf?" the young lad asked excitedly, hopping from one foot to the other.

"What on earth, boy? Where did you hear that?" He chuckled at his wide-eyed innocence. He was an inquisitive and kind-hearted little fool who idolized him.

Ruffling his shaggy brown hair and sending the boy on his way, he looked around at the men in the courtyard. Gossip spread like wildfire and seeing several men making their way inside, there was a good chance Silas would have already heard the news by the time he got to him.

Entering the dimly lit keep, he made his way to the great hall. As he strode through the doorway, the smell of piss, stale beer, and rotten food was enough to make his stomach churn. The hall was definitely in need of new rushes on the floor. Silas was seated in a large chair at the far end of the room. His large frame slouched down in the chair, giving the impression he was bored of the tale the men were recounting.

The men, trying to impress Silas, made up unbelievable testimony, fumbling over each other and changing the story from one account to another. He stood back, shaking his head in disagreement every time the men exaggerated something new. He supposed they thought there was safety in numbers, but they should have known better.

Silas suddenly bolted upright in his chair.

"SHUT UP!" he roared. As he predicted, Silas saw right through the outrageous story of Kenna being devoured by the massive wolves. Furious, Silas pushed up from his chair, tossing his goblet of wine into the face of the bravest idiot closest to him.

Then he started swinging. First arms, then chairs, candlesticks, and whatever was near and effective in punishing the offenders. Growling at the men, his anger seemed to grow in intensity, and Sampson knew he needed to stop the attack.

Cam had followed on his heels into the hall, and seeing Silas' rage gasped in shock. He grabbed Cam's shoulders and turned him toward the large doors, giving him a slight push. It was all the hint Cam needed, and he took off running out of the hall. He had to give him credit. For as gangly as the boy was, his long legs served him well in speed.

Silas, catching Cam's movement out of the corner of his eye, looked up to see Sampson standing there. This pause allowed some of the men to escape and find somewhere to hide. Silas pointed to those still standing and promising to come back for more stormed out of the great room. He followed close behind, giving orders for the men to make themselves scarce.

Turning down a dimly lit hall off the main keep, Silas made his way to a small office he kept for private meetings. He followed him in and closed the heavy door behind him, placed the lock bar in the door to ensure the conversation not be interrupted.

"She isnae dead" Silas blurted out, his glare intense

on the candle on the desk, confirming his suspicions about the girl. "She shifted." he said matter-of-factly.

"Ye still believe she is one of them?" he questioned Silas, his tone indicating his doubt.

"Dinnae be a fool Sampson!" Silas hissed. "Ye ken the stories as weel as I. Aye, I dinnae just believe. I ken she IS one, and I've just gotten my proof!" Leaning over the desk, Silas held up the shreds of Kenna's bloody clothing in his face for him to inspect.

"I've been waiting for this! Now that she has developed her gift, we will marry. Her uncle has sworn the oaf, Audric, was their Alpha. If Kenna is his true heir, she will be the next Alpha, the rightful one. She will be mine to control. And the Camerons. Weel, they willnae have a choice but to follow her."

Silas appeared to escape into his own thoughts as he laid out his plan. He began stroking the clothing, and he knew he had to snap him out of his madness.

"How do ye plan on finding the lass? She is sure to be long gone. If she truly shifted," he added. "Dinnae they heal quickly?" He continued to question Silas, hoping he had forgotten his anger toward the other men for delivering the news of Kenna's loss, instead getting wrapped up in his knowledge of the wolves.

"YES! Can't you imagine??" Silas' excitement was growing, and he moved around the small room erratically. "Imagine large McLindon men mixed with the wolves! Strong and untouchable, able to heal from a battle wound in the blink of an eye. We will be unstoppable!"

He knew this was what Silas craved all along. He wanted an army of men to defeat any enemy. Unfortunately, he knew the men he controlled only followed Silas out of fear, not true loyalty. Silas was dreaming of an army Sampson wasn't sure his men intended to provide. However, marrying Kenna enslaved the Camerons to him as well and ensured his heirs also bore the wolf's blood. The man would be unstoppable for sure.

Chapter Two

Liam and his men approached the bushes slowly, unsure of what awaited them. An ear-piercing scream, followed by a chilling howl, had called them off their hunt. Heading in the direction of the noise, they spotted a trail of dark red blood. Following the trial, they came upon an area near the edge of the woods littered with low-growing shrubs.

The fresh snow made it difficult, but they made out a body hidden in the underbrush. Blood was smeared across the snow where the body had obviously been dragged and left for dead. Wolf tracks intermingled with the footprints in a large circle around the area.

Chopping the bush back with their swords, the men were careful not to disturb the body. A collective gasp escaped their mouths when they saw the girl, certain she was the source of the scream.

Hair, matted down with blood, mud, and snow, covered her face. Her body had been beaten so badly it was impossible to tell if the purple color was from bruising or the cold. Curled into a small ball on her side, it was obvious she had tried to use what was left of her clothing to cover her exposed skin before the loss of blood had caused her to pass out.

He ordered his men to tend to the girl and wandered away to examine the surrounding area. Shaking his head, it was hard to imagine what the young girl had been through. He assumed she was young, anyway. Her body was so small, she must be just a child.

Whoever did this must suffer the consequences. This had happened on his land, and he intended to deliver swift justice. Bending to examine one of the wolf tracks, Liam placed his hand over it for comparison. It was much larger than his palm, unusual for a typical wolf.

As Fergus began to wrap Kenna's body, a small groan escaped her lips.

"Liam!" he yelled, "Ye best come quick!"

"What have ye found?" He rushed back over to see if his friend had discovered a clue as to the evil who had done this.

"The lass is still alive. Barely" Fergus said grimly.

"Impossible," he argued as he bent over to push her hair off her face and see for himself. An odd familiarity hit him as he looked at her.

"It can't be," he mumbled to himself.

"Sorry?" Fergus stepped closer to hear what he had said.

Standing, he wiped his bloodied hands on his trousers.

"Wrap her up. Carefully," he added, "and I will carry her with me." He moved to ready his horse for the journey home. It was only a couple of miles back to the castle, but it wasn't an easy trek.

Upon hearing the girl was still alive, some of the men tried to rouse her out of her unconsciousness.

"Leave her be," he ordered. "She'll want to be unconscious for the journey home." Grumbling their agreement, they went back to wrapping her in warm blankets and temporarily bandaging any bleeding wounds. Once she was ready, Fergus gently lifted her limp body into his large arms.

He was a beast of a man but as mild mannered as they came. He didn't feel the need to use his size to bully and intimidate others. The girl looked even smaller and more fragile in Fergus' big arms.

"She must be a strong lass to survive that." Fergus flashed a look of warning as he passed her to him where he sat in the saddle.

Once she was settled across his lap, he nodded toward the area where her body had been lying.

"Wolf tracks." He ran his hand through his hair and looked down worriedly at Fergus.

"Rouge?" Fergus wrinkled his brow trying to answer his own question. "No, I dinnae think so. Maybe young, uncontrollable."

He looked down at the small figure in his arms.

"Let's get her to Hannah. She'll know what to do for the lass. We'll come back tomorrow at sunup." He turned his horse toward home while Fergus and the others gathered the scraps of shredded clothes and followed quickly behind.

He held her body close to his to keep the jarring movement to a minimum. The ride was not an easy one on a normal day, but add in snow and a near dead lass, and it was damn near impossible, he thought to himself. It wasn't far to the castle, but the way was full of jagged hills, rocks, and caves.

The landscape was useful as a means of protection but perilous when performing a rescue. The girl groaned several times during the trip but never woke. She was getting paler by the minute, and he fought to maintain a steady pace. He wanted the journey to be as smooth as possible. In her condition, she was certain to have broken bones, and he didn't want to make Hannah's job any more difficult by jostling the girl around. Even after all of this, it would be a miracle if she survived at all.

The castle loomed ahead, illuminated by the brightness of the full moon. It stood high on a steep hill overlooking the Cameron lands. Climbing out of the forest below, he was awestruck by its presence. It was an impressive silhouette, offering a feeling of safety to those welcome within its walls. To those on the outside, it was impenetrable and terrifying.

He let out a sigh of relief as they approached. The lass was still breathing, although it had become ragged and shallow. Fergus had caught up and ridden past him to alert Hannah. As he crossed through the gate, he saw them both waiting inside. He handed the unconscious girl gently down to Fergus and dismounted quickly, eager to have her back in his arms where he knew she was safe.

He watched Hannah look at Kenna's limp body as the plaid wrapping her fell away. She had tended many battle wounds and had treated many women whose husbands thought they had gotten out of line. Her eyes widened in horror, looking from him to Fergus and finally to the lass.

Nothing could have prepared her for this tiny girl and her broken body. Shaking her head, she gently smoothed the girl's hair and looked at him with sad eyes. He nodded his silent agreement, wondering how a person treated such a delicate creature this way? Gathering her wits, she began barking orders to several servants standing and watching nearby.

"I've a room ready next to your own," she directed him and followed close on his heels. As they made their way through the keep, she instructed any maid they passed to bring items to the room. Making their way up the stairs and down a dark stone hallway dimly lit with only a few sconces, they finally reached a room at the end of the hall.

The heavy door was cracked, but he gently kicked it farther open with his foot and made his way to the bed in the corner of the room. Laying the small, weak body on the bed, he remained bent over her, pushing her hair away from her face trying to see her clearly. Studying her features, her full lips and her slightly upturned nose, something in him knew behind the bruising and swelling of her eyes they were wide and childlike, green with flecks of gold.

Swatting his back with a towel, a gentle reminder she needed to tend to the girl, Hannah pushed him aside.

"She's a bonny lass, I know, but I must work! Now, out with ye!" She tried to turn his body toward the door, barely moving him. He looked down at her and smirked, causing her to sigh and throw her hands up in defeat. Giving him a resigned smile, she pointed toward the door, and placing a quick kiss on the top of her head he obliged.

She was like a grandmother to him, and he knew the lass was in good hands. If Hannah was not able save her, then there was no saving her. He had seen her work her magic many times, delivering every babe, treating every illness, and tending every wound no matter how severe, since he was a boy. Only once did he remember her being unable to heal someone from an illness and only because she hadn't been allowed near the patient.

During Laird Audric's illness, only his wife, Lady Evelyn, had been allowed by his side. Audric had swiftly gone from a vibrant, strong leader to a shell of a man in body and mind. His last days were spent bedridden, coughing up blood and gasping for breath.

Only his wife had been allowed in his chamber. This was one reason her guilt was so easily accepted by the clanspeople. Once the rumor spread she had poisoned him, he remembered how quickly they had been ostracized. Lady Evelyn, her brother Judson, and the young daughter, Kenna, had all been forced from the clan.

He stopped mid-stride as the realization hit him. Turning on his heel, he charged back into the room. Hannah looked up at him as he strode into the room. He felt the color drain from his face, and she hastily shooed everyone from the room. Closing the door behind them, she slowly turned toward him.

In a shaky voice, Liam looked down at Hannah.

"Is it her?"

Hannah hesitated. Looking up at him, her eyes glistened with unshed tears.

"Aye. The lass has returned to us," she whispered.

He made his way over to a cushioned chair by the large fireplace and collapsed into it.

"Why? Do ye think she's returned to claim her place? She is the rightful Alpha after all." He looked at Hannah for answers.

Taking a deep breath, she looked into his face. Her tone reminded him of how she comforted him as a child.

"I think she's come for help. Nothing more. We will know soon if she possesses the gift."

Her calmness took away some of the sting of his discovery, but he still remained unsure.

"I smelt it on her," he confessed, and Hannah's lips formed a grim line. He continued, as if he was remembering a dream.

"At first, I thought it was a rogue wolf. Or even a young one who had just come into their power. But it was too strong. When I held her against me, I smelt it."

"I suggest we let her rest and heal. When she wakes, we will get our answers. If she is wolf, as ye believe, she will heal quickly, so I best get to work." She pulled him to his feet with more help from him than she realized.

"Go freshen yerself and get a bite to eat. Ye've had a long night. I'll wake ye if she rises."

For the second time of the evening, he placed a kiss on her head and left the room, distracted as he made his way down to the kitchen. He knew his mind could not rest until he had answers. He hadn't been born into this role. He was Laird Audric's cousin by marriage, but he was the only one in line with wolf blood that didn't already have one foot in the grave.

He had worked hard to prove he was the right choice and had gained the respect of the Cameron clan, not just as their Chief, but as their Alpha as well. He did not intend to give up his clan without a fight. And if she was anything like her mother, he'd definitely keep a close eye on her. Kenna was the true heir and Alpha, but did she know it? And if so, had she returned to force it from him?

Questions filled his head as he stepped into the

small doorway in the kitchen. Breathing in the smell of stew and fresh baked bread, his stomach growled in anticipation.

Nissa, the old kitchen maid, poured him a cup of ale and a bowl of stew and set it in front of him on the small table. Eating it hastily, he thanked her as she refilled his bowl. He had never really noticed the woman, and as she reached over the table to pour him another cup of ale, he leaned back to get a good look.

The graying strands of her hair stuck out from under her kerchief. Thin beads of sweat formed around her hairline. Her plump face filled out her wrinkles, making her look slightly younger than he imagined she actually was, and her upper lip held a thick mustache.

She turned to smile at him and to ask if he needed anything else. The smile made him cringe as he noticed her badly decaying teeth—the few left in her head. Smiling at her to hide his disgust, he thanked her and dismissed her. He wondered why he had never really noticed her before.

Fergus walked in, passing Nissa as she walked out. He quickly got out of her way and ducked into the low kitchen.

"De ye ken that woman?" He narrowed his eyes at Nissa's back as she walked away.

"Aye, old Nissa. She's a nasty looking woman." Fergus gave a teasing shudder. "But," he added, "she is a damn fine cook."

"Wonder why I've never noticed her before now." He tried to place her face in his memories.

"Weel, she has never married. Maybe because ye've never seen a husband or son. Ye dinnae spend yer days about the kitchen. Ye just ne'er crossed paths, I recken." Fergus dismissed the conversation.

He sat staring out the window, his mind racing with unanswered questions.

"The lass is Audric's daughter." He spoke bluntly and took Fergus by surprise.

"Truly?" he asked.

"Aye. I ken it when I saw her, and Hannah ken it as weel." He was surprised by how well Fergus took the news, not seeming worried or concerned.

"So, she's returned. Wonder where the lass has been to have been beaten so badly. What do ye think she wants with us? To come home?" Fergus asked the same questions he'd been asking himself. He didn't know the answers, but when she woke, he would see he got them.

Chapter Three

Several days had passed since Kenna was brought to the keep, and whispers and rumors had started to circulate among the people. It didn't take long for word to get out the true heir had returned. Liam was aware of the eyes everywhere he moved, wondering what he was going to do. It seemed like they were all on edge waiting on her to awaken.

He had already decided what needed to be done. She was not welcome. Once she was well enough to travel, he would ask her to leave the Cameron lands. He knew his decision was harsh, but he could not afford to risk her coming back and trying to take over as Alpha.

Hannah thought they must wait until she had woken to see if she had the gift, but he already knew. As did any other who possessed it. He smelled the wolf on her skin. He knew those tracks around her body had been hers. She had shifted to make it look like an attack. What she was running from though, he had no idea.

Obviously, she had been beaten, punished, but for what reason. Had she tried to poison someone too? He knew he wasn't being fair. When he had known Kenna as a child, she had been kind and loving to everyone. Of course, so had her mother, he thought snidely to himself.

He wandered out to the courtyard where several of

the men were gathered round watching a few honing their battle skills and learning new ones. He could do with a little exercise. He picked up a broad sword and expertly swung it in the air.

"Who's up for a little challenge?" he asked the small circle of men.

The men all looked down at their feet, shuffling their shoes in the dust.

"Come on. Anyone?" he prodded. No one stepped up to the challenge, knowing they were no match for his skill.

"I'll take ye on." Fergus strode up to the men with his sword in hand. Clamping a hand on Liam's shoulder, Fergus ducked under the wooden fence and entered the practice area. The grass had been worn away from the years of dueling in the enclosure.

Fergus raised his arms to encourage the men to cheer for him, but they all jeered and booed. Fergus was a favorite among them all, but they had heard the gossip and knew Liam was concerned about the lass being the true Alpha. They were not about to give him the idea they were not behind him completely.

Being a cousin of Audric, he was next in line to rule the clan once the immediate family had been banished. Still a boy when Audric died, he had to be taught many things. Fergus had groomed him to lead the clan, and when the time came he took control as Laird and Alpha. Fergus had taught him how to control his shifting, how to fight and protect the clan.

At the time, he was reluctant to take the Alpha role, knowing Kenna was the rightful heir and the rightful Alpha by blood. If and when she returned, they had no say in the matter if Kenna stated her claim to the clan.

Everyone, including Liam, would be forced to obey her. Now that he had claimed the Alpha role, he'd be damned if she or anyone took it from him. He planned to make sure she was gone before she realized it was hers to claim. A part of him, however, felt a twinge of guilt for being so hasty.

Laughing, he entered the fenced ring.

"Ye sure ye want to be doing this, old man?" he teased Fergus, and the cheers from the men only encouraged him more. The two began to pace around the ring, and Fergus was the first to take a swing. Quick on his feet, he was able to dodge the swing easily. It was like watching a dance.

Both men were large, but Fergus had him beaten in size by far. Fergus was thick and muscled while Liam, tall and broad, still had a leanness about him. He moved much faster than Fergus and was darting around him, striking small blows from every direction. Huffing with exertion and frustration, Fergus spun around trying to catch where he anticipated Liam next.

He managed to get behind him and grabbing Fergus' long braid, pulled his head back exposing his throat. He brought his sword up across Fergus' chest. "Ye had enough yet?" he teased. The teasing spurred Fergus to life. With a *roar*, he threw him off and across the circle. Liam landed hard on the ground, the air knocked out of him. Turning to the face the crowd, Fergus raised his arms in victory.

The boos and taunts turned to cheers, and Fergus turned back around to Liam scrambling to his feet. He charged at Fergus, hitting him square in the chest. Wrapping his arms around Fergus' waist, he pushed him back several yards.

Swatting at Liam's back, Fergus let out a boisterous laugh.

"Ye still fight like a child!" Fergus only succeeded in instigating him further. He was done laughing, however. The exertion had helped relieve some of the anxious energy he felt.

He was ready to confront Kenna. Pushing Fergus away roughly, he backed up swinging his sword in front of him.

"A child? We shall see how badly a child beats you shortly." He charged at Fergus. A low *growl* let Fergus know he was ready to end this. Fergus was not going to let him win easily though. He definitely had to earn it. The swords had long been forgotten in the dirt. The two men were wrestling, locked in each other's arms when the crowd suddenly became quiet.

His head was closest to the ground, and he saw the skirt blowing in the wind before Fergus. Letting himself go limp, Fergus began to laugh and boast. When no boos came from the crowd, Fergus also looked up and quickly let go of him.

Hannah was standing at the fence patiently waiting on the game to be over. Quickly jumping to their feet, he rushed over to her.

"Has there been any change?" he asked, impatience showing on his face.

"Come with me." Hannah glanced at the crowd and appeared to not want to give information away around gossiping clanspeople.

Making their way through the crowd, a few brave souls followed them into the keep. Stopping at the entrance to the main hall, Hannah turned sharply, causing the group to come up short.

"Be gone. All of you!" She fussed at them in a grandmotherly tone. "Ye all have work to be done. This only concerns William."

She hadn't used his full name since he was in trouble as a child, and he instantly knew this was serious. The group slowly dispersed, and she led him to one of the two fireplaces warming the large room. Although there were several large tables in the center of the hall, those were reserved for mealtimes.

Small tables and chairs were positioned in front of the fireplaces for the men to gather after meals, and Hannah settled into one of the chairs, staring into the fire and smoothing the apron over her skirt. Her shoulders sagged a little, and for once he saw the age catching up to her.

Her hair had long gone gray, but he had never seemed to notice. Now he noticed the wrinkles around her eyes and mouth and the sagging skin around her cheeks and chin. Her eyes, however, still had a spark he loved and feared. She was the only person he was scared of, but also someone he truly loved. He would be lost when the time came for her to leave this world.

Pulling a chair beside her, he sat facing her. Reaching over to take her hand, he tried to calm his anxiety so as not to worry the woman.

"Hannah, what is it? Has she spoken to ye? Do ye ken why she is here?" She gave him a soft smile and placed her hand on his.

"Nay, love, but she did wake." His eyes widened and he started to rise, intent on speaking to her.

"Only fer a brief time," she added as she tightened her grip on his hands, urging him to sit back down.

"But she didnae speak?" he asked again.

"Nay. Her throat wouldnae allow it. The poor lass was near strangled to death, and the bastard's hands still mark her neck," she whispered through gritted teeth, beginning to get upset.

He shook his head and pulled his hands away from her, running them through his thick dirty-blond hair. Too anxious to sit, Hannah jumped up and began pacing in front of the fire.

"Remember when ye were a laddie?" She looked at him and continued. "Ye used to play with Kenna?" He winced at her name.

They had been friends, he remembered, nodding. He remembered the pain he felt when she had been forced to leave. It was more than friendship and was when he recognized the affection he'd had for her. He was a couple of years older than her but had known he'd loved her even though he didn't really understand what love was. She had left without even a tear in her eye, and he had run to the stables with his eyes overflowing.

"I think she's returned here fer ye. Fer yer help. She knows ye wouldnae deny her," Hannah stopped pacing and stood still in front of him.

"She ken coming here, we had nay choice but to help her." He looked up at Hannah, the hurt and anger evident in his voice.

Hannah knew he was referring to her Alpha blood. She was the rightful Alpha, and if she wanted his help, he would have no choice but to help her.

"Ye are right about that," she agreed. "However, I dinnae get the sense she is of the same mindset. I think she's hoping ye will do it out of kindness. And from whatever ties remain from yer childhood. Surely ye will

allow her to explain herself before ye send her away."
Standing and crossing his arms across his chest, he gave
a heavy sigh.

"I WILL speak to her next time she wakes." He
looked her in the eye, making sure she understood very
clearly his intent. "Fer her sake, I hope ye are right.
Questions need to be answered before she is allowed to
stay here. First and foremost, I need to ken where she
came from, who she was running from and why. Fergus
and I are planning to take some of the lads back to
where we found her to search for any signs. We should
be back by dark."

Placing a kiss on top of her head, he strode out of
the hall to find Fergus and gather a few men.

Fergus wasn't hard to find. He had known right
where to look. He had seen Fergus making eyes at one
of the ladies during their game earlier. He found them
both, her sitting on Fergus' lap with her plump arms
wrapped about his neck. He was whispering in her ear,
his face all but buried in her ample chest. They had
snuck away behind the stable to a pile of fresh hay not
yet been laid out for the horses, not really hiding from
anyone, but definitely not wanting to be disturbed.

Clearing his throat as he walked up, he hoped to
avoid the awkward task of pulling Fergus away.
Unfortunately for Liam, Fergus kept on nuzzling the
woman's neck and she kept on giggling. He cleared his
throat again, a little louder this time.

"I hear ye boy. Ye dinnae have to keep doing that."
Fergus didn't even look up from her neck but pulled her
closer to him instead.

"Fergus, gather a few of the lads. We will go back
to the woods before dark." He turned and walked away,

leaving Fergus to say his goodbyes to his wife. The two were still flirtatious after many years of marriage. He admired the relationship they had and hoped one day for his own. He also knew Fergus was cussing him as he walked away for interrupting his afternoon.

About an hour later, Fergus and several others met him in the courtyard. Mounted and armed, the group set out to search the area Kenna where had been found. The snow had stopped falling a couple of days before and was more ice than powder. Now, instead of worrying about sinking in the snow, they worried about slipping on ice.

The journey to the forest took only a couple of hours, and when they reached the wooded area where Kenna had been hiding under the shrubs, they separated and began scanning the area for any signs of her attackers.

The men Fergus had gathered were not a random few. They were all born with the wolf gene, and the group together was a strong force. If any trace was left of Kenna's attacker, they would surely find it. A few of the men shifted, but he and Fergus stayed in their human forms. He moved to the edge of the wood line. Kenna had come from the direction of the McLindon territory.

About a mile away from the forest, the McLindon land bordered the Cameron territory. They had wanted Cameron land for as long as anyone remembered but had never been strong enough to take it. He had never actually met a McLindon and never wanted to. He had heard of their Laird's cruelty.

Surely, even Silas McLindon wasn't capable of all Kenna had endured. He knew better though. He was almost positive it was Silas who had dealt Kenna the beating. Walking the line of trees, careful to stay hidden in the shadows, he looked for any sign of the McLindons. It didn't take long before he found what he was looking for.

Hanging from a low branch, a small piece of cloth rustled in the wind. He held it between his fingers, wiping off the dirt and mud caked on the fabric. As it came clean, Liam recognized the plaid. Gripping the fabric in his fist, he promised himself he would make the man pay for what he had done to Kenna.

Fergus knew from the look on his face that he had found something. Liam's jaw was set firm as he gritted his teeth. Not saying a word, he held his palm out, showing him the cloth.

"Well, seems about right." Fergus gave a sarcastic grunt. Letting out a shrill whistle to the others, they mounted their horses and led the way back to the Cameron keep.

Chapter Four

Kenna's throat burned as if she had swallowed hot coals. Her head was pounding, and her limbs felt as though they were made from lead. She heard movement around her and thought she made out faint singing as well. In too much pain to move, she lay still trying to decipher what was going on around her. She tried to think back to the last thing she remembered.

She remembered crawling under a bush to escape Silas' men, but she must be dead. She was warm and lying on soft cushions, not freezing in the ice and snow. Of course, if she was dead, she shouldn't feel this much pain. She tried to open her eyes, but they felt as if they had been rubbed raw with dirt and sand. She groaned weakly, feeling a desperate thirst. What she wouldn't give for a drink of water! Although she wasn't sure she could swallow it.

As she began to stir, a damp cloth with cool water wiped the beads of sweat forming on her forehead. She turned her head slightly, as much as the aching would allow. The cool cloth felt amazing on her fiery skin, soothing her eyes and lips.

She turned her face toward the cloth, welcoming the dampness on her parched lips. Her lips parted, and a few drops from the cloth trickled into her mouth. It was not enough to swallow but felt like Heaven to her dry, cracked lips and parched tongue. Her eyelids began to flutter as she tried to wake.

Groaning at the bright light in the room, she tried to focus her eyes and take in her surroundings. The ceiling was high with large wooden beams spanning the length of the room. The walls had been left the original stone instead of covered with a mud stucco like Silas' keep.

She liked the stone better, she thought. The bed she lay in came out from the wall, directly across from a heavy wooden door. A small table was to the left of the bed, holding a small wash basin and pitcher. To the right, the large stone fireplace filled the wall, and the fire burning warmed the room to an almost uncomfortable heat.

She made out the figure of the older woman bending near the fire. Opening her mouth to ask where she was, she found no sound came out. Surprised, she tried again to get the woman's attention and still made no sound. Preparing herself to try again, she stopped when the woman turned toward her bed.

Balancing the teacup and pot on a small tray, the woman looked amazed to see her awake.

"Och, child! Dinnae try to speak!" She rushed over, careful not to spill the tea.

A faint memory washed over her as she drank the thistle tea and honey. She had been given it as a child to cure almost anything. Smiling at the memory, she knew it also put her back to sleep, and she welcomed the rest.

The woman was strong for her age, and she noticed how she held her firmly and securely with one arm while offering her a few more sips of the tea with the other. She gently laid her back onto the pillows.

"There now," she said in a motherly voice. "Not

too much too soon".

As she adjusted her on the pillows, the old woman gently turned Kenna's chin, exposing her neck. The bruising on her throat had turned from the deep purple to a yellowish green, but the shape of the hand and fingers that had wrapped around her slim neck were still clear.

"Och, ye poor lass. Yer throat must feel raw. My tea is powerful, and ye should be back to talking soon. Ye needn't fear me or anyone else here. Ye are safe."

She rose from the bed, and she watched as she went to the window to open the curtain. Turning back for her approval, the woman pulled the curtain back to allow the light of the day to enter the room. It was cloudy, as usual, but a breeze carried fresh air into the stuffy room.

She watched as the woman leaned out, taking in a deep breath of the sweet air, and came over to sit at the small table by the bed.

"Ye've been through it, lass" she *tisked*. "But dinnae fash now. We'll get ye looked after and on the mend," she said cheerfully. Obviously not expecting an answer, she continued rambling.

"I'll admit though, I'll be glad when yer voice is back. I'm a tad bit anxious to know how ye came into this predicament." She motioned over Kenna's body.

"Ye want another sip of tea, dearie?" She nodded, feeling some relief from the dehydration her body had suffered. After a few more sips of the tea and another good washing of her face, the woman lifted her gently again to plump her pillows and adjust her blankets. As she settled back in, the woman moved again to the window.

Looking down, she spoke in a hushed tone, going on about the lives of the people she saw moving and working below. Her tone was soothing, and Kenna closed her eyes. She felt the woman's gentle hands brush the curls from her face.

"Welcome home, lass," she whispered. Her words sunk in as she succumbed to the tea's effects.

"She knows," she thought, unable to fight the sleep her body was eager to welcome.

Hours passed, and when she woke she saw the woman had not left her side. A delicious smelling broth sat beside her bed, still warm and steaming in the bowl. She tried to push herself into a sitting position. The woman rushed over to help her, and once she was comfortable sat beside her on the bed, facing her.

"Och, lass, I expect it will take several days for all the swelling to go down, but ye look a sight better than ye did when ye first arrived." She smiled kindly at Kenna, and although Kenna was hesitant she found herself offering one in return.

"My name's Hannah, lass. I'm a healer. You're safe now, child. But—" Hannah paused, and Kenna's eyebrows raised as her shoulders sagged. She prepared herself for the worst, and Hannah reached a hand out, patting her own in comfort.

"When you're ready," she continued, "Laird will be wantin' to speak with ye."

Of course he would, she thought. Was she even able to speak? She wasn't sure but gave it a try.

"My…" Her words caught in her throat and, clearing it, she started again. "My name is Kenna," she said weakly. She was surprised her throat didn't seem to hurt that bad. The tea she drank must have worked wonders.

"Well, of course it tis!" Hannah looked at her like she was talking nonsense. "Would ye like some broth, dear?"

Nodding, Kenna pulled the thick wool blankets up around her. She was naked, she realized, except for several bandages covering her body.

"Dinnae fash, lass. No one has seen ye except I ta bandage yer wounds." Hannah's confession offered her a little comfort, and she wasn't sure why, but Kenna felt like she could trust the older woman.

"Lass, the first question he is going to ask is who did this to ye. Is it something ye can answer?" Hannah spoke slowly, but she understood what the woman was asking. Did she remember and was she willing to give up the bastard's name, knowing the Laird would most likely go after him.

"I came from the McLindon's, but I am nay one of them. I have grown up there, but it was never my home." She spoke quietly, and Hannah looked at her with sympathetic eyes.

"And have ye come home, lass?"

She met Hannah's eyes.

"I'm nay sure I'll ever be home, but they willnae touch me here." Her voice was almost a whisper as she sipped the warm, salty broth. It soothed her throat but did even more for her soul. She felt like she was home but would not stay if she wasn't welcome. Once she was healed, she must move on, putting as much distance between her and Silas as possible.

"Do ye feel up to speaking with the Laird? He can be a bit gruff sometimes, but dinnae fash, his bark is worse than his bite." Hannah winked at her. She trusted the woman to make sure she was feeling up to it before she was presented to the Laird, she felt certain.

Offering to change her bandages, Hannah took the broth from her and set it on the table. She had already had one of the young servant girls bring up a suitable dress since the clothes she had arrived in were in rags. Helping her to the edge of the bed, she began unwrapping the bandages, gently washing, and treating the wounds.

She had stitched several areas, including the gash near her temple. Speaking to her about her wounds, Hannah appeared rather proud of the work she had done. She was certain the areas she had stitched closed would barely leave a scar.

She touched the area at her temple gingerly. It was still tender, but Hannah was right. The stitching was small and tight.

"All done, dear." Hannah finished replacing the bandages that needed it but only a few areas remained fresh. She had healed remarkably well and quickly. Examining her body, she looked at Hannah quizzically.

"How long have I been here?"

A knowing smile crossed Hannah's face.

"About four days. Ye've healed verra fast, love."

Hannah brought the clothing over next, and she admired the simple yet amazing quality of the dress. She allowed Hannah to help her lift the chemise over her head, allowing it to fall down her body. The thin material was soft and warm from being near the fire. The overdress was next, and it was a pale green linen.

Stepping into the dress, she turned to let Hannah fix the lacing running from the top of her hips up the back of the dress. The dress fit like it was made just for her, and she smoothed the front of the dress, admiring the tiny thistle flowers stitched around the wrists in a darker green.

Once she was laced in, Hannah placed a belt around her waist. The belt hung on her hips and was made of pewter discs connected with a thin silver chain. In the center of each disc was a greenish-yellow stone. She ran her fingers over the smooth stone.

"They say the stone is the color of a wolf's eye." Hannah came around to face her. "I've never seen the large ones they say roam the woods. But 'tis what they say." She felt the woman eyeing her suspiciously. She looked down at the belt again.

"If 'tis true, they must be verra beautiful creatures." She rubbed the large stone and looked up at Hannah and smiled. Nodding her agreement, Hannah held out her hands and offered her a small leather purse to attach to the belt.

In it, Hannah had put a small linen square with a small thistle embroidered in the corner. Tears began to well up in her eyes. It was lovely, and she had never been gifted anything like it before. The compassion Hannah had shown her was overwhelming, and before she knew what she was doing she reached out to hug the woman.

After a few moments, Hannah patted her on the back and pulled her over to sit in front of the fire. Behind her, Hannah began brushing her dark auburn hair, the loose curls hanging down her back. Hannah pulled pieces back from each side, securing them with a leather cord. With a broad smile, she stepped back to admire her work. A loud knock sounded on the door causing both women to jump. Exchanging a glance with

Hannah, Kenna knew it was time for the Laird to seek his answers.

Chapter Five

Liam stood in the doorway, his arms folded across his chest. His presence was intimidating but Hannah stood her ground, giving Kenna a sense of protection. Hannah gave him a stern look before allowing him to enter but stayed put between the two. "Kenna, dear, this is Liam, Chief of the Camerons."

Her eyes widened. She knew Liam instantly as a flood of memories came rushing back. He was no longer the young boy she remembered, and her heart beat faster. He was a fully grown and very handsome man. His dark-blond hair was cropped short and only accentuated his pale blue eyes. His nose had a small bump where it had obviously been broken and healed too quickly before being reset. His jaw was strong, even though it was obvious he was gritting his teeth.

"Hello, Kenna," he greeted her slowly. "I'm pleased to see ye are doing much better than when I last saw ye." She nodded suspiciously, holding the chair by the table to steady her nerves.

"Here, lass." Hannah started fretting over her, trying to make her comfortable. "Come sit down. Liam has a few questions he'd like to ask ye. Dinnae fash, he is a lot softer than he looks." She whispered the last, giving Liam a warning look.

"I'll be happy to answer anything I can," she cleared her throat and answered cautiously. She knew though, there were some answers she could not give and some he already knew the answer to. She smelled the wolf on him and knew he sensed it on her as well. He smelled of the woods and fresh snow to her, and she wondered what her scent was for him. Blushing at how intimate the thought was, she looked down quickly at her feet.

"Hannah, do ye mind getting us some wine? I'd like to speak to Kenna alone, please." Liam smiled sweetly at Hannah. She knew Hannah was displeased at being asked to leave, but the woman knew not to argue with their chief in front of an outsider. Hannah shuffled to the door and turned to smile back at the pair, but the smile did not reach her eyes. Kenna didn't miss the warning look she shot Liam before she slipped from the room.

"Now then." Liam sat on a stool across from her, his hands folded in front of him. "I'd like to show ye something." He reached into his sporran and pulled out the dirty scrap of fabric he had found in the woods, holding it out to her.

"This was found snagged on one of the trees near where we pulled ye out. Do ye recognize this plaid?"

She reached out shakily to take the cloth. Running it between her fingers, she nodded.

"And these are the ones who were chasing ye?" He obviously already knew the answer but wanted her to confirm it. Again, she nodded.

"This is who attacked ye?"

She looked up with tears in her eyes. The memories still fresh in her mind. The fear she had felt came back up to the surface, and she knew Liam heard her heart pounding.

She spoke in a soft but clear voice.

"Ye ken the answers to the questions ye ask. Mayhap ye should ask me something ye dinnae already ken." She paused, looking at him intently before continuing. "The why."

He sat back, crossing his arms across his broad chest.

"Ok. If yer willing, tell me. Why?"

She held her head high, and taking a deep breath, began recounting the past years of horror she had endured under Silas. As she bravely told him stories of her past, she tried to hide the fear and anger in her voice.

She told him how her mother had been kept separated from her, drugged into believing they were happy and being treated like the nobility they were. She spoke of how Silas reminded her of the favor he had done by taking them in, all the while beating her to the brink of death.

She gave details of the years of abuse the other maidens suffered at his hands, too many unable to survive his torturous appetite. By the time she had finished, she was shaking with exhaustion.

He had stood during her tale to stalk the room. She watched him pace, clenching and unclenching his fists.

When her atrocious tale ended, he offered her a cup of wine to ease her throat and her nerves. They both knew the other's secret, and inhaling deeply, he looked her in the eyes.

"Kenna, did you ever shift in front of Silas?"

Taken aback by the directness of his question, she took a moment to regain her composure before answering.

"Never," she replied quietly. "He only wished to use it for evil."

"It was ye. In the woods," Liam said matter of factly, and she nodded in confirmation.

"Silas' men are terrified of the woods and the wolves they've heard tales of. I ken they'd believe I was attacked. It was the only way to escape them. I couldnae go any farther in the shape I was!"

Her voice had risen to near hysterics trying to defend her decision to come onto Cameron land. Trying to calm her down, he raised his hands in defense to quiet her. It was too late though. Hannah returned and burst into the room. Hannah gave him a scathing look before rushing over to pat Kenna's shoulders.

Smiling gently at Kenna, the old woman sat her down, treating her like a child.

"There, there lass, what has ye so distraught? I ken I promised ye he wouldnae be coarse." She shot Liam another threatening glare as he tried to hide his smirk.

"Weel, before ye rushed in so, the lass was explaining just how she escaped McLindon's men and how we happened upon her. I'm sure that has been verra upsetting for her," he tried to ease Hannah's mind.

"O'course it has!" Hannah again patted Kenna's head like a puppy.

He sighed and started to question her again under Hannah's watchful eye.

"Kenna, do ye remember anything of yer life before ye went to Silas' keep?"

Kenna took a deep breath. This was the question she had feared most. Yes, she remembered. She just wasn't sure she would be welcome if she said so. If she lied, though, Liam would know, so having no choice, she nodded.

"Aye. I do remember some, my friends and how happy we were."

She locked eyes with Liam, hoping he remembered her and their friendship as well.

"I remember the wonderful people and how my father and mother loved everyone as weel." She eyed Liam and Hannah nervously as she mentioned her mother. She was cautious of their reaction. Liam, a true Laird, showed no emotion, but Hannah gave an audible humph in disgust.

Turning to face Hannah, she held the older woman's hands in helrs.

"Dinnae believe what ye've been told. My mother loved my father verra much," she pleaded with Hannah. "She'd never have done what they accused her of. It had to have been someone else."

Hannah sighed and looked toward the window.

"Kenna, when yer family left, there were a lot of questions left unanswered. Whether yer mother was guilty or nay, it was easier to think the murderer had been removed from our lands and is why everyone accepted her guilt. If ye ken something about it, ye must tell us."

She heard the hope in Hannah's voice. Perhaps she thought enough of her parents to know Lady Evelyn was not capable of murdering her father. She wished she could convince them of her mother's innocence, but it had to wait.

Liam and Hannah sat quietly waiting on her answer. She shook her head. All she knew was her mother had not killed her father. She was certain of it.

She just wished she knew who did.

"Ye are welcome here, Kenna, and I want you to feel free to move around the lands. Ye are nay a prisoner here. Ye are our *guest*." Liam stressed the last, and Kenna understood that while she was welcome, he had no intention of allowing her to stay permanently. Standing to leave, Liam gave a satisfied smile to both her and Hannah.

"Thank ye fer speaking with me. We will talk further when ye are feeling up to it. If ye are feeling stronger, I'd like ye to join us fer supper as weel." Nodding his goodbye, he turned on his heels and strode out the door, leaving the two women alone.

****

Sighing, Hannah walked to the window. Kenna wondered what she was thinking, but she didn't have to wonder long as Hannah began sharing her own memories.

"I ken yer mother and yer father verra weel. When yer father died, I saw the grief in yer mother's face. I ken she wouldnae have done what they accused her of. She ken her herbs weel. After all, I had taught her. And she never used them to hurt someone, least of all kill someone she loved so."

Turning back to Kenna, she had tears in her eyes. She sensed the woman wanted to ask her own questions as well. While she had started to trust the woman, she wasn't sure if she was ready to open up completely. She was uncertain how Liam felt about her mother's guilt. Until she was guaranteed of both her and her mother's safety, she would keep her guard up.

Wringing her hands, Hannah bent in front of Kenna.

"Ye ken dearie, he didnae ask what he truly wanted to."

Kenna figured as much.

"He's afraid I've come back to claim my place as heir."

Hannah remained silent, waiting for her to continue.

"Ye have all helped me more than I ever hoped. I have no intention of threatening his position as Laird."

Hannah's shoulders relaxed, and she smiled.

"Well, he will be glad to hear it. Although he willnae give up without a fight, mind ye. He has grown into a good leader, and these people love him. They will stand beside him."

She caught the pride and the slight warning in Hannah's tone.

"I'm glad to hear it. I can see how much ye admire him."

Hannah returned her comment with a smile and nod.

"Aye, I am verra proud of the man he has become. It's as if he's my own son. I've watched him grow from a brokenhearted lad to a strong and brave leader."

"Brokenhearted?"

"When Audric died and yer family was sent away, he was crushed. He lost everyone he had respected. Everyone he looked up to. And," she paused, "his best friend. A friend who left without so much as a goodbye. Aye, he was heartbroken and angry. 'Tis why he is so cautious now that ye've returned."

Hannah poured her another glass of wine.

"It's about supper time. I'll leave ye to yer thoughts. When ye are ready, there will be a place set for you at the Laird's side." Hannah made her way to the door as she stared into the fire thinking about the young boy she had left behind.

"Hannah", she called after the older woman. Hesitant to speak, she hoped Hannah understood what she was about to say.

"Aye, lass," Hannah turned back.

"I have nay intention of claiming my place as Alpha. I needed help, and the Camerons generously offered it." Pausing, she thought about how to continue. "Had they not, however…well, I ken my birthright. Make no mistake, my years of being controlled by someone else are over."

Hannah stared at her wide-eyed, and she knew she had caught the meaning behind her words. She had not come with a plan of enforcing her birthright but knew they had no choice but to obey her if she chose to do so—and Hannah knew as well.

Raising her head high, Hannah gave her a slight smile and sighed.

"Weel, lass, it seems ye have a verra cunning mind. 'Tis a good thing for a woman to have. I do hope we will see ye at supper," and bowing slightly, she backed out of the room.

As the door closed, she let out an exhausted sigh. She had held it together but wasn't sure how convincing she had been. She wanted to seem powerful, instead of the scared, weak girl she felt like inside. She had felt the tension between herself and Hannah. She knew Hannah would alert Liam to her warning, and she expected some tension there too.

She was growing to like Hannah and hoped she forgave her for her revelation. It had to be said though.

She needed them to know she needed their help and hoped they continued to willingly give it. Her fears returned as she thought about what should happen if they refused. If she truly did have to use her power, did she even know how?

Chapter Six

Kenna made her way winding through the maze of hallways down to the banquet. The boisterous noise and laughter grew louder as she neared the great hall. Her stomach was in knots, and she wasn't sure she'd be able to eat, but after her confession to Hannah she needed to face Liam. Hannah surely conveyed their conversation, and he was probably furious with her.

The large wooden double doors were propped open, and she paused before going in. The smells wafting through caused her stomach to almost betray her as the bile rose in her throat. Ducking behind one of the large doors, she gripped her middle and fell against the cool stone wall. Trying to settle her nerves, she took several deep breaths and wiped her sweaty palms on her skirts. When she felt steady enough, she pushed away from the hard wall, leaving the safety of her hiding place and entered the doorway.

At once, a silence fell across the hall as the men stared blankly at her. The women looked at her with distrust in their eyes. At the end of the hall, she saw Liam seated at a long table with several other men. On his right was a very large man, their heads bent close in a conversation obviously not intended for everyone to hear.

Trying not to make eye contact with any clansmen, she kept her head down and made her way down the makeshift aisle being created as benches were quickly scooted away from her. She walked quickly toward Liam's table, trying to blend in. She caught Hannah's eyes first, and forcing a nervous smile at the woman she watched as Hannah set down the pitcher of ale she had been carrying and wiped her hands on her apron.

"Well, dearie," Hannah announced loudly for everyone to hear and gaining Liam's attention. "I am pleased to see ye were feeling weel enough to join us tonight." Hannah came to stand face to face with her. Even though the woman hunched slightly, she noticed they were almost the same height. Gripping her shoulders, Hannah pulled her into a tight hug and placed a kiss on her cheek. She knew it was for show and felt the tension coming from Hannah as she was steered to the table and to the chair on the left of Liam.

Liam and the large man to his right stood until she was seated. Nodding a greeting to her, they returned to their own seats and conversation. Hannah began to place food in front of her and poured her a cup of wine. She gently touched Hannah's hand as she set the cup in front of her.

"Thank ye, Hannah," she spoke softly and hoped Hannah would hear the sincerity in her voice. She truly was grateful for all that Hannah had done to help her. Hannah's lips were a tight line, and the woman made no movement. Unsure of what to make of her reaction, she waited until she felt Hannah relax under her hand and was rewarded with a small smile and slight nodding of Hannah's head. Releasing Hannah's hand with a smile of her own, she took a sip of her wine and felt her nerves calm as she allowed herself a look around the room.

Some of the older faces felt familiar, and she tried to place them in her memories. The room had returned to normal, full of loud conversations, laughing, and even singing. Everyone seemed so happy and comfortable here. It was certainly different than any gathering she had witnessed in Silas' home. The food was better as well!

Her stomach felt much better since her nerves had calmed, and she realized how hungry she was for real food! She had not had much other than the broth since arriving and dove into her plate eagerly. Hannah had given her generous portions of roasted lamb and fish, stew, cheese, and bread. Platters full of meat pies, figs and dates, cheese wheels, and walnuts lined the long table. It was a feast like she had never seen, and she looked around the room wondering who or what they were celebrating.

As she devoured her food, she spied Liam watching her out of the corner of his eye. Embarrassed, she slowed her eating and patted the corners of her mouth with the linen cloth beside her plate. She was genuinely delighted to be there.

"Kenna." Liam addressed her and waited until she had swallowed before continuing. "It's good to see yer appetite has returned. When ye gather yer strength, I'll take ye riding through the Cameron lands. I thought ye may like to see the village."

"Yes! I'd like that verra much! Thank ye!" She leaned forward eagerly, for a moment forgetting her manners.

"When ye feel up to it, head down to the stables. Fergus here"—he tilted his head toward the large man—"will get ye a suitable mount." She eyed Fergus hesitantly. His size was intimidating, but he ate his leg of lamb so delicately she almost laughed out loud. He was definitely a contradiction, but she was learning most everyone she met here was. Fergus grinned slightly at her before going back to his meal.

"I'm feeling much better and think I can manage. I will come tomorrow morning if it suits ye?" She raised her eyebrows toward Fergus. Not looking up from his food, he offered her a grunt in return, which she took as a yes and returned to her own plate. She was excited about the possibility of getting out of the keep tomorrow, but as she ate her fill exhaustion settled over her. Pushing back from the table, she rose to excuse herself. She thanked Liam for the delicious meal and tried to stifle a yawn.

"Get some rest then. Tomorrow will be a long day, and ye will need all the energy ye can muster," Liam instructed. She knew he doubted she was up to the task, but she was anxious to see her lands. As she walked out of the hall, she felt the eyes on her back.

****

Liam watched as Kenna left the hall, all eyes following her as she went. Not taking his eyes off her back, he leaned to Fergus.

"Do ye think she is capable?" He knew he'd get an honest answer from his old friend.

"Aye. Most definitely." Fergus replied. "A lass like that, regardless of any supernatural abilities," he paused a moment shaking his head. "She'll do ye in fer sure if ye let her."

Liam laughed. He'd meant capable of riding and making the journey, but Fergus had seen otherwise. He agreed, however, and he'd be damned before he'd let a lass undo him! Clamping a hand on Fergus' strong shoulder, he excused himself as well.

He followed Kenna from the hall, careful to stay back. He wanted to ensure she went back to her chambers and wasn't wandering the keep. The castle was sometimes dangerous for a lass alone at night in dark hallways. Plus, he wasn't too keen on her having full access to the castle unsupervised. Kenna was almost to her room when she paused in the hallway.

Realizing she had stopped outside his own door, Liam ducked behind a stone column. His door was open. Hannah must have gone in to tidy up or leave him some wine, he thought. He watched as Kenna turned to look into the room. Her expression looked surprised but then turned to disappointment at whatever she had seen inside. He wondered what she had seen.

She quickened her pace to her room, and once he had seen her disappear inside he left the cover of the column and made his way to his own chamber. The events of late had taken their toll, and he was eager to get some rest. Thinking the wine help may him drift off to sleep, he was taken by surprise when he entered the dark chamber.

A pretty, well-endowed lass sat by his window, looking out. He recognized Margo's blonde curls instantly. Turning, she gave him a sly smile and a little giggle. The lacings on her bodice had all but come undone, and her breasts threatened to spill out. Suddenly, he wasn't as tired as he had been a moment earlier. Margo had been his companion for a few months, and he always enjoyed their time together. But it was all in fun, nothing serious. While she was only a year younger than him, she was very immature.

He expected never to be able to have a serious conversation with her or look to her for anything other than a little amusement. He felt guilty thinking this way and knew he should send her away and end this. His body, however, was thinking otherwise. One more night, he convinced himself and shut the door, stripping off his shirt.

He slipped out of his chambers before the sun rose, long before Margo woke. He was done with their trysts and must break the news to her. She would be heartbroken of course. He knew she was hoping for a future with him, but Margo was not like him. She did not possess the wolf, never understanding how it dictated his life.

He walked slowly down to the stables after passing through the kitchen to grab a pastry to break his fast. He enjoyed the early mornings best. The fog was thick, and everything was just waking up. It was still quiet except for the grunting coming from the stables. He visualized the breath coming from the horses' nostrils in the crisp, cold morning.

He wanted to make it down to the stables and have a word with Fergus before Kenna arrived. He knew she was eager to get away from the keep. He had felt the tension from the clansmen and knew their eyes would be on her every move, his own eyes included. At least until he was certain of her intentions, that she kept her promise not to use her leverage as the Alpha heir to force control on his clan.

Fergus was sitting on a wooden stool, gripping a horse's hoof tightly and cursing as he cleaned the shoe.

"Ye just try it, ye son of a bitch!" he yelled at the horse who had obviously tried to kick away from him.

Fergus had already worked up a sweat on his brow struggling with the animal, as well as trying to keep his large frame balanced on the small stool. It was quite comical, and Liam let out a laugh, earning him a scowl from the exasperated man. Wiping his brow, Fergus stood and stretched his back, letting the horse go and walking out of the stall still cursing the beast.

"I'm guessing that won't be the one you put Kenna on," Liam said sarcastically.

"Nay, but I should put yer ass on it for nay helping me!" Fergus ladeled a gulp of water from the barrel nearby. Liam looked around and saw no sign of Kenna yet.

"I want ye to ride with us today. I'm taking Kenna around the village and I'd like ye ta help me, uh…get to know her a little better." He fumbled over the words, but he trusted and valued the man's opinion. He knew Fergus to be honest with him even if he didn't like what he had to say.

"Ye mean ye want me to find out what she's up to!" Fergus, of course, saw right through his intentions and had been expecting it.

"Aye, weel, I had already planned on it, of course. Ye cannae

go unsupervised around the village. People will talk." Fergus gave him a side glance and he nodded in agreement.

****

Kenna approached the stables easily overhearing the two men talking. She didn't want to appear as though she was eavesdropping, so she tried to approach loudly. It was unmistakably hard to make noise on dew-soaked ground with soft leather boots. Trying a different tactic, she began to hum softly, a tune her mother had sung to her as a child. She slowed her walk as she remembered the song and how wonderful her life had been with the Camerons. Tears started to swell in her eyes, and she quickly blinked them away. Today was bound to be emotional enough, seeing her past and being questioned by Liam. Gathering her composure, she entered the open stable doors and was greeted warmly by Fergus.

"Morning, lass. Yer up with the sun this morning."

"Seems I'm up *before* the sun," she joked lightheartedly.

"Ay, weel 'tis a wee bit dark still, but it will lighten up as the day goes." Fergus seemed convinced but she wasn't so sure. The sun was trying to peek through the clouds, but the sky threatened another snowfall.

Liam led two horses from the stalls and brought them to stand in front of her. Immediately, the horses began pawing the ground and snorting in protest. He held the reins tightly, quieting them, and she backed away uneasily. The horses must sense the wolf in her, she thought, yet they were not scared of Liam. She looked between the horses and Liam quizzically.

"Aye," he said, understanding her puzzled look. "They've been trained to not fear us. A healthy respect between beasts," he said teasing her.

"They will be fine. Here." He grabbed her hand and, using his own to guide her, helped her stroke the horse she was to ride. He was a beautiful animal and once he calmed, his gentleness shown through.

"This is Angus. He's a little older and will do well fer ye." He stepped back, allowing her to pet the animal alone.

Suddenly, she was lifted from behind and plopped into the saddle. Fergus stood beside her laughing. Before she knew it, she was holding the reins in her delicate hands. The men had each mounted their own horses and were leading her through the stable doors.

A cold, misting rain had already started to fall as the group set out from the gates of the keep. It was not a long ride to the village, and she was looking forward to every minute. She could finally relax and not worry about looking over her shoulder for Silas' wrath.

She was excited to meet the villagers, and she hoped it triggered some memories for her as well. A narrow dirt trail acted as the road for villagers coming and going from the keep. It had been worn by years of travel. There were fields of heather growing high on either side of the road and while it looked lovely during the day, her mind raced with the dangers that hid in the tall grass after the sun went down.

As if reading her mind, Liam looked over his shoulder at her. The authority in his voice was clear. His words were not a suggestion, but an order.

"Never leave the keep at night unattended. Wolves are nay the only dangers ye may encounter once ye are outside our walls."

She shivered, and immediately her mind went to Silas. She'd gladly face any danger in the woods compared to what she had witnessed with him. The thought gave her courage, and she sat straighter in the saddle.

They continued to ride in somewhat silence. Occasionally, she asked about the landscape or comment on livestock grazing off the path. They passed a few fields being tended, and at each one the clansmen waved as they passed. Surprised at their greeting, she was pleased to see how happy they were to see Liam and Fergus passing by. Silas' visits to his people were always a dreaded event and usually ended in violence.

The landscape didn't change much until they came to a rocky hill. The grasses gave way to dirt and rocks as they climbed the path in single file. When she came to the top of the hill where Fergus and Liam had stopped, she saw the small village sitting at the bottom of the other side. The small, round homes were scattered around in a sort of circle, and she thought the thatch roofs made them look like toadstools. She giggled to herself quietly at the thought of Fergus the giant looming over the village.

In the village center, there was a massive stone pit with a fire blazing and several people standing around warming their hands. The light rain had gotten heavier and colder, and Kenna shivered, noticing the bite in the air.

"Let's get moving. It will be warmer down there, and ye can warm by the fire." Liam nudged his horse forward, and her and Fergus' mounts followed suit. Welcome greetings were shouted from the men and women as they grew closer, and she could sense the loyalty and feeling of family coming from them.

They dismounted and approached the fire. A space cleared between the villagers to allow her to move closer and warm herself. Nodding to the men in thanks, she eagerly stretched out her hands to warm them over the fire. Removing her wool gloves, her hands started to thaw from the cold. Suddenly, someone grabbed her hand, and she was pulled away from the fire.

"Och, lass! This will never do." A woman stood

before her shaking her head.

"Agnes," Liam exclaimed cheerfully, obviously happy to see the woman. Coming from behind Kenna, he planted a kiss on the woman's rosy cheek and smiled sweetly down at her plump face.

"This is Kenna. She is—"Liam paused briefly"— our guest. I thought I'd bring her along to see the village." Liam was pleasant, but she caught his meaning behind the term guest. He had no intention of her staying longer than necessary. She felt her heart sink a little at this realization, and she wasn't sure just why.

"Well, welcome to ye lass, and let's get ye into somewhere warmer afore yer fingers fall off!". Smiling at Agnes, Kenna allowed her to pull her along. She liked the woman instantly. She followed her, with Liam on her heels, into a small hut. Inside, a warm fire was roaring in the fireplace, and a lovely smell filled the home. A stew was obviously bubbling over the fire. She looked around the room, noticing there were herbs hanging from the beams along the ceiling to dry. A small table with benches lined one wall where a single plate and cup sat. She pitied the woman being all alone. This was surely why she was so eager for their company.

Agnes poured her and Liam a cup of warm tea, which they graciously accepted. "There now, lass, that should do ye good. 'Twill warm the hands and the belly." Taking a long sip of the tea, she began to cough. It was strong with peppermint and she wasn't expecting it as it burned a little going down.

She wasn't much of a drinker, but she imagined this is what a shot of whiskey would feel like in your belly. Taking the cup from her, Agnes' eyes narrowed as she looked at Kenna's hands. She set the cup down and returned to hold her hands in her own, examining the lines of her palms. Just then, a gust of wind blew in through the door as Fergus stood in the doorway.

"Weel, I see nay much has changed around here. A mon can't be gone more than a few days before another mon moves in on his woman." Liam smiled and kept playing along.

"Ye were supposed to be gone longer. I hadn't even gotten more than a peck on the cheek." He stood and squeezed Agnes from behind in a big bear hug.

"Och, you two!" She pulled away from Liam and wrapped her small arms around Fergus. He bent to her, and Agnes gave him a kiss which made Kenna look away blushing.

"Weel, that's more like it!" Fergus playfully slapped Agnes on the behind as she turned to pour him a cup of tea also.

Kenna relaxed at their playfulness. The love surrounding her in the home was evident as Fergus made himself comfortable. She was glad Agnes was not as alone as she thought and warmed herself by the fire while the others sat around the table in a businesslike manner. She listened as Agnes began recounting events in the village while Liam and Fergus made mental notes to visit the sick, settle disputes and any other needs Agnes brought to their attention. She was fascinated by all of it.

Agnes obviously played an important role to Liam, and she wasn't sure why, but hoped the woman liked her. Her thoughts drifted off as she stared into the warm fire waiting for them to finish their business. Just as she was drifting off, a loud, high-pitched scream pierced the quiet morning air.

Sitting up straight, she watched as Liam and Fergus jumped up at once, looking like soldiers at attention. Agnes rushed past them and through the door. She sat motionless, unsure of what to do and not wanting to be in the way. Another scream broke free, and Agnes ran back inside, gathering herbs and her medicine pouch. A lass was in labor and had been through a rough pregnancy. Grabbing Kenna's arm and pulling her along, Agnes insisted she needed a woman's touch and Kenna would be of great use to her. She felt her knees almost buckle at the thought of what may happen to the lass or the babe if she screwed up! Agnes would need all the help she could get to deliver the baby and take care of the mother.

Liam agreed to head back to the castle and fetch Hannah. Hearing Hannah's name, she breathed a sigh of relief. She knew Hannah's skills firsthand and was certain the young girl and the babe were going to be well taken care of. Following Agnes into the cold, she watched Liam swing himself onto his horse and ride away.

Chapter Seven

Liam rode hard back to the keep for Hannah. From the sound of the lass' screams, the babe was coming soon. His mind wasn't on the babe though. He was focused on Kenna. He wasn't sure he wanted to leave her with Agnes just yet. He had seen the way she examined the lines on Kenna's palms. Lines only someone with wolf blood had. Deep set and a lifeline seeming to never end. Agnes knew for sure, as she was wolf herself. She was also a wonderful healer and midwife, and he had often thought her wolf senses enhanced her gift. She would have recognized Kenna's scent right away, but standing so close to him, Agnes might have mistaken it for him. The lines, however, confirmed her suspicion.

He reached the castle in record time, barely beating the snowfall that had grown out of the rain. It was getting heavier and heavier and may make for a treacherous trip back to the village if they didn't hurry. He unmounted and headed straight for the kitchen. He knew Hannah well and expected her to be overseeing the preparations for supper.

Just where he thought her to be, bent over a large pot on the fire, he found her barking instructions to several cooks. Others were bustling around the kitchen preparing various dishes, and as his large frame entered the doorway they suddenly went silent. Looking up from the stew she had been hovering over, Hannah's smile disappeared when she saw the look of seriousness on his face. Nodding to the other girls to take over the meal, Hannah followed close on his heels as he led her to the hall.

"Agnes has an urgent need of ye in the village," he sputtered out and hoped she didn't ask for more detail as he wasn't sure he knew what to say. She didn't. He was thankful Hannah knew Agnes well enough to know if she sent for her, the situation was dire. He followed close on her heels as she rushed from the room to her study and began gathering herbs and bottles and tossing them into a big leather bag. He only seemed to be in the way in the small room and was glad to step outside the door when she swatted him aside. When she finished gathering what she needed and headed out the low doorway, he pulled the door locked behind them and raced after her.

He had not spent time getting a mount ready for Hannah. As far as he knew, she had never ridden alone. He got her settled first and climbed up behind her, urging his horse forward. Hannah's body tensed as he rode swiftly through the falling snow. It would be icy for the journey home, but right now the snow was fresh and still soft, and the horse's hooves were surefooted as they made the trip. The village scene had changed slightly since he left, and a crowd was now gathered outside the door to the hut. He joined the other men around the fire while several women swarmed Hannah and ushered her into the home.

****

The door opened and brought with it a welcome blast of icy air. The small home was cramped and hot from the fire roaring in the large fireplace. Several village women were being too nosey to help and only added to the claustrophobic feeling. Kenna smiled with relief when she saw Hannah's motherly form enter the home. Agnes was too busy tending to Elin, the sweet lass about to become a mother, to give any instruction, so she hid in a corner, unsure of where she was needed most. Hannah pushed through the bodies to stand beside her.

"Well, dearie, let's put ye to use, shall we?" Hannah handed her a bowl with directions to gather water from the rain barrel outside. Opening a window slightly to allow some fresh air inside, she then proceeded to find jobs outside of the home for the other women as well.

She welcomed the opportunity to step outside and took a deep breath of the fresh, cold air. She closed the door quickly behind her as she eyed the curious men gathered round the home. Liam gave her a quick smile. Returning his grin with a shy one of her own, she tried not to spill the freezing water before she slipped back inside.

She balanced the water carefully and made her way to the bedside. Elin moaned in pain as another contraction hit, contorting her body to try and relieve the pressure. Sitting on the bed beside Elin, she held her shoulders tightly, helping to prop the young woman up to a more comfortable position. She drenched a cloth in the cold water and dabbed Elin's temples and neck hoping the cool water helped ease some of the pain. Huffing deep breaths, Elin relaxed slightly before the next contraction hit. They were coming on fast, and Kenna grimaced as Agnes lifted Elin's dress.

"I'm going to check to see if I can feel the babe's head," Agnes reassured Elin, and Kenna gripped her tighter, feeling the tension in her as Agnes patted her knee comfortingly and then went about the chore. After a few moments, Agnes let out a sigh of relief, and she felt Elin let her full weight relax into her, letting out a sigh of her own.

"Aye." Agnes smiled at both her and Elin. "Yer babe has finally turned! It willnae be long now." Leaving them for a moment, Agnes huddled near the fire with Hannah. Kenna listened to their whispers. Agnes was worried they may have to deliver the baby surgically because the babe had not turned, and everyone knew the delivery was risky. Not many survived births such as this, mother or babe, and was the reason she had sent for Hannah so urgently.

Another contraction hit, and Elin gasped in pain, gripping Kenna's hand tightly. She tried to soothe the young woman as Hannah rushed over, wiping Elin's brow.

"'Tis time, lass. Do as Agnes tells ye, and all will be fine." Hannah spoke in a soft voice, trying to soothe Elin's fears. She was glad the older women remained so calm. It was keeping her fears at bay as well, but they were just under the surface. She didn't want to see anything happen to the babe or Elin.

Elin pushed hard for several minutes, but it felt like hours. She wanted to hear the babe cry, knowing that sound would let everyone know all was well. The babe arrived, however, without making a peep, and her heart sank. Something was wrong. She looked down at Elin and offered a soothing smile, wiping away the sweat-soaked hair from her brow.

Agnes had quickly handed the babe to Hannah, and she was by the fire, bent over the child. Seconds felt like hours, and she watched as Hannah stuck a finger down the baby's mouth, pulling out blood and mucus. A loud wail finally broke the tense silence, and a collective outburst of cheering, laughter, and tears of happiness erupted from the ladies in the room. Elin, exhausted from the birth, gathered the baby to her chest as Hannah handed over the wrapped bundle.

"Well done, lassie. You have a strong son." Hannah beamed at Elin and patted her cheek, then moved back to allow the mother time to bond with her newborn.

Opening and closing her hand to stretch her cramped fingers, Kenna beamed at the new mother. Settling Elin back against some pillows, she smoothed her hair and wiped her face one last time before heading outside to allow Elin's family in to see the new babe. Smiling to herself, she walked outside, wiping her hands on her skirts and taking a deep breath of fresh air. She expected it to be nightfall, but to her surprise it was only midday, and she was glad to see Liam still standing around the large fire circle.

"Weel, it's nice to see a smile on yer face." Liam stood from his seat on an overturned barrel to approach her.

"It's a wee lad," she grinned at him. "He's beautiful. And Elin...she is a strong lass! I ken her husband will be verra proud of her." She nodded toward a man who had brought the child outside and was holding it up for the other villagers to see.

"Aye, he would have been," Liam agreed, and she looked at him puzzled.

"Elin's husband, Collin, was a carpenter like her father, James." he said, nodding to the man. "Collin was killed in an accident in the woods several months back." She gasped as Liam continued. "A weak tree he had been chopping fell the wrong way and landed on Collin's back."

"Och, the poor lass." Her heart broke for Elin. She had been through so much! "Did she ken about Collin?" she whispered quietly to Liam.

"What do ye mean?" he asked, looking at her puzzled.

"Weel…" she started slowly. "The bairn. He is one of us. I smelt it instantly, but it didnae come from Elin."

He stood straighter, his brows pulled together as he thought for a moment.

"I'm nay certain if he ever told her. It will be awhile before the babe starts to show any signs, but she will need to be prepared. It shouldnae be a surprise to her though. Collin was verra strong. His body tried to repair itself from the accident verra quickly, but his lungs were already filled with blood. He passed during the night."

She remained quiet as Liam told her of Collin's fate. Her heart broke imagining how Elin must be feeling. They trekked through the snow back toward Fergus' home as villagers started to disperse and things were settling down to normal.

The fire was welcoming, and she hurried over to warm her cold hands and feet. Neither Agnes nor Fergus had returned, but Liam made himself at home. He brought out a loaf of bread, along with some fresh churned butter and cut both himself and Kenna a generous slice. Her stomach let them know just how hungry she was with a loud growl. Gripping her belly, her cheeks reddened, and he laughed out loud.

"I figured ye to be starved by now," he said as he handed her the slice of bread. She took it gratefully, nibbling it slowly. He turned to butter another slice, and she shoved the rest in her mouth just as Hannah walked in the door. She nearly choked on the food trying to gain her composure.

"'Tis all right, dear, I willnae tell him ye need to eat." Hannah patted her on the back and gave her a wink. Hannah sat down at the small table and accepted the slice of bread Liam offered.

"Agnes has asked for us to take Elin and the babe back to the keep. To watch over them. I told her ye would be glad to find a position for Elin. Since Collin passed, she will need help with the babe her mother and father cannae give." Liam nodded his agreement.

"Aye, she will need us as the babe grows into his ability." He paused for a moment, glancing toward Kenna and back to Hannah.

"Does Elin ken? About the babe?" Liam voiced her question to Hannah.

"Aye, the lass told Agnes Collin made certain she ken before they wed. He didnae feel it right to spring it on her after they were married. Much less, after they had a bairn. He wanted her to have the choice. O'course, she didnae think anything about it. She loved him."

Hannah had a wistful look on her face as she spoke, obviously remembering a love of her own. Good, Kenna thought. At least it won't come as a shock to her when the babe starts to show signs of his gift.

"Will they be going today?" Liam wondered aloud causing her eyes to widen. Surely not, she thought to herself. Elin needed to rest. Her mouth gaped open as Hannah answered.

"Aye, 'tis early enough in the day the journey shouldna be too bad. It's a short journey. Fergus'll take us in the wagon to keep the lass and the bairn warm enough." Glancing toward Kenna, she continued. "If it is alright with you, lass, we will need yer horse to help share the burden," Hannah appealed to her sympathetically. Of course she would give up her ride for the young girl, but before she had a chance to answer, Liam interjected.

"Aye, take it. My horse can easily carry us both and whatever we collect from the clan." Confused at his response, she spoke up.

"Are we nay heading back as weel?"

"Nay," Liam laughed. "We came to take care of business, nay deliver wee bairns," he explained. Dismayed, she sighed. She was exhausted. The morning had lasted a lifetime and had taken every ounce of her energy. Now he expected her to finish the day's tasks with him. Before she thought on it too long, Fergus opened the door, and his large frame blocked any light peeking through the clouded sky.

"Wagon's ready. Agnes will need ye ta help load the lass and the babe," he directed to Hannah. Turning to Liam, he pointed to Hannah, taking the blame off himself.

"She told me ta go ahead and ye'd go along with it. I've added extra blankets to yer mount." Then, directing the rest towards Kenna, "Ye should be fine to return to the keep before nightfall, but if ye need a place to stay, yer more than welcome to stay the night here," he said a little gentler. She nodded her thanks as Liam clapped him hard on the shoulder.

"Thank ye, Fergus. We'll get on then." She watched as he kissed Hannah on the cheek, bid them safe travels, and headed outside. Caught up in how quickly everything was happening, she didn't follow right away, and Hannah ushered her to the door.

"Ye best follow him afore he leaves ye. Even if ye wanted ta stay, he wouldnae be too happy about that." Taking Hannah's advice, she picked up her skirts and quickly followed after Liam, who was waiting by the large animal to help her up.

"Should I nay go back to help Hannah? I'm sure I'd be of more use to her than to ye." She sputtered in protest.

"Hannah has things well under control." He hoisted her up and into the saddle before she argued any further.

"Besides," he continued, "I'd like ye to see where ye came from. I doubt ye saw much more than the keep as a child." He was right, she thought. Her mother and father never wanted her to wander too far from the keep, and she did not remember ever seeing the hills beyond its walls. She was grateful for the opportunity to see her lands, even if she had no plans of claiming them.

They rode quietly for a while, and she took in the surrounding countryside. It was beautiful the way the mountains rose behind the forest, their tops hidden by the clouds. The snow had stopped falling for the time, but the air still bit with cold, and Liam wrapped a blanket around her.

"Yer shivering is making my own teeth chatter," he teased her, and she gave an embarrassed giggle, relaxing a little. Pulling her closer, his breath blew hot on her neck. She felt the heat coming from his body as he adjusted in the seat and found herself enjoying the closeness of him, scooting back against him even more. His body reacted to hers and he became hard against her. Instinctively, she moved closer to him, and he quickly adjusted the blankets, forcing one between their bodies.

She was surprised to find herself enjoying the effect she had on him and wondered what other things she may enjoy with him. The thought sent a thrill of excitement through her, and knowing he heard her heart pounding in her chest a rush of heat came to her cheeks. Trying to get the thought out of her mind and steady her racing heart, she fixed her eyes straight ahead.

On the outskirts of the village were a few more homes with larger fields in between. The homes were a welcome sight, and she hoped they would rest and stretch their legs for a while.

As they approached, she heard shouting coming from one of the fields. Two men, who were both claiming rights to one field, were arguing loudly while their wives looked on. Neither man budged on the matter, and now Liam was having to step in. If needed, he would take control of the land, as was his right as Laird.

He dismounted, and she saw both men rushing over to him, each walking quickly to beat the other and eventually breaking into a run to be the first to reach him. She tried not to giggle at the childish behavior. Liam held up his hand to silence their stammering arguments as they both reached him at the same time. Once they were silent, he addressed them calmly but firmly.

"Ye will each have a chance to voice your concerns. In private," he stressed eyeing the men. They were obviously distrusting of each other, and she imagined them both as pouting children as they simultaneously huffed and crossed their arms over their stocky barrel chests.

Stifling a laugh, she dismounted and noticed two women standing at the entrance to one of the homes, shaking their heads at the men. Clearing her throat to get Liam's attention, she placed her hand on his arm and tilted her head toward the women.

"Perhaps we may trouble ye for a drink of water before ye begin yer discussions?" She hoped he caught on to her idea to speak to the women first. Thankfully he did.

"Aye, of course. Gentlemen," he said, turning to the men, "please see to it there is enough firewood to keep Lady Kenna, and yer women as well, warm while we settle this matter?" He took her hand in his arm and escorted her toward the women. Leaning down to whisper to her, his warm breath moved the hairs on the top of her head, sending little shivers over her body.

"That should keep the lads busy fer a while."

Closing her eyes, she tried to focus on the task at hand and not the nearness of his body. The ladies welcomed them into one of the small thatch-roofed homes, and they were greeted with a blast of warm air from the fire. They seated themselves around a small table while one of the women poured their drinks.

Just as she had suspected, once the women were

together, the root of the issue was discovered. The two men were brothers, and the wives explained that one of the brothers had wanted to use the field to introduce a new crop, and the other wanted the field to stay unharvested, allowing the soil to regain its nutrients. Each brother had claimed a right to the field, either by birth or living proximity to the field. Now the snow had come, and nothing had been planted.

Kenna saw the concern on Liam's face. She knew the farmers in the village also fed those in the keep, in exchange for the land and the Laird's protection. The land itself ultimately belonged to Liam as Laird, but for decades upon decades no Laird had enforced it. The land had stayed in the same farming families over time. Once the women had finished their explanation, Liam stood and stretched.

"Kenna, perhaps ye should remain in the warmth of the fire. I shouldna be too long." Leaving her with the women, he stepped out into the cold to settle the matter with the men. When she turned to face the two women, they both stared at her with smiles on their faces. She sensed the speculation about her and Liam in their minds and tried to steer the conversation elsewhere.

"How long have ye been married to the brothers?" she asked, trying to start small talk. They were more interested in her though. Sitting down at the table, both leaned in to begin questioning her. She shrugged off each question until they asked if she was there to marry Liam. Her eyes widened at the question.

"Oh goodness, NO!" she exclaimed. "Yer Laird and his men helped me in the woods." She didn't want to go into the details of her ordeal, but she didn't need to. Gossip spread in the village, and the women had already heard about her and her attacker. They began fawning over her, and even though she tried to dissuade their attentions, she found herself enjoying their company. By the time Liam had returned with the men, the women had told her all about the villagers.

When the men returned, each brother had their arm around the shoulders of the other. Squeezing through the door, they each planted a kiss on the cheeks of the women. Warming his hands by the fire, Liam turned to Kenna.

"We'd best be on our way. The snow has started again and will make it near impossible to get back to the keep after nightfall." Standing, she hugged each of the women and thanked them for their hospitality, promising to come visit again soon. Once they were mounted on the horse, Liam turned in the direction of the keep.

"I thought ye had more business to handle." She knew it would be dark soon, as it was getting late and the clouds now covered the sky.

"Aye, I do, and it will have ta wait fer another time. Night will be here soon, and it isna safe to travel out here at night." A shudder ran down her spine as she remembered what he had said earlier. Other dangers besides wolves lurked in the fields. She instinctively scooted back into him, causing him again to bury the blanket between them.

Chapter Eight

Kenna had been quiet for most of the ride, and the silence was deafening to Liam. He wanted to know what she was thinking about. Her mood had shifted since leaving the village. A sadness seemed to have crept over her, and her shoulders sagged. It surprised him how in tune he had become with her. Anytime she was close, his senses seemed heightened.

"Ye must be exhausted, lass. I ken ye weren't quite expecting all we encountered today." He tried to break the silence, hoping she hadn't fallen asleep in the saddle.

"Aye," she said so quietly he may have missed it if his hearing wasn't stronger than most. "But I enjoyed it verra much. Everyone was so lovely." He smiled at the sincerity in her voice.

"I dare say they feel the same about ye." He was glad the villagers had all taken a liking to her, especially Agnes. Fergus had surely told her of Kenna's past and the suspicions of her mother. Liam wouldn't have blamed her if she had a much different reception, but Agnes had treated her kindly and by the end of the morning was actually very fond of the lass.

"Elin will be happy to see ye when we return. Hannah said ye were a great comfort to her. She was glad ye were there to help."

"Elin is a sweet lass. I ken she will be a verra

74

loving mother. I just wish she didnae have to do it alone." She trailed off, growing quiet again.

"She willnae be alone. We will be there for her and the babe," he responded. Surely Kenna did not think he would leave Elin to raise a child with the wolf trait alone. He would be there for the baby, raising him and teaching him what it meant to have the wolf's blood.

"I'm sure Elin will be grateful to ye. And the wee lad as weel. I didnae have guidance. Even though I ken about the wolves, it was a terrifying time when I started to change. I've only shifted a few times, each time still scares me."

He felt her shudder as she remembered. His heart went out to her, having to go through it without anyone there to help her. Clearing his throat, he changed the subject, hoping to help her escape those memories.

"I'd actually like to speak with ye about Elin, about her role at the keep." he continued.

"With me?" she wondered, obviously confused. "I'm nay sure I can be much help. I've only just met her."

"Weel, I'd like Elin to be your maid. Ye may be with us for a while yet, and ye seem to have taken a liking to each other."

"Liam," she hesitated. Hanging her head, her voice was a whisper. "I cannae stay. I must return to Silas." He pulled hard on the reins, causing the horse to whinny and rear back. Screaming, Kenna grabbed the saddle horn to keep from falling as he jumped down off the horse. He pulled Kenna down to him and grabbed her shoulders.

"Are ye daft, woman? Do ye nay remember how ye came to us? The beating he gave ye?! Ye cannae go back to him!" he yelled at her. She had tears in her eyes as he shook her shoulders.

"I dinnae have a choice," she cried to him. "He has my mother! I left her there all alone to face him. There is nay telling what he has done to her!" She was hysterical. Pulling her to his chest, he stroked her hair trying to calm her.

"Ye did what ye must to survive the…demon." He knew no better word to describe Silas. Anyone capable of his cruelty was surely not of this world. Pushing her away, he looked at her face and wiped her tearstained cheeks.

"Ye willnae go back to him. I willnae allow it."

"I must!" she sobbed. "I ken ye think she poisoned my da, but I promise ye she isnae capable of such a thing. She is kind and loving. She loved him!" She pleaded her mother's innocence.

"I ken she didnae do it. Someone wanted her to be blamed." She was crying and stumbling over her words as she tried to convince him.

"Kenna, I willnae allow ye to go after yer mother. It is too dangerous." Pressing a finger to her lips as she tried to protest, he continued. "I will go for her." Her eyes widened as she looked up at his face.

"Nay! Ye cannae fight him alone!" she insisted.

"I dinnae intend to go alone. My men will join me." He spoke matter of factly, hoping to end the conversation.

"I ken they willnae be agreeable to it but will follow ye anywhere, and I am grateful." She reached up to place a hand on his chest, her cheeks flushed from her tears. Her touch made his stomach flutter, and he wanted to pull her in and kiss her urgently. Fighting the desire, he pushed her away and helped her back onto the horse, climbing up behind her.

"Kenna," he questioned after they had gotten back on the snow-covered road. "Ye said yer mother was left with the McLindon all alone?"

"Hmmm," Kenna muttered in agreement.

"When ye left us as a child, didnae her brother accompany ye? Has he passed on since ye left?" Kenna sighed downheartedly.

"Nay, he is verra much alive. When we arrived, we were all separated. My uncle, Judson, was always seeking the McLindon's approval. I didnae see him much after we arrived. It saddens me to think he is influenced by such a cruel man as Silas."

Suddenly, she turned in the seat to face him, catching him off guard.

"Mayhap he will come back with ye as weel!" she said excitedly.

"I will do my best, lass," he promised, giving her a hopeful smile.

Night was coming quickly, and the snow and wind had picked up. He urged the horse on to reach the keep before they were caught in the weather. As they rode, he couldn't shake his suspicions about her uncle. What drove Silas to allow him in his inner circle? They were outcasts. What did Silas gain from taking them in? He must speak with Hannah when they returned. Surely she remembered the man.

When they arrived at the castle, the snow had turned to ice and was now a frigid, swirling storm. A group of men met them as they came through the gate into the courtyard. He jumped down, helping Kenna unmount. Hannah met them outside and quickly ushered them into the warmth of the keep.

As Hannah led Kenna away, he joined the men in the great hall. He needed a drink and something to eat. He enjoyed spending time with his clansmen and hearing the news of the day, but once he filled his belly, he excused himself to his study. He entered the room and was surprised to see Hannah already waiting on him with a pitcher of ale.

"Ye must have exhausted the poor lass. She barely kept her eyes open while we dressed her in dry clothes." Hannah chuckled as she recounted the events.

"I woke her to eat a bite, but the lass fell asleep as soon as she climbed into the bed. I tucked her in warm and left the tray in case she wakes. I'm sure she will be starving."

Liam smiled at the thought of Kenna's childlike behavior. He knew Hannah saw the weariness on his face as well, and she looked at him sympathetically.

"It's been a long day fer ye, lad. Have ye had yer sup yet?" Ever the mothering type, she made sure he didn't neglect his stomach.

"Aye, thank ye. And it was delicious as usual." He patted his stomach to make sure she knew he was full. Walking around the room, eyeing his possessions scattered on the shelves, Hannah wiped imaginary dust from the shelves.

"What did Kenna think of our land? Seems ye both had quite the day." She was fishing for information, and he saw an opportunity to get a little from her as well.

"Aye, it was eventful fer sure. Hannah, what do ye remember about Kenna's uncle, a man named Judson I believe?" He hoped Hannah may be able to shed some light on the man. He had an uneasy feeling.

"I remember him, aye. But nay too well, to be honest. He wasnae a verra outgoing man, kept to himself. I do remember he wasnae verra loving to his sister. Lady Evelyn doted on the man, and he treated her and the lass like a nuisance. I didna ken why she even bothered bringing him with her when she married Laird Audric..." Hannah trailed off to her own memories. Obviously she remembered more than she thought she did. He kept it to himself. He didn't want to interrupt her thoughts but was getting the notion the man may well be behind the Laird's death. Hannah, deep in her memories of long ago, occasionally smiled or scowled at something in her mind.

"Hmph," she grunted, her lips pursed and her eyebrows pulling together in concentration.

"What is it, Hannah?" He was impatient and hoped it was something telling.

"Maybe nothing, but..." She tried to focus on the specific memory. "I remember a woman he had scorned right afore they were forced out." She got quiet, even behind closed doors, as if she was giving away the woman's secrets. Whispering, she leaned in toward Liam.

"They shared affections." She gave him a wink. "But from what I heard tale, Judson had promised marriage and then spurned her when they left." Hannah put her finger to her lips as if she was giving away a secret. His interest piqued, he prodded her on.

"Do ye remember who the woman was? Is she still here in the keep?" He felt sure if she was still here, she probably still carried some resentment toward the man and may be willing to tell him anything he wanted to know.

"Oh, aye! She's still here. In the village. She never wed after he left, although, ta be honest, she wasnae much ta look at. Her name is Nissa."

"Thank ye, Hannah." He rose and walked over to her, planting a kiss on her chubby cheek. "Ye have given me a lot to think on."

"Why do ye ask about the man? Has he sent word to Lady Kenna?" she asked distrustfully. Liam raised his hand to settle her and shook his head.

"Nay, nay. She said she must return fer her mother. She was upset, saying she had left her mother all alone with the McLindon. When I reminded her of her uncle being there as weel, she mentioned he had become close to Silas." She contemplated what he was saying, her brow wrinkling in concentration.

"It struck me odd that the McLindon was so willing to take in a Cameron outcast, much less allow him to get close." He tapped his fingers on the wooden desk, thinking over the situation.

"I agree, 'tis odd behavior for sure. What are ye going to do about Kenna? Ye cannae let her go back to the man!" Her voice rose in worry.

"O'course I'm nay gonna let her return!" he assured her. "I'm going ta go! Fergus will go with me and some of the others of course. We will fetch her mother and keep them both safe here."

"Ye nay longer think she is here to claim her birthright?" she asked him curiously.

"Nay, but I will have them both here where we can keep an eye on them. At least 'til we get to the bottom of Audric's death. Her uncle had something to do with this. I ken. I feel it in my bones. I must speak to Fergus right away. I want to leave tomorrow evening." She nodded in agreement. He opened the door, setting off to find Fergus.

****

Closing the study door behind Liam, Hannah shuffled hastily to her own room. She wanted to check on something now that he had her thinking about the time of Kenna's banishment. Hannah had taken care of Audric up until a few days before his death. During those last days, only his wife, Lady Evelyn was allowed by his side. Hannah had kept a journal of his illness and hoped she still had it.

Searching through her shelves of books and dried herb bottles, she felt it. A small, leatherbound journal she had hidden behind several bottles. Flipping through it, she found what she had been hoping for, notes she had taken of her suspicions regarding Audric's health. Reading over her scribbling, she found what she was looking for.

Poison. She had suspected it long before Evelyn had taken over the task of feeding him. She had noted his nails changing color, his gums turning white, and even the whites of his eyes being discolored. She knew Liam would want to know this and gathered her journal to go find him.

Liam was seated with Fergus at one of the large tables in the great hall. It was late, and several snoring bodies lay sleeping around the large fireplaces at each end of the room. As she hurried toward the men, she lifted her skirts, trying not to trip over the sleeping bodies. Reaching them at last, she plopped the book in front of Liam, out of breath.

"What's this?" he asked, opening it to the page she had marked. Holding the worn journal up to the light of the fireplace, he only took a minute to read her scribbled handwriting. His mouth gaped open at her findings, and he eyed her questioningly.

"'Tis my notes," she said in a hushed whisper. "I had been feeding and caring for Laird Audric. I had noticed some verra strange symptoms, and when I started to suspect something more was afoot, I jotted down my worries. Then, one day out of the blue, I was nay allowed near him. Only Lady Evelyn was permitted to care for him. Only now does it seem odd *who* my instructions came from. I didna remember until ye mentioned him, but Judson was the one who insisted Evelyn care for Audric." She took a deep breath, gripping at her chest. She collapsed in exhaustion in a seat across from Liam.

"Whew! Feels like a weight has been lifted from my chest!"

Liam and Fergus exchanged a meaningful look. They both knew Liam was right to suspect Judson of having framed Evelyn. Now they needed to get her to the Cameron keep to confirm it. Fergus stood, having already agreed to go with Liam. Clamping a hand on his shoulder, Fergus looked down and told him to get some sleep.

"I'll gather the others, and we will leave tomorrow night."

Hannah stood as well, kissing the top of Liam's head. He was like a son to her and after seeing what Silas had done to Kenna, wolf or no, she was worried for his safety. Patting her hand, he looked at her sweet face, her eyes glistening with tears.

"Dinnae fash over us. We'll be home afore ye ken with Lady Evelyn in tow." She smiled halfheartedly.

"Och, lad, ye ken I will worry always." Patting him on the arm, she left him to make his plans.

****

The next morning, Hannah was bustling around the great hall when Kenna came down to break her fast. She smiled at the lass and nodded her head toward Elin. She watched as the two young women embraced. Both Elin and the babe were doing well, and she knew Liam had made the right choice in assigning Elin to be Kenna's maid.

"Good morn to ye, Lady Kenna. What can I get ye to break yer fast this morning?" She set a plate of sausages, boiled eggs, figs, and dates down on the table.

"Oh thank ye, Hannah! But I am nay too hungry yet. I'll be glad to hold the baby while Elin eats her fill though." She smiled hopefully as Elin handed the plump lad over eagerly.

She spied Liam watching Kenna with the babe. She watched as he smiled at himself and made her way over to him.

"Ye ken, lad, one day, she will make a fine mother." She winked up at him.

"Aye, she will make a good wife and a fine mother." He looked down at her before adding, "For someone in the future. I'm nay looking fer a wife."

A blush came to Kenna's cheeks when she turned to see them both watching her. Liam looked away quickly while Hannah smiled between the two. Of course Kenna had overheard, she thought to herself but knew the two were fighting the inevitable. She patted him on the arm as he headed off to go find Fergus.

Kenna placed a quick kiss on the baby's cheek as she handed him back to his mother. Jumping up, she wound through the crowded hall catching up to Liam just as he was leaving.

"Hello, Kenna. Ye slept well, I take it. I ken yesterday was verra taxing."

"Oh aye, thank ye! I'm feeling better than ever. Liam," she touched his arm gently, stopping him in his tracks.

"May I have a word with ye? In private?" Her voice was low. Unsure of what more she wanted to ask from him, he nodded.

"I was just about to go down to the stable. Care to walk with me?" They walked through the kitchen, each grabbing a hot roll from a basket.

****

Kenna shivered when they stepped outside. She had forgotten her overcoat, and the snow had continued through the night. Large snowbanks had formed outside the doorway. She rubbed her arms to try and keep warm and was thankful when Liam wrapped his plaid around her shoulders.

"I ken ye said ye would free my mother from the McLindon, for which I am truly thankful." She paused, waiting on his reaction.

"Aye, I thought it was already decided. What more is it ye ask?" He sounded as though he growing impatient and unsure how to say it delicately, she blurted out the words.

"And…I want to go with ye!"

Liam, who had turned and started down toward the stable, spun on his heels to face her, but before he said anything, she pushed on.

"I ken I can be of help to ye! Another wolf will give ye even more advantage!" She pleaded with him desperately, but he shook his head in denial.

"Kenna, I ken ye are strong. Nay many men, much less a lass, could have survived what the beast put ye through. But ye have only started to discover yer gifts. It is too dangerous for ye to join us—this time," he stressed. Gently gripping her shoulder, he tilted her chin up to look at him.

"I promise ye, I will deliver yer mother safely to ye. And then, we will get to the bottom of who really killed yer father. If the bastard is still in this keep…" He shook his head. If he did catch them, what he'd do wasn't for Kenna to hear. He didn't want her to think of him the same way she saw Silas, as a monster.

"Dinnae ye fash about this. She will be with ye before tomorrow eve." He meant it. He would do whatever it took to get the woman away from Silas. Turning Kenna back toward the keep, he continued to the stables. He needed to find Fergus and finalize their plans. He couldn't afford for anything to go wrong, and he refused to break his promise to Kenna.

Chapter Nine

Silas shoved the limp body toward Sampson.

"Take care of this," he sneered with disgust. He had hoped the girl would entertain him enough to keep his mind off Kenna's disappearance. She had failed. She didn't even put up a fight. Just pleaded with him to stop. It didn't take long for him to tire of the pleading and, once his lust had been satisfied, had no use for the pathetic girl.

He held the lass gently, glaring at Silas' back as he strode away. Rearranging the girl's body in his arms, he mistakenly allowed himself a look at her face. She was young, too innocent for what she had endured. He didn't recognize her face and assumed she was new to the keep, probably looking for servants' work. Silas had a reputation for taking in any young lass looking for work. Unfortunately, none usually survived to discourage others from the job.

He laid her still warm body gently into a plaid, wrapping it around her. Placing his hand over her eyes, he forced them closed and folded the plaid to cover her face. He was growing tired of disposing of Silas' cast-offs. The lack of value Silas had for human life was exhausting to him. The people Silas killed had families who cared for them, he thought to himself. They never had the chance to say goodbye.

Laying her body across the back of his horse, he

mounted and swiftly rode out of the castle grounds, the girl's long hair falling out of the plaid and trailing behind. He carried her to the same place he always took them. His own private mausoleum. No one knew the countless number of bodies he had buried there. With each one, he offered as much dignity and respect as possible in the secret burial.

He dismounted and removed the stone from the small opening in the side of the hill. A deep cave had formed thousands of years ago, making the perfect area for what he needed. Placing the body in the cave, he offered a quick blessing for her soul and slid the rock in place, once again concealing the cave's dark secrets.

Heading back toward the McLindon keep, he fought to forget the grisly task he was awarded. It was no use. He truly feared there was no humanity left in Silas, and he worried for the McLindon clan. They were being led by a violent, uncontrollable madman. Nothing stopped his obsession with Kenna and the power he sought. The castle gates were in his sight, and he dreaded entering through them. He longed for a peaceful life and tried to imagine it, surprised when he pictured Evelyn with him.

Unfortunately, that was not in his cards, he thought as he saw Silas was waiting on his return. As soon as he was through the gates, a stable hand took his horse and Silas, spinning on his heels and heading inside the castle, did not wait for him to follow. He trudged behind as Silas led him to his private study.

Inside, Silas took a seat behind a thick wooden desk, staring into space. Studying Silas, he doubted the man even remembered the lass he'd just buried or what the monster had done to her, and the thought chilled him to the bone.

Unable to sit still for long, Silas didn't seem to notice Sampson's distance toward him as he stood and paced the room, tapping his fingers on each piece of furniture he passed. Speaking matter of factly, Silas showed no remorse for his actions.

"Kenna will be wanting to see her mother."

He wondered if the man really had lost his mind. He spoke as if Kenna were still at the keep. Trying to bring the man back to reality, he countered.

"I'm nay sure the lass survived. The scene we came upon was quite gruesome."

"She survived, I'm certain of it." Silas had come to stand beside him, cornering him in the room.

"She's a verra fast healer, ye ken." He winked at him, hinting at Kenna's wolf blood and once again giving him an uneasy feeling.

"If she sought the Camerons, and I'm certain she did, she will use them to retrieve her mother as well. She is their Alpha, after all," Silas said with certainty.

"Ye think she will force them to come for Evie? If Evie returns with the Camerons, they may kill her." His heart sank as he thought about her leaving. He had come to care for the woman but was shocked as he began to realize the depth of his feelings for her.

"Aye, of course the lass will be wanting her mother to join her. It doesnae matter if they banished her. Being the Alpha heir, Kenna controls the whole Cameron clan." Silas' tone was filled with hatred and jealousy.

"They can do what they want with her mother. Dinnae fash, she is naught to us. Kenna is the key. We must get her back." He knew Silas was forming a plan in his mind. Afraid he planned to use Evie as bait, he found himself hoping Silas was wrong and Kenna had not survived his attack.

Another thought entered his mind as he thought about defending Evelyn. He was confident in his battle skills, but if Silas was right, fighting a pack of wolves was not something he was prepared to do. He knew, however, that he must fight to protect Evie. The Camerons had banished her, and it seemed he now had to protect her from Silas as well, who intended give her up to them without a care.

"Mayhap we should attack first," he offered. "We will go retrieve the lass. She is yer betrothed, after all. I will bring her back to ye."

"Nay." Silas shook his head dismissing the idea. "If she has taken over as Alpha, ye will never be able to separate her from her clan. They will have nay choice but to protect her. She must come to us on her own and knowing her mother is here, alone, is all the invitation she needs. She will return, and then she will be back where she belongs."

Pausing, Silas turned to examine him. The scrutiny made him uncomfortable and finally, after several minutes, Silas spoke again.

"Ye've grown fond of the woman. Of Evelyn. Have ye?"

He was taken aback by Silas' words. He had hoped to hide his affection, knowing it could only be used against him.

"Aye, she is kind and gentle." He saw the smirk on Silas' face as he spoke. "But...she is weak. I see no reason to involve her in our plans." He tried to persuade the man to forget Evie, but Silas' eyes lit up in excitement.

"Precisely! Kenna will want to protect her and will return, whether alone or with the Camerons, and we will be ready for a fight. We must not allow her to leave again." Locking eyes with him, Silas clamped a hand on his shoulder. He stiffened. He tried not to think about what those hands had done to the girl he had just buried. Giving Silas a quick nod of understanding, he hoped the man was satisfied to end the conversation.

Silas strode over to his desk and poured two cups of ale. He pretended to sip the ale, his trust in Silas long gone. He knew Silas had been the mastermind behind Audric's death. Silas liked to dabble in poison and experimented on innocents. He was certain he had given Judson poison for Audric. The man was too stupid to have thought of it himself. Or to have known what to give the Laird to go undetected. Silas also knew of his own affection for Evie, and he needed to be more guarded.

"Nothing will interfere with my plans. I will claim the Cameron lands and have control of their clan. Their wolf blood mixed with our strength will make me unstoppable." Silas' eyes glazed over as he spoke, seemingly drunk on the power he sought. Sampson knew that controlling both the McLindon and Cameron clans, Silas would be one of the most powerful Lairds in the country and invincible to overthrow.

He left Silas' study with a sense of dread. He did not have trust in Silas but had no choice but to go along with his wishes. He trusted the Cameron clan to accept Kenna back in, she had done nothing to deserve banishment, however, he prayed for Evie's safety. Was it possible for Kenna to demand they let Evie back in?

Did Evie know about the wolves?

If the tales he heard were true, they offered her more protection than he ever provided. Even if she wasn't accepted back into the clan, he thought, she had a better chance of surviving on her own than staying here with Silas. If Kenna refused to produce the Cameron lands for Silas, he was sure to kill both her and her mother anyway.

****

Silas sat thrumming his fingers on the desk, lips pursed in concentration. Judson slipped into the small office, closing the door quietly behind him. Judson's constant presence was a nuisance he endured, but hopefully not for much longer. Once he wed Kenna, he planned to get rid of the man. Until then, though, he must tolerate the coward. And his sister. Shuffling over to his desk, Judson wrung his hands nervously, stammering over his words.

"I…I have g…gotten word from a Ca…Ca…Cameron about K…K…Kenna." Leaning forward, now eager to hear what he had to say, he motioned for Judson to have a seat.

"Oh really? I wasnae aware ye still had any contacts there." He looked at Judson intently. He knew Judson had been keeping information from him. Judson shook with nerves as he looked down at his hands.

"Weel, it isnae one I'm verra proud of. The kitchen maid, Nissa. She and I, weel, we were…" Judson hesitated, and he held up his hand to stop the explanation. He certainly didn't want to hear the disgusting details of their intimacy.

"What did the hag say? Did Kenna return to them?" He was growing impatient.

"Aye, she di...did, sssssir. She returned and wa...wa...was on death's door, she said." Judson's eyes lit up as he delivered the news, clearly hoping he earned Silas' favor for the information.

"But the old nurse, Hannah, helped he...heal her, and now she is acting like the lady of the ma...ma...manor." Judson's tone had grown more confident and turned into disgust, laced with jealousy. He knew jealousy is what had driven Judson to kill his brother-in-law and now helped him force Kenna back.

"Has she mentioned her mother?" he pressured Judson for more information.

"Nay. A...a...at least n...n...nay to any of the maids. Nissa did s...s...say that the Cameron Laird and his ma...ma...man, Fergus were p...p...planning something. They have been prepa...pa...paring fer a journey." Sweat beads formed on the old man's forehead. Sitting back in his chair, he thought on the matter. He was certain the Camerons were coming for Evelyn. Or him.

"I want ye to get close to this woman again. I need to ken Kenna's position in their clan." Judson shuddered at the thought, and Silas didn't miss his unease. Smirking, he teased the man further, wanting to see just how uncomfortable the old woman made Judson.

"Ye dinnae mind being close ta the woman, de ye? I ken ye weren't a braw man, but I didnae take ye fer a sissy." Standing straighter, he cleared his throat before speaking.

"I've n...n...never shied away fr...fr..from the comforts of a woman. I'll be more than ha...happy ta see what else she ha..has ta say." Judson failed to sound convincing, and he chuckled as the old man backed out of his study, closing the door behind him.

****

Evelyn knew something had happened to upset Silas. He had been marching about the keep for the last few days with even more of a scowl, and additional guards had been placed outside her chamber door. The castle, however, was inexplicably quiet, and she had heard none of the usual whispers of gossip from the servants. As she prepared herself for the evening meal, she knew she would be seated by Silas. She would make it a point to ask about her daughter's presence.

Kenna had not been at the supper the past several nights, and she missed her daughter's company. The evening meal was the only time during the day they were allowed to speak to each other. She knew Silas kept Kenna busy during the day, grooming her to be the next Lady McLindon. He had told her Kenna filled her day taking music lessons and learning how to manage the home and the servants. She hoped Kenna found happiness in these duties and longed to teach her what she knew as well. Silas never allowed it though. He wanted her to learn only from the women who knew the McLindon ways, or so she was told.

They were outsiders, after all, and she was thankful to Silas for inviting them in and preparing to make them part of his clan. Silas was a handsome man, tall with broad shoulders and a rugged, square jawline. He didn't have the kindness in his face like his man, Sampson. He was rugged too, but she thought his face softer and more appealing. Still, though, she didn't understand why the other women in the keep and surrounding village kept their distance, other than to be respectful of

Kenna's betrothal to him.

She was grateful to her brother, Judson, for arranging the alliance between Kenna and Silas, but she sensed the dislike Kenna had for the man each time they were near. She prayed her daughter opened her heart to him. She felt certain once Kenna and Silas were married Kenna may bring a smile to the man's constant scowl.

A knock on the door brought her out of her thoughts, and she opened the door. Expecting Sampson, who escorted her down to meal every evening, she was disappointed when one of the guards, who hadn't taken the time to introduce himself, stood rigid on the other side. Greeting him sweetly, she was awarded with a grunt in return as he turned stiffly and led her down the dark halls.

When they entered the large room, Silas was seated at the center of the long table which ran the back length of the room. The table was positioned to look out over the rest of the room. Silas' head was bent in conversation with Sampson, seated to his right. Looking up as she entered the room, Sampson offered her a warm smile, which she returned, a slight blush coming to her cheeks.

She liked Sampson and was always happy to see him. He had been kind and welcoming to her and Kenna when they first arrived, and she felt a kinship to the man. Her brother, Judson, however, was a different story. The hate was evident on Sampson's face anytime Judson was near. And unfortunately, Judson kept very close to Silas. In fact, she noticed, Judson was seated to Silas' left, where she was usually seated.

She made her way over to the table and Judson,

eyeing her critically, looked away, not giving her a second thought. She stopped beside him, unsure of where to sit. One of the kitchen maids took notice of the situation and quickly pulled out a chair beside Judson for her. Once seated, the maid brought her a cup of wine. The wine was sweet and delicious, but she wanted to be careful not to drink too much.

It always seemed to make her drowsy, and she did not want to miss any of the conversation going on around her. She wanted to be sure she did not feel the wine's influence too much tonight as she wanted to ask Silas where her daughter had been. If she had been ill, she needed to tend to her. And if she had begun her change, well, she would do her best to explain it to her as well. Silas would need to know the truth before he married her. It was quite a shock when she found out from Audric.

Silas' eyes were on her as she ate her meal. Looking up at him, he smiled slyly at her. He raised his own cup in a toast, encouraging the maids to pour her more wine. Her cheeks were flushed, and the heat spread down her neck and onto her chest. Surely, the one glass of wine had not affected her so strongly.

Everyone had finished eating, and she heard the entertainment begin, or so she thought. She heard the men's raucous laughter and women squealing, but the room started to spin, and she was feeling quite tired. The young maid began to pour her another cup of wine, and she tried to place her hand on the cup to signal to the lass she did not care for more. Before it could be stopped, the girl had poured the wine onto her hand, making a mess along the table.

Standing quickly, she intended to help the lass

clean it up, but the room spun around her, and she felt herself falling. Large arms caught her before she hit the stone floor. She was sure it had been Sampson who had broken her fall and looked up to see his handsome face close to hers. She smiled up at him and relaxed into his arms, allowing her eyes to close.

Picking her up gently, Sampson carried her out of the dining hall. Opening her eyes with a quick gasp, she remembered she had wanted to speak to Silas about something. She glanced back over Sampson's large shoulder. The young maid was trying to clean the spill, but Silas grabbed her arm, pulling the girl away with him. She had a fleeting thought she should be concerned but did not understand why. Ignoring the feeling, she laid her head on Sampson's shoulder and closed her eyes again. She'd remember tomorrow what it was she needed to speak to Silas about. It must not have been that important.

Chapter Ten

Evelyn woke from what seemed like an eternity of sleep. Her eyes felt heavy, and her head ached from the lingering effects of the wine. She opened her eyes to a darkened room. The heavy drapes had been pulled shut to block out any light, and she was unsure what time it was.

Moaning, she rolled to her side and tried to sit up on the side of the bed. The room spun around her, and she held onto one of the footposts to steady herself. When the spinning had stopped, she opened her eyes, daring to look around the room and quickly came to her senses. This was not her room! Where had she fallen asleep? How had she gotten here?

She didn't remember any details after supper last night. She tried to remember, but nothing came to her. It was like she had blacked out the entire evening. She knew she had gone to supper with the intention of asking Silas something. Had she asked? Had she gotten the answer she was looking for? What was the question she had wanted to ask?

Her head throbbed and massaging her temples she stood slowly and walked to the window. She pulled back the heavy drapes, but instead of light flooding in like normal, the only view she had was another castle wall. The darkness was daunting, and she realized she had been moved into an interior chamber in the keep.

The room was much larger than her own bedchamber, however it was sparsely decorated. The only furniture in the room was the bed and a small table and a single chair near the fireplace. She had never seen this room, but she imagined there was a good deal to the castle she had never seen. She was only allowed access to certain areas for her safety, she had been told.

Her clothes had been laid over the chair, and she looked down to see she was only wearing a thin nightdress. Hugging herself, she wondered who had undressed her and shivered at the thought. There weren't many she trusted in the keep.

Poking the embers in the fireplace to stir the dwindling flame to life, she hoped to bring some warmth into the cold space. Climbing back into bed, she pulled the covers over her as a knock on the door made her groan again as her head pounded in sync. The door opened, and her half-brother shuffled into the room.

"Weel, my dear sister, I'm glad to see ye are awake. I wasnae certain we would be seeing ye this day. How are ye feeling? Hopefully better than ye look, woman!"

Judson seated himself at the table beside her bed and patted her hand in a loving gesture. The gesture didn't reach his eyes though, and she suspected he was not there on his own accord. He rarely acknowledged her around the keep, much less came to visit her in her chamber. She eyed him suspiciously.

"How long have I been asleep? I dinnae remember changing." She motioned to her dress lying on the chair.

"Oh, it hasnae been more than a day. Dinnae fash

over it, dear." He dismissed her, but she continued to question him.

"Why am I nay in my own chamber? Who brought me here?" Her voice was becoming louder in a panic, and he silenced her by putting a finger over her lips.

"Evie, I can explain everything. 'Tis for yer own good. Sampson, o'course, helped bring ye in this room after sup last eve. Ye had too much wine. Again," he added, hanging his head in embarrassment. She didn't remember having that much, but then again, she didn't remember much from the night before.

"Silas requested ye be brought to this room. For yer protection."

"Protection?" She looked at him quizzically. "How is this chamber any safer than my own?"

"Silas didnae want to alarm ye, but unfortunately, Kenna is…" He paused for a long moment.

"Is what?" she insisted in a high-pitched tone.

"Gone. She is gone, dear." The drugs Silas had been slipping in her wine kept her subdued and oblivious. Looking at him with large eyes, she forgot about her headache and sat up straight, trying to clear her mind. She wanted to focus on what Judson was saying, but her mind still seemed fuzzy.

"Gone?" she repeated, hoping she had heard him wrong. She couldn't bring herself to think of Kenna as dead. Her gut told her otherwise.

"What do ye mean she is 'gone'? She isnae dead?"

"Nay, nay. At least," Judson paused. "We dinnae think so. She has been taken prisoner." Judson watched her intently before continuing.

"She was taken by the Camerons. They came fer her, Evie. To make her pay fer Audric's death." Judson hung his head and spoke quietly. Guilt overcame her, and she looked down at her hands.

"She was just a wee bairn when Audric died! She didnae have anything to do with it! They came fer her and nay fer me?! I must go to her!" Her voice rose in her urgency.

"Unfortunately, dear sister, Silas fears they will come fer ye as weel. He is beside himself with worry over Kenna's safety, and of course yers also. He wants nay more than to have his betrothed safely back in his arms." Judson gripped her hand. His actions seemed sincere, but his voice did not. She heard the contempt in his voice, and she was unsure why.

Her eyes started to fill with tears. Her daughter was the most important thing in her life, all she had left from her husband and a life she had loved. She must not let the clan who banished them take revenge on an innocent child.

"Silas believes they plan to put Kenna to death fer Audric's murder. It will ensure his bloodline is wiped out and nay heir will try to reclaim the clan." His words made her gasp with shock at the idea.

"Nay! They willnae! She is innocent!" She gasped as her panic built.

"Without being wed, Silas cannae offer her his protection. She is still a Cameron and they can, and will, do what they want to the lass. Once she is returned to him, Silas has vowed to wed her immediately. Then we will all have the protection of the McLindons."

She nodded in understanding and reached out to grip his hands in hers but noticed he pulled away from her. Confused, she brushed it aside to plead with him. The shock of Kenna's absence was wearing off, and she began to form her own plans. She had to do anything to save her daughter. Even if it meant sacrificing herself to the Camerons, the clan to whom she had pledged her loyalty and her heart years ago.

"We must get her back. I will go. I will offer myself in her place. After all, it's me they want to punish. They wanted me put to death before. Only old Hannah was able to talk them out of it."

"Nay, sister. Ye cannae risk yer own life, although the McLindon is certain they will come fer ye as weel. 'Tis the reason fer this chamber. Fer yer protection. However," he paused as he seemed to rethink his plan. "If they do manage to breach the guards, ye are our only way to ken if Kenna is still alive. Aye, ye must go with them. Allow them to take ye, and together, escape back to us." Judson went to the window and opened the drapes more.

"We will all fight, Evie, to keep ye safe. But if the Cameron is too strong, Silas cannae afford fer the McLindon people to suffer." Her shoulders sagged in disappointment at his words.

"I wouldnae want them to suffer either. Dinnae fight to protect me. His people come first. I will bring Kenna back to him, where she is safe." She was convinced Silas was a caring and fair Laird.

"Get some rest, my dear. Ye will need yer strength in the coming days." Patting her hand, he tucked her into the bed like a child and slipped quietly from her chamber.

****

Kenna had been gone more than a week, and Judson knew Silas was getting anxious for her return. He smiled to himself, proud of the convincing role he had played of the distraught uncle and caring brother. Silas would surely see him favorably after his performance. He had convinced Evelyn to return Kenna to Silas. She even thought it was her idea! Now, he must conquer the next task he had been given.

He had sent word to Nissa of his affections for her. He dreaded this of course, but it was necessary to Silas' plan. They had exchanged love letters and made plans to meet in the forest between the McLindon and Cameron territories. He made sure the meeting place was on McLindon land, though. If anyone was going to be killed over this tryst, he wanted to make sure it was Nissa and not him. He'd better start drinking now, he thought, if he was going to be able to get through making love to her again.

The woods were freezing, and his teeth chattered as he waited under the tall, icy trees. His need to be useful to Silas overpowered his hesitation, and now he found himself in the middle of the night in a dark forest waiting on the one person he hoped to never see again. The one person left in the Cameron clan who knew his part in Audric's death.

A loud rustling in the trees behind him made him jump, but he knew right away it was Nissa. Any animal would have been much quieter. He turned to see the large woman struggling to get through the branches, her layers of clothing getting snagged on one as she freed herself from another.

As she plodded toward him, he didn't think it was possible, but the woman seemed to have gotten uglier. Her hair was thin and grayer than the brown it had been when he last saw her. Her wide, round face broke into a smile when she spotted him, revealing just how few teeth were left in her mouth. This was going to take more effort than he thought.

She opened her arms wide and did her best to run through the thick snow toward him. He forced a smile and welcomed her into his arms. She was breathing heavily and smelled of rotten teeth and unbathed body. Pulling her away from him, he hoped his smile wasn't the grimace he felt in his mind.

"Nissa, dear, ye are still the bonnie lass I remember!" The blush on her cheeks deepened, and she gave him another toothless grin.

"Och, Jud," she said, using her pet name for him. "Ye flatter an old maid! 'Tis good ta see yer handsome face after all these years." She held his hands and pulled herself closer to him for a kiss. Trying to mask his disgust, he obliged her with a peck on her cheek, but she wanted more, nuzzling her face against his. He wasn't sure if the hairs he felt were from his own scruff or the long ones that stuck out from the moles on her cheeks and chin.

Breaking free from her grasp, he turned and pointed to an area he had set up for their rendezvous. He had piled branches of soft evergreens to form a bed and spread blankets over them for comfort. He had brought along a satchel of breads and cheeses and a canteen of wine. He hoped the wine made her pass out or at least helped him get through the terrible deed. Either way, he was sure he hadn't brought enough.

Nissa squealed in delight when she saw the bed he had made for them. She quickly made herself comfortable and patted the area beside her for him to join her. He laughed nervously and brought out the wine, taking a large swig for himself before offering it to her. She eagerly took the canteen and chugged several large gulps before wiping her mouth with the back of her hand and letting out a large, unladylike belch.

"I've missed ye, Jud." She whispered loudly to him as he sat beside her. Best to get it over as quickly as possible, he thought. Nissa rubbed her large bosom against his arm, stroking the side of his face with her chubby hand.

"I've missed yer touch," she continued, taking his hand and placing it on one of her breasts.

"I...I...I've m...m...missed y...ye too," he stammered as his nerves began to take over and she moved his hand over her breast, encouraging him to fondle her.

Much to his dismay, he found himself becoming aroused as she ran her hand up his thigh and grabbed him through his pants. She began to massage him teasingly, and soon he was stripping off his own pants to allow her access.

He was both disgusted and proud of his response to her advances. Her hand stroked him up and down. Reluctantly, he admitted to himself he enjoyed her petting. She was skilled at pleasuring men, even though not many men wanted her touch.

Suddenly, she pushed him onto his back.

"I'm ready fer ye," her husky voice told him selfishly. He cringed inwardly but let her ease onto him.

Nissa rode him hard, making sounds he'd only heard animals make. Closing his eyes, he let his imagination take him to someone else, and it wasn't long before he yelled out in his release. Nissa, sweating and panting, giggled and collapsed beside him, taking another swig of the wine.

"'Tis been awhile, huh, Jud? Dinnae fash, twill come back ta ye soon." She teased him, massaging his limp manhood and nuzzling her head into his neck. "I've missed ye so," she continued. "'Tis been so lonely without ye."

Offering her more wine, he put his arm around her, pulling her close. This was his chance to get her talking about the Camerons and Kenna.

"Aye, Nissa, I've missed yer company as weel. Ye always did ken how ta please me." He took a drink of the wine himself, hoping to drown the memories of their intercourse. Sitting up, she eyed him devotedly.

"I'll come stay with ye, Jud. I'll come to the McLindons if ye want me ta!" She was serious! She was resolved to give up her place at the Camerons to be with him.

"Nay, Nissa dear. Ye must stay. The McLindon Laird….Weel, he would seek yer talents as weel." Judson squeezed her breast to make his point, and she moaned against him, hoping for another round. "He isnae a gentle man. Ye need ta stay. Fer yer safety," he stressed.

She nodded in agreement.

"Aye, I ken the rumors, and I saw what he done ta yer niece…" She trailed off, shaking her head. This was the opening Judson hoped for. Nissa had seen Kenna, she had returned to them.

"Ye've seen her?" Judson asked, his voice full of fabricated hope. "I was afraid she was dead!"

"Nay, she isna dead! She is alive and weel." Nissa laid her head on his shoulder, hoping to comfort him with her news.

"Although," she added snidely, "she is acting like she is the lady of the keep." The jealousy in Nissa's tone was evident, but he had heard what he needed to hear. Kenna must have used her Alpha gift to take over the clan.

"'Tis a relief she is weel, though. I can ease her mother's fears.'

Nissa looked up at him, placing her hand on his cheek.

"Ye are a kind man, Judson. 'Tis lucky I am ta have found ye!" Before he knew what was happening, she was kissing him deeply and fondling him. Against his will, his body responded, and she pulled him down on top of her, eager to go again.

Chapter Eleven

The horses stamped their hooves, and the steam from their noses was visible in the night air. Liam hoped using the darkness of night helped hide them as they breached the McLindon keep. He wasn't worried about failure—he was confident of their success. His concern was only for Lady Evelyn's safety. He had promised Kenna to return with her mother, unharmed. He didn't want to break this promise, but Silas was an unpredictable man. Liam feared he may have already hurt or killed Evelyn to spite Kenna.

The group of men Fergus had assembled were standing with the horses waiting on him. He approached slowly, looking at each of the men and realizing not one of them was wolf. Looking quizzically at Fergus and then around at the men.

"This is the group ye've gathered?" he asked, skeptical.

"Aye, and then some." Fergus assured him all was well. Taking his man's word for it, he mounted his horse to lead the men out of the gates. Taking one last glance around, he noticed a strawberry-blond lad seated on a horse, hiding near the back of the group. Sighing downheartedly, he watched as the boy tried to control the beast. He tossed his reins to Fergus, dismounted, and walked back to the boy.

"Niall, what are ye doing here?" He took the reins

from the boy's hands to steady the beast. "Ye cannae go with us. Yer mother willnae forgive me if something happened to ye."

He tried to be gentle with the lad. He was only sixteen, and the boy's father was his cousin. He had died of pneumonia a few winters past, and he had since looked after the lad as he'd promised. He'd be damned if he was going to let the boy get himself killed on this errand.

"Dinnae send me away! I can do this! I can be of help to ye!" The boy pleaded with him.

"Please, Laird," he whispered, using his formal title in hopes he saw him as a capable young man instead of his cousin. Liam was silent for a while, thinking over the situation. He didn't expect the boy to be in too much danger if he did go, but accidents happened, and Niall used the silence to his advantage.

"I want to make my father proud. He'd want me to go. He'd expect me to be here with ye. With him if he were still alive." Niall hung his head in sadness. "Ye ken he would," he added quietly.

Sighing, Liam looked hard at Niall. The boy was right.

"Ye will do EXACTLY as ye are told. At all times. Do ye hear?" Niall nodded, and reluctantly he agreed to let him go. Knowing Niall was not a wolf, his commands as Alpha had no power on Niall. However, he was still his chief, cousin or not. Niall had no choice but to obey his Laird or face punishment and humiliation when they returned.

He rejoined Fergus in front of the men, and Fergus tried to hide his grin as they left the keep. Plodding through the thick snow, he looked back to see Niall had finally gotten his horse under control and was keeping up with the group.

"The lad will be just fine. Let him be," Fergus insisted, reassuring him he had made the right decision in letting the boy tag along. The full moon reflected against the snow and lit the way as they crossed small hills and valleys, eventually coming to the edge of the thick forest. The forest was a barrier between the McLindon and Cameron lands, and when they emerged on the other side they needed to be ready for anything. As they entered the forest, rustling came from around all sides as gigantic wolves came from the trees. He smiled to himself as he thought about Fergus sending them ahead to scout. Fergus truly was a battle-minded and trustworthy friend. He was glad to have him by his side.

The wolves joined the pack of men, trotting alongside the horses, their backs as high as the stirrups. He recognized each one as he looked around. Some were childhood friends, others a little older. There was a blacksmith, a few farmers, and even the village clergy among them. He said a silent prayer that these men all came back unharmed.

The moonlight didn't penetrate the trees, and the darkness enveloped the pack as they went deeper into the woods. Finally, the group came to the outer edge of the forest. Clouds had moved over the moon, and snow had once again started to fall. The air bit at their faces, but the anticipation of what was to come heated their blood.

Ahead of the men, the large span of open, snow-covered ground offered no protection. He was grateful for the clouds as it gave them the needed disguise to cross the McLindon lands. Looking up at the sky, Fergus pulled his mount up beside him.

"Let's hope the clouds hold. Moving through this"—Fergus nodded at the snow—"willnae be fast going."

He looked down to two of the wolves, a barrel shaped brindle wolf and a taller, slimmer black wolf. James and Thomas, the two were friends from childhood. They had all gone through the shift together, and he trusted them with his life. They moved ahead of the group, scouting for any signs of trouble. The men unmounted, leaving the horses hidden in the forest, they had no need for them in the keep.

After a while, a howl from James and Thomas echoed through the night signaling all was clear. The men slowly left the safety of the trees and moved silently and stealthily across the open space. The journey was long as they moved through the thick snow, but they made it without incident, and he breathed a sigh of relief when they finally reached the other side of the clearing.

Unfortunately, he thought, going back would be even worse. The snow was turning to ice and coming down even heavier. And if he were being realistic, he thought, they may be returning with injuries or worse.

The McLindon keep was in sight, and it was an imposing force but did not have the comfort and warmth which emanated from the Cameron keep. This was a fortress, cold and unfeeling. He hoped finding Evelyn proved not to be too difficult. Not one of the group had ever been inside the McLindon castle, and no one knew what they should expect.

The land around the keep had changed slightly to a

more traveled ground, and the snow had a hard time sticking to the muddy, wet dirt. Sparse trees scattered the land and using these as cover, the group formulated a plan. Splitting into two groups, Fergus leading one and he leading the other.

He made sure to send Niall with Fergus. He trusted Fergus to keep an eye on him. He also knew he must not let himself be distracted by his own feelings toward the boy. Not being wolf, Niall's sense of sight and smell was much dimmer than his own. He was not able to anticipate danger as easily. For this reason, he sent Niall with his own sword, taking the small dagger the boy had brought for himself.

He led his men around the left side of the keep. Outside the walls, ivy grew covering the stone. There were no guards walking the parapets and no one at the gate. It was eerily quiet and seemed like an open invitation, too easy, and had him on high alert. They needed to find Evelyn fast and get out as quickly as possible.

Hidden among the overgrown ivy, a small wooden door led through the outer wall of the keep. It had rusted off the hinges and was hanging loosely. Pushing it open was easy, however it made a loud creaking sound, and he cringed, hoping the keep was truly as empty as it felt and no one heard it. His group included three men and two wolves. He could shift if need be, but finding Evelyn was his priority, and he must be able to communicate with her.

The group slipped silently into the courtyard, creeping along the left side of the outer stone wall. He spied the other group doing the same along the right. Still not one soul had been seen from the McLindon clan. The courtyard was dark and quiet. The ground was thick mud, and empty livestock pens lined one side. The smell of manure was overwhelming, and he knew his men would be eager to be done with this task.

Suddenly, a door burst open, spilling light into the courtyard, and the two groups quickly backed against the walls into the shadows. A drunken man stumbled into the middle of the grounds, belching loudly before dropping his britches and pissing in the middle of the grounds. Struggling to retie his pants, the man stumbled, falling into the cold mud and passing out in the frigid night air.

Through the open doors, the groups heard raucous laughing and jeering, along with crashing and banging. Motioning for the others to stay put, he slowly crept through the courtyard and slipped undetected inside.

The scene in the hall turned his stomach. Bodies lay all over the floor, passed out in their own vomit. Men were fighting amongst themselves, turning over benches and smashing each other into tables. Wailing and screaming came from women as men forced themselves upon them. Those who escaped one man only found themselves being attacked by another. It was vile and heartbreaking to think Kenna had been exposed to this life, and the scene only intensified his desire to find Evelyn quickly and get her out of there.

He returned to his men. The two groups had become one again.

"We must nay waste time finding Lady Evelyn. It shouldnae be too hard." He looked around, reassuring the men. "Everyone seems ta be drunk or passed out." He tapped Fergus on the chest.

"Ye stay with the men downstairs. I'll go up and

see if I cannae find her. The wolves can stay out here in the yard and keep guard. I dinnae think we will need too much manpower tonight." He shook his head at the pandemonium happening in the hall. The behavior would never be tolerated in his keep. Realizing there had been no Laird in the hall, he wondered where Silas was hiding. He had been so distracted by the chaos and was suddenly on high alert. It may have been a trap.

"Be on alert." Voicing his fears to Fergus, he confided, "I dinnae see the McLindon, and it was too easy for us to enter." Fergus agreed.

"Aye, something is amiss. Watch yer back."

"Aye. And ye as weel. Dinnae let the lad out of yer sight," Liam continued, motioning toward Niall, and the boy's cheeks reddened in embarrassment and frustration. He knew the boy wanted to prove himself. However, doing what his Laird commanded and being careful was a better example than any bold move. He wanted obedience, not bravery, a fact Niall needed to remember.

He waited until the men had surrounded the courtyard, hidden in the shadows. Then he made his way into the great hall, trying to blend in with the drunken mess. Picking up a cup and stumbling around, he pretended to slur his words and bumped into other drunken bodies. A narrow stairwell was in the far corner of the hall, and he worked his way around the room and slipped up the stairs seemingly unnoticed.

The stairwell wound to the second floor and onto a walkway that was open to the great hall below. He saw where holes in the handrail had not been repaired and wondered how many men had been pushed through during a drunken brawl. Several doors lined the walkway on the other side. Hesitating, he hid behind a wooden beam in the wall.

The walk was straight, only turning at the very end. It offered nowhere to hide. Taking his chances, he stepped out into the open. He stopped at each door, using his keen hearing to listen for whatever was behind the door. He had made it to the third door when he saw a man turn onto the walk heading toward him. With his head bent, he headed straight for Liam, looking at the floor as he walked.

Deciding to meet the man head on and hopefully avoid suspicion, Liam stumbled toward the man, bumping into him. Slurring his words, he gripped the man's shoulders, apologizing, pretending to be drunk and looking for his room. The man looked up at him, and catching himself, he swallowed a gasp of recognition. He would know the face anywhere. He was face to face with Kenna's uncle. Judson, using his pause to his own advantage, pushed him away and turned, running back down the hall.

Liam chased after the man as he turned left, down another dark hall lined with closed doors. Was he leading him into a trap? The hall led to a dead end, and the man turned, scoffing at him.

"Yer wasting yer time," the man spat angrily. "Ye will nay find what yer lookin' fer." It was all he did to keep from beating the man senseless. Something in his gut told him the man was pure evil.

"Who are ye?" he demanded, stepping closer to the man, wanting him to confirm his suspicions.

"Ye fool! I am nay concern of yers. I am Lady Evelyn Cameron's brother." He rose up haughtily until Liam snickered disgustedly.

"Weel, *half*-brother," he sneered, shrinking back down. "Name's Judson."

"Where is yer sister? Where is she?" He grabbed the man by his bony shoulders, shaking him forcefully.

"Ye dinnae have ta break me!" He winced in pain, and he let loose his grip on the man. Judson backed away from him, cowering against the wall.

"If yer looking for Evelyn, I'll take ye to her. She makes no difference ta me." He heard the hatred in the man's voice and wondered what had happened in their childhood. From all of the stories he had heard, Evelyn had always made sure Judson was taken care of, including bringing him into the Cameron clan when she married Audric.

"Why are ye doing this?" He wasn't sure he should trust the man. "What's in it fer ye?"

"Dinnae follow me then. Tis up to ye. If ye dinnae follow me, ye will never find her." Judson started heading back down the hall but didn't answer his question, and Liam hesitated. He might be leading him to a trap, but he was right. If he didn't follow the man, it only wasted more time. He decided to follow him, all of his senses heightened for signs of danger.

Judson stopped at the end of the hall. To their right was the staircase he had just come up. Another long hallway stretched out in front of them. Dim sconces were lit along the wall every several feet but didn't do much to break the darkness. There were no windows along the hall, and even though they were on the second level he felt like they were winding through a dungeon in the belly of the castle.

Turning down the hall, Judson stopped in front of a door.

"In here. She willnae fight ye." Judson stepped away from the door, backing out of his way, allowing him access to the door. Pausing, he narrowed his eyes at the man.

"Ye didnae answer me. What's in it fer ye if I take the lady with us?

Judson looked apologetic.

"She is my sister. I ken she misses her daughter. If she's still alive." He looked skeptically at Liam.

Leaning over the man, snarling down at him, he hissed.

"If she's dead, tis nay by our hand. Yer Laird made sure of that!"

"Aye." Judson cowered away from him. "He is a brutal man. If Evie stays here with the McLindon, she is in more danger than anything ye can do ta her." He wasn't sure he believed the man's sincerity, but if it got Lady Evelyn out of danger, then so be it.

"After all," Judson continued, "it's Kenna Silas wants. He doesnae care what ye do with her." He nodded his head toward the door.

"Where is yer Laird? Where is the McLindon?" He wanted to get Evelyn and get out quickly. No one would find him in this maze of hallways if this were a trap.

"Dinnae fash about him. He willnae be bothering ye tonight. Silas isna here." Judson tilted his head again to the door, urging him to open it. He noticed the door had a bar on the outside unlike most doors. This was designed to keep her in, not keep someone out. Removing the bar, he knocked quietly before he pushed the door open.

Inside, a pretty woman sat on the edge of the bed.

Evelyn had barely aged since he'd seen her last. The resemblance to her daughter, however, had gotten even more noticeable over the years as Kenna had blossomed. Kenna's auburn hair suited her temperament better, he thought to himself. Evelyn's light hair seemed to fit the calm demeanor she displayed.

She sat, unmoved by the men entering the room, staring straight ahead. Judson stood back toward the doorway as he moved carefully to her.

"Lady Evelyn." He bent to look her in the eyes, and she blinked, looking at him, although he was not sure she actually saw him. "I'm here ta take ye to yer daughter." At the mention of Kenna, Evelyn seemed to wake slightly and see him for the first time. Her eyes widened, and she looked around, spying her brother by the door. Seeing him, her posture relaxed slightly.

"Evie, this is Laird Cameron." Judson spoke slowly, but the hatred was evident in his voice. "He has Kenna." Looking back at him, Liam's eyes narrowed. He felt like Judson was trying to convince her Kenna was in danger. Before Judson continued, he interrupted, explaining himself to Evelyn.

"Kenna is safe at the Cameron keep. We'd like to take ye to join her there. Tis where ye belong," he added. He wanted Evelyn to know he believed she was innocent of Audric's murder. She looked to Judson for approval, her eyes wide.

"Evie, go fer Kenna," he ordered.

Evelyn didn't say anything, she simply nodded.

"Ye'll come as weel," she asked Judson. Shaking his head, Judson refused.

"Nay, I cannae. I have sworn allegiance a long time

ago to Silas. After we were sent away from the Camerons." He shot a look at Liam, the comment stinging in its intent, and he was fine with leaving the man behind. He didn't trust him and did not want the man back in his keep.

As he moved toward the door, pulling Evelyn along with him, Judson moved swiftly beside him. A burning sensation tingled along his shoulder. He looked down to see blood spreading onto his shirt, a clean slice through the sleeve. Glancing around, he saw that Judson, had dropped the dagger still stained with Liam's blood and had disappeared. The man seemed to slip into the dark. He realized he and Evelyn were stuck. He had no idea how to get back to the main hall. He had fallen for the man's trap. Confused and wounded, he worried he may not get out of the keep before McLindon returned.

Picking up the dagger, he turned it over in his hands. He was shocked to see the Cameron crest on the hilt of the weapon. Claiming it, he tucked it into his boot and began to lead Evelyn down the maze of hallways.

As they neared the end of one hallway, he heard the commotion coming from downstairs. Following the noise, he finally found the stairwell and held Evelyn close to him. As they made their way back down to the great hall, the chaos filled his ears, and he smelled smoke. He had been right. It was a trap, he thought!

Grabbing Evelyn's hand, he rushed down the narrow stairwell to see the great hall had erupted in violence. Fergus and several of his men were fighting off unskilled attacks from McLindon men. The tapestries hanging along the wall were soaked with ale, although he doubted it was intentional, and had caught fire, filling the room with smoke. Had it all been a ruse? Now he and his men were trapped inside.

Spinning on his heels, he scoured the room for Judson, but the man was nowhere to be found. Evelyn stood in a daze, eyes wide, but no expression on her face. Knowing he needed to get her out of harm's way, he grabbed her arm and, seeing Fergus through the smoke, pulled her along toward him. She came along without a fight, and he again wondered how much of the scene she was aware of.

"Weel, looks like ye couldnae stay out of trouble." He yelled to Fergus to be heard over the commotion.

"Aye! Seems ye couldnae as weel. Ye do ken yer bleedin', aye?" Fergus yelled, as he swung his gigantic fist at an angry face, grunting with force as he made contact with his target. Liam pulled Evelyn out of the way as the man fell face first.

"Aye. 'Tis just a scratch." Rushing her outside, he had never seen a clan so unruly and fighting so unorganized. It seemed every man for himself. The riot had moved into the courtyard, and several of his men fought alongside the wolves. The wolves were a ferocious sight, and it made him proud. Looking through the haze of smoke, his heart sank when he saw Niall holding his arm and leaning against the stone wall, Liam's sword by his side. Pulling Evelyn along, he went to tend to Niall, an idea forming in his mind.

"Niall! Are ye hurt, lad?" The injury matched his own and wasn't too severe, nothing Hannah couldn't stitch. Niall would be eager to do his bidding, and this was an important task. Ripping a piece of the lad's shirt to tie around the wound, he spoke to him calmly but firmly.

"I need ye to keep Lady Evelyn safe with ye until we can get out of here. Can ye do that, lad?" He looked at him earnestly, and Niall nodded his head and sputtered.

"O'course I can! She's safe with me!" He rustled the boy's hair.

"I ken." He smiled at him and pulled the boy to his feet, handing him the sword. "Stick to the wall and get through the door. Then I want ye to find cover and wait fer us ta join ye." Niall placed his good arm around her for protection and gave him a serious look.

"I willnae let any harm come to the lady. Ye have my word." Smiling at the boy, he watched as the pair made their way in the shadows to the small door hidden in the ivy.

The smoke was billowing out of the doors to the great hall, making it near impossible to see inside. Liam felt his body wanting to shift and ducked inside the hall, using smoke for cover. Allowing the wolf to take over, he embraced the tingle traveling down his spine, and the shift happened in seconds. He was transformed into an enormous wolf covered in a light-brown fur. He let out a howl to alert his men to get out if possible. As he did, he felt a strong thud across his back. One of Silas' men had hit him across the back with a wooden bench from inside. The bench had been burned so badly it broke easily across his back.

Turning to see the culprit, he grabbed the man by the back of his tunic, slinging him across the room. Running through the room, he continued to dodge blows by other men using swords, clubs, fire pokers, whatever they got their hands on. He needed to get his men out quickly. He found Fergus where he had left him, still swinging, and nudged him, alerting him to his presence.

"Weel, it's about time ye joined the fun," Fergus joked with him. He quickly realized it was not a ruse, and the McLindon keep really was as chaotic as it appeared. Silas' drunken men were no match for the Cameron wolves or their warriors. Nosing Fergus to push him toward the door, he let another howl loose, alerting his men to get out. They had what they came for. Fergus whistled a signal as well, and they moved around the room, fending off clumsy attacks in order for their men to escape. Soon, no other McLindons were advancing on them, and he and Fergus made their way out of the hall and outside into the courtyard.

As the smoke cleared, the scene was worse than he had expected. Bodies were strewn about the courtyard in unnatural positions. Several men were nursing wounds which would never heal. Quickly surveying the dead and dying, he was glad to see none of his men were among them. He picked up Niall's scent, and following it towards the side gate where they had entered he heard another whistle from Fergus.

His man had already ushered the remaining men out of the keep, and they were making their way back toward the cover of the forest. He ran swiftly through the snow toward a tree filled with ice-covered branches. His straw-colored fur blended with the snow and the night, hiding him from anyone who followed them out.

He looked back at the keep, studying its defenses. Again, he wondered where Silas had been. It had been too easy to get Evelyn out, and the small fight the McLindons did attempt only ended in their own destruction. A true Laird never left his keep undefended, although Silas cared none for those men he had lost. Their lives meant nothing to him.

The smoke billowed into the sky, and against its silhouette he saw movement along the parapet walkway. Letting his eyes adjust, he peered closer and realized there were three men looking down toward him. He recognized a familiar form and knew it was Judson. The man was bent over, standing with Silas and another larger man.

Silas had been within the keep's walls the whole time, never helping his clansmen. Seeing the men standing side by side, Liam realized he and Judson had been working together all along. He had suspected Judson, but now he wondered if Silas had been the mastermind behind Audric's death. Disgusted at the men, he left his hiding spot and ran for the woods.

****

Sampson was shocked at what he was seeing. It was true! All of the stories he'd heard as a child and Silas' crazy plan—all of it was real. The wolves were real! He wouldn't have ever believed it if he hadn't seen the Cameron Laird in both his human and wolf form. And now, he thought to himself, the wolves had Evie.

He turned to see Silas looking smugly at him.

"Do ye understand now? Ye've seen the strength and abilities of the wolves. We would be unstoppable."

"Ye dinnae think they will kill her? Evelyn?" he questioned Silas wide-eyed at what he'd just seen. It was Judson who answered him, however.

"Nay, Kenna willnae allow it." He answered quickly, and Silas turned to look at him, causing the man to tremble. "She l...l...lives." He looked at Silas, proud of the information he provided. "And the Ca...Ca...Cameron Laird was qu...qu...quite offended when I s...s...said he'd hurt her."

"So, Liam has allowed Kenna to return. And," Silas added, "is obviously doing her bidding. Tis it nay as I predicted?" Silas turned to Sampson, not waiting for an answer, and left him standing there, watching the large wolf leave the cover of the tree and run toward the woods.

****

Once he had made it back into the cover of his forest, Liam allowed himself to shift back into his human form and evaluate the condition of his men. Several had been injured or burned in the fire, but all were accounted for, and the wounds could heal quickly.

Niall had done as he had promised and hadn't let Evelyn out of his sight. She still seemed to be expressionless and had not yet spoken. Looking the boy over, he was pleased to see his arm wasn't broken, only bruised and a cut that needed stitching. The lad was proud of his battle wounds, he thought, and was glad they were not more serious.

The group mounted the horses they had left in the woods and started making the journey back to their own warm keep. Fergus threw Liam's torn clothing at him.

"Thought ye may need these fer the journey home." He had picked up the tattered, soot-stained clothing on the way out of the hall.

"Thank ye," he mumbled. He knew Fergus had done it more for decency than for Liam's comfort, but he had thought to get them, and he was grateful.

They rode in silence for a while. He had allowed

Niall to escort Lady Evelyn back, as he had taken on the role of her guardian, and they followed close behind.

"I thought it was to be an ambush. I ken we have a few injuries, but nothing more than a tavern brawl. Why de ye think?" He questioned Fergus, knowing he should have some idea but unable to figure out why the McLindons had not fought harder. Fergus nodded.

"Aye, it was too easy with no one to guard the place." Fergus thought for a moment before continuing. "From what I can tell, the McLindon clansmen were fighting just ta fight. They dinnae have any sense of loyalty to their Laird."

He agreed. He never imagined the Cameron clan being disloyal to him. They supported each other and would defend him to the death, and he them. Fergus nodded toward Evelyn and voiced another question Liam had been asking himself.

"Do ye think she seems a bit off?" he whispered, not wanting the others to overhear.

"Aye. I've been thinking the same thing myself. She hasnae spoken since I found her, even with all that was going on around us." Letting Fergus in on what he had witnessed, he continued.

"I saw McLindon watching as we left with her. He ken we were there and did nay ta stop us. Kenna's uncle was with him as weel. I dinnae ken what he has planned, but I feel certain her uncle is involved in it." He grew quiet and thought about how the man had spoken to Evelyn.

"Her brother led me to her." Fergus' eyes grew large in surprise as he explained how Judson had shown him the way to her chamber. "He told her we *had*

Kenna and to go fer her."

"Had her?" Fergus laughed. "Like a prisoner?"

"Aye. 'Twas right before he attacked me." He sneered, rubbing his arm, and Fergus laughed at the thought of the weak man taking on Liam. He continued recounting the events, talking more to himself than to Fergus.

"Kenna isnae a prisoner. She belongs with the Camerons, and I'll see to it this time she stays."

"Ye have grown fond of the lass." Fergus smirked as he spoke, and Liam shook his head. "Weel, either way, lad, we will protect her. Let him try to come fer the lass. Or her mother. We shall be ready fer them. Although, I dinnae think we need to prepare too much if we just saw their battle skills."

Both men erupted in laughter, gaining looks from the others. Growing quiet, they rode the rest of the way to the keep mulling over what had happened at Silas' keep. Knowing the situation was more serious than they let on, Liam's anger grew. He realized the man had no loyalty to his own clan. He knew Silas hadn't given up, and he swore to do whatever was needed to protect Kenna and the Cameron clan from his violence.

Chapter Twelve

Kenna had been pacing the room, anxiously waiting Liam's return. Hannah had suggested a bath to help her relax and had sent some maids up to prepare it. Sipping the tea Hannah had also sent, she watched as steam rose from the water. The young girls emptied buckets of hot water into the large wooden tub.

Baths were a luxury she had not been afforded when she was with Silas. She had been given a small basin that was refilled with clean water every few days. Many times, she held the basin out of the small window in her room and fill it with fresh rainwater. It wasn't steaming like this, but at least it was clean.

As the girls poured the last bucket in and excused themselves, she dipped her toe in the water, testing the temperature. Unable to resist, she immediately shrugged off her robe and sank into the hot, soothing water. Rose petals floated in the water, releasing their fragrance in the air. This was truly special treatment, and she wasn't sure why she was being treated like a lady, but letting the thought slip from her mind she sunk deeper into the tub.

Closing her eyes, she felt the water rise to her chin. Her muscles finally began to relax. She had been in tight knots for so long it was a welcome relief to feel the tension ease away.

The tub seemed to fit her perfectly, she thought,

wondering just how old it must be. The hand-scraped wood had been rubbed smooth with use over the years and felt like slick river rocks under her skin. No slipping on this though, as the wood seemed to cup her body, cradling her in place. It wasn't long before she had fallen asleep.

A log snapped in the fireplace startling her awake. The water had turned cold, and her fingers and toes were shriveled from soaking for so long. Elin, the young widow who was assigned to tend to her needs, was bent over the fire poking the logs trying to stoke the remaining embers to life. A pot of water hung from the iron hook, heating over the coals.

"Dinnae fash about the water," she grumbled sleepily, starting to stand. Elin jumped at the sound of her voice and hastened over to the tub with a robe in hand.

"I'm so sorry ma'am! I didnae mean to wake ye!" She smiled at Elin, shaking off the notion the girl was a bother.

As she slipped into the garment Elin held for her, the door was suddenly thrown open, forcing away any grogginess she still felt from the warm bath. Liam burst into the room, angry and intimidating. On his heels was Hannah, sputtering about a bath and indecency. The pounding of his boots seemed to make the whole room shake, including Elin, who was trembling with fear.

As she stepped out of the tub, her back still to Liam, he roared with anger.

"EVERYONE OUT!" Elin jumped at his tone and tried to scoot past his big frame blocking her way to the door. Unable to get by, she wrung her hands, and Hannah bustled around the room, gathering loose garments and water kettles. Unhappy with their pace, he let out another bellow.

"NOW!"

Elin wasted no time squeezing past him and quickly out the door. Hannah, however, paused on her way out to give him a stern look, clearly displeased with his behavior. He followed her to the door, stopping her before she left.

"Hannah." His tone was much gentler with her. "I need ye ta look after a few of the lads. Nay any major injuries, but a few may need some stitching and some of yer salves." Hannah nodded, patting him on the chest and shoulders.

"Are *ye* nay injured?" she worriedly questioned him.

"Nay more than a few scratches. The men are in the hall."

"Aye, I'll see to them." She heard the door close behind the woman as she left and knew she was alone with Liam. She jumped slightly hearing the wooden bar dropping into place, locking them inside.

"We willnae be interrupted. Ye will be answering some questions, lass." She stiffened, worried about the men who had been injured or lost.

"The bastard has nay conscience." Liam spoke more gently. "He had nay concerns for his own clan. I ken now he has nothing to lose, nay loyalty from his clan."

Her back still to Liam, she stared into the fire. She had tried to warn them. Now he had seen for himself. She took a deep breath, causing her shoulders to rise and fall in defeat. The thin linen fabric of her robe was transparent in the glow of the fire, and the very feminine curves of her body were visible through the wet fabric. The loose curls of her long hair hung past her shoulder blades, and when she moved the scent of roses filled the room. Sighing heavily, he turned to pace around the room. He leaned over the tub and began laughing at his reflection.

"'Tis any wonder wee little Elin went running," he jeered. "I must look like the devil himself!".

He began stripping off his boots and clothes. Hearing the water moving in the tub, she spun around to see him washing the blood off of his face and arms. She quickly turned away, wrapping her thin robe around her body. When she faced him again, he was leaning back against the tub, his eyes closed. Her breath caught in her throat as she looked at him. He was beautiful, although too large for the tub. His veins ran down the sides of his neck, and her gaze followed them down his arms, along the tops of his hands.

The muscles in his forearms flexed as he gripped the edges of the tub. Aware that she was standing there, staring at him, she regained her composure and cleared her throat.

"What the bloody hell do ye think ye are doin'?" she demanded.

"Taking a bath," he replied, his eyes never opening.

"Right now?" Her irritation did not escape him, and he opened one eye, glancing toward her. Without a second thought, he closed his eye and let his head roll back to rest against the tub's high back.

"Aye. There is nay sense wasting good water. Could stand to be a wee bit warmer though," he teased her. Underneath the light tone, the exhaustion sounded in his voice, and she decided to let her resistance drop. Moving to the fire, she lifted the pot of water Elin had been warming for her and carried it over to the tub. She tried to keep her distance to avoid seeing any of his exposed body but did not succeed. He must be so powerful in battle she thought, human or wolf, mesmerized again by his body. Walking up behind him, she watched his chest rise and fall in the water. She set the pot on the floor beside him and moved across the room, putting as much space between them as possible.

"Was it bad?" she asked in an almost whisper, scared of the answer she would get.

"Aye," Liam replied but gave no further explanation. She felt her eyes fill with tears, knowing she had caused all of the losses they had suffered.

"How many were lost?" She looked up hesitantly.

"Lost count. It doesnae matter," his cold tone frightening her. Unsure of why he showed no emotion and feeling guilty for her hand in the matter, her own temper began to flare.

"How can ye be so callous?" she said angrily. Rising to sit up straight in the tub, he looked at her and suddenly he seemed much larger, making her feel very small. Uncomfortable, she rushed around the room, gathering her clothing.

"The families must be told and taken care of!" She turned to glare at him and continued.

"Why are ye still sitting there?" She had thought he cared about these people!

He looked at her in confusion.

"This is what ye wanted! Why do ye care about their families?"

"Wanted this? These people protected me and

fought for me. Why would I ever want to see them killed?" Her chin trembled as she fought to keep her emotions under control.

"Protected ye? Is that what ye call what they did to ye? When we found ye, lass, ye were on the brink of death. I dinnae call that protection. Besides, yer mother is safe with us now. Why do ye care how many we took out to get her here?"

His words caught her off guard. As she processed what he was saying, the relief came crashing down on her and she held onto the bed to steady herself. Her mother was safe! It wasn't Cameron losses he was talking about.

"Ye are all all right?" she asked him quietly.

"A few minor injuries, but aye, we are all home safely." He started to stand out of the tub. She felt the heat rush to her face as she realized she was about to see all of him. Turning away quickly, she let the reality of what he had said sink in. Her mother was here. *Safe.* She clinched her stomach as her insides started to roll. Her leaving had left her mother alone with Silas, putting her life at risk.

"I must go to her!" She spun around storming straight for the door. Half-dressed, with only his trousers on, he grabbed her shoulders to stop her.

"Nay dressed like that." He looked down appreciatively at the damp robe clinging tightly to her body. She was hiding nothing by hugging the robe tighter. He saw every detail of her naked body underneath the wet material.

"Dress and I will take ye to her," he sighed. "But once ye have seen she is weel, ye and I will speak privately, aye?"

She nodded, and raising the bar on the door he opened it and slipped into the hall.

"I'll wait in the hall until ye are ready."

****

A few moments later, she stepped out into the hall. She had dressed ,and her curls were piled on top of her head, leaving a few hanging down around her face and neck. She could feel his eyes scrutinizing her, and she instinctively smoothed her dress. Her wounds had all but healed, with only a small scar near the top of her forehead, along her hairline still a bright pink.

"Ye look lovely, lass. Yer mother will be pleased." He tried to reassure her, taking her hand through his arm.

They walked down what seemed like an endless hallway, making many confusing turns, and she began to wonder if they'd ever get there. She certainly could never find her way to her mother on her own. Why were they keeping her so far away from her, she wondered. Sighing heavily, she pursed her lips and shook her head. Looking down at her, Liam snickered at her pouting. After a few more turns, he stopped suddenly in his tracks, causing her to stumble and tighten her grip on his muscular arm.

"We are here." Liam had stopped in front of a small door. Stepping aside, he urged her forward. Collecting herself, she prepared for the worst. She knew her mother surely had been beaten, possibly as bad as herself. Her mother was older though, and not having the wolf gene, her wounds may be more severe.

Kenna knocked on the door, and a sweet, high-pitched voice called at her to enter. Hesitantly, she opened the door a crack at first.

"Come in," her mother said timidly. Hearing the soft voice, she flung open the door. Evelyn stood in the tiny room by a small table, looking as elegant as always.

"Oh, Mother! Ye are all right!" Kenna was overcome with emotion and pulled her mother in for a tight embrace. Her mother stood stiff, and Kenna pushed away, forcing Evelyn to look at her.

"Kenna?" Evelyn blinked, uncertain of what she was seeing.

"Aye." She had tears in her eyes as she gripped her mother's shoulders. Evelyn shook her head slightly, seeming to come out of her trance.

"Och, Kenna! Ye are weel?" Evelyn questioned, looking her over for any bruises or wounds.

"Aye, I am verra weel." She kissed her mother on her cheek. "And now ye are safe as weel."

"I am so glad to see ye are safe, love. I have been worried. And I am nay the only one." Looking over Kenna's shoulder, Evelyn eyed Liam suspiciously. Kenna turned to see his face, but her mother pulled her into an embrace and whispered in her ear.

"I do need to speak with ye. Alone."

She pulled away and kissed her on the cheek. Turning toward Liam, she smiled sweetly.

"Thank ye fer showing me the way to my mother's room. I'm sure I willnae have trouble finding my own way back." She knew she had to rely on her wolf senses to help find her way out of this maze but didn't want to give Liam a reason to hang around. She needed to hear what her mother had to say.

"I'll let ye get reacquainted, lass, but I'll be waiting outside the door to escort ye back." He nodded matter-of-factly as he backed out of the small doorway. It was no use arguing the matter. Sighing, she shut the door behind him and sat beside her mother on the bed. Evelyn had been given one of the servant's quarters, much smaller than the room she had been given. While not uncomfortable, the room was not exactly fitting of her mother's status. Of course, she knew the Camerons were going to be very skeptical of her mother since they were all convinced she had poisoned their Laird.

Focusing on her mother, it was her turn to look for any signs of abuse.

"They've nay harmed ye?" she questioned, concern flooding her voice.

"Nay, dear. Why would they?" Evie asked curiously.

"I thought…with my leaving the way I did." Kenna trailed off.

"Ye mean running away?" Evelyn looked at her with a disapproving eye.

"Mother! Silas McLindon is evil! I've seen what he does to the other girls! I ken what he's done to me!" Pleading with her mother, she tried to convince her she was right to escape Silas.

"He is yer betrothed, Kenna. Ye must return to marry him." Evelyn's voice was flat.

"Ye dinnae ken how he treated me. I can assure ye it wasnae the same as he treated ye. Silas kept ye in a lovely room, fed ye feasts, and treated ye like a lady! He beat me and threatened ta kill me every day!" She was near hysterics, and Evelyn continued to shake her head in denial.

"Mother! Surely ye are nay so blind? Look at me! I still bear his scars!" She held out her arms to her mother, not believing her mother had been oblivious to Silas' cruelty. Evelyn seemed to be siding with Silas. What was going on with her? Kenna felt defeated.

"I was beaten and starved. I was his prisoner!"

"Och, Kenna. He cares for ye and will be a good husband." Evelyn repeated the words, but there was no feeling behind them.

"Never," Kenna whispered. Wringing her hands, she backed away from her mother in the small room. Evelyn reached out for her, urging her to sit again.

"He is yer betrothed. Ye must return to him. Ye have a contract."

Shaking her head, she swore she would never return to Silas.

"We're nay welcome here, Kenna. This clan...they banished us, and thanks to yer uncle he convinced Silas McLindon to provide a home for us. I ken ye dinnae remember much. Ye were just a wee lass." Her mother fell quiet, withdrawing into her memories. Returning to sit beside her mother, she held her hands and tucked a loose curl behind Evie's ear.

She noticed the hair around her temples starting to gray, and the fine lines around her eyes and mouth had grown deeper. Her mother was only forty-two years old and was still very beautiful. Her reputation, however, never allowed her to remarry. After being accused of killing her husband, Evelyn had been seen as evil and a curse on any clan.

"Mother," she said slowly, speaking as if she were talking to a young child. "Liam is a fair Laird, and the clan respects him. They will follow what he says, and he has welcomed us."

"They will follow YE!" Evie looked at her with a

sudden spark in her eyes. "Ye are their rightful leader!" Evie pleaded, grabbing her hands in urgency.

"NAY!" Her forceful tone startled her mother, and Evie's eyes widened. Shaking off her mother's hands, she stood from the bed and smoothed her skirts, trying to regain her composure. She knew the words Evelyn spoke came from Silas. They were not her own.

"I willnae force control on these people. They have offered me protection, and ye as weel, if ye will take it! I willnae betray them! Liam is Alpha here, and I will gladly step aside and support him." She trembled with emotion as she spoke.

Evie blinked wildly at the outburst. Rubbing her temples, Evie seemed to be waking up from a deep sleep. When she felt like she had finally come to her senses, she held Kenna's hand gently.

"I didnae ken ye even remembered this clan. I'm glad ye did." Evie sighed with a gentle chuckle. "Ye have found yer place back among yer people. I ken yer da would be verra proud." A sadness entered her eyes as she continued. "I cannae stay here with ye though. I must return to the McLindon keep."

She started to protest, but her mother quickly put a hand up, silencing her.

"They dinnae see me the same way they see ye." Evelyn explained. "To them, I am responsible for yer father's death. I hope ye ken I wouldnae have done such a thing. I loved him dearly." Evelyn closed her eyes.

"I must return," Evie continued. "If I dinnae return as promised, Silas will come. Ye ken as well as anyone. He will come for us both, and these people will suffer greatly. I see it clearly now."

She shook her head fiercely in denial as Evie spoke and pulled her into a tight embrace. A knock on the door interrupted their reunion. She had forgotten Liam had been waiting outside to escort her back through the keep. Pulling out of their embrace, both ladies began wiping their tears and straightening each other's hair. Suddenly, she longed for the simple mother and daughter actions they had been denied for so many years.

Another bang on the door reminded her Liam was growing impatient. Smiling at her mother, she turned to scowl at the door.

"I'm coming," she growled. She knew what she must do. She intended to return with her mother. She was determined not to put her in harm's way again, nor subject these kind people to Silas' punishment. Giving her mother a tight hug and a quick kiss on the cheek, she promised they would speak again after Evelyn was well rested.

Pushing open the door, she saw Liam standing with his arms folded across his chest and a stern look on his face. Shoving past him, she used her shoulder to knock against his arm. She growled in frustration hearing him chuckle behind her as she rubbed her arm where she had hit him. Catching up to her quickly in the darkened hall, he grabbed her elbow, spinning her around to face him. The look on his face told her he was ready to defend his clan, not just against Silas, but against her as well. Crying, she instinctively tucked herself into his chest. She felt him relax, and gently he rubbed his hand along her back. A few minutes later, she pulled away from him, wiping her eyes.

"I must leave here," she whispered, unable to bring

herself to look at him. "I have put yer clan in danger by coming here. Ye have taken me in and cared for me. Ye are my family. I willnae see them butchered by a madman."

"Nay, lass, I cannae let ye do that. If ye return to the McLindon, he will use ye against us. I ken that his is plan now. He will use yer Alpha birthright to control those of us who have shifted. I cannae allow that. But..." He looked down at her and lifting her chin to look at him, he continued, "I protect those who have pledged their allegiance to me, as Laird. And Alpha," he added. "That includes ye...and yer mother, if ye wish. This is yer home, and ye belong with us."

She gazed up at him, eyes round with surprise. "My mother as weel?" she asked him, hesitantly.

"Aye, I heard ye speaking to her. I didnae mean too, but...weel, I cannae help it." He smiled sheepishly pointing to his ears. The wolf allowed for much keener hearing than a normal man.

"I ken she wasnae responsible for Audric's death. Unfortunately, it means either the real murderer is still here or..." He trailed off, looking into the empty darkness.

"Or we took them with us." She finished his sentence. They had traveled with a group of men who had pledged their allegiance to her uncle after Audric's death. Surely one of those men had not put her and her mother in danger intentionally. If so, she thought, she had no choice but to return to Silas. She must face him and find out the truth.

"I am a Cameron, and this is my rightful home," she said to Liam. "But I cannae...I willnae be responsible for putting these innocent people in danger.

Ye dinnae ken what Silas McLindon is capable of!"

"I think I have a good idea." He stroked her temple gently where only a thin scar remained, reminding her of the condition they had found her.

"I am betrothed to him. We have a contract. Silas willnae give up until we are wed." She did not see any way out of the situation. None which spared the lives of the people she had grown to love.

Sighing, he cleared his throat.

"There is another way. Although I am nay certain ye will be in favor of it." She pushed back from him, eyeing him hesitantly.

"Yer marriage contract isnae valid." He spoke hesitantly. "I have been looking for this loophole since we found out about yer betrothal to the bastard. It was actually Fergus who pointed it out."

"Why are ye talking nonsense? The contract's been in place as long as I can remember. Since I was a babe."

"Since ye were young, aye, but nay since ye were a babe. Hannah said yer uncle made the contract with Silas before yer father had passed. If so, it wasnae his right to do so." Her eyes widened, and she cursed herself for daring to hope he might be right!

"Even then, once Audric passed," Liam continued, "the decision fell to his successor." Smiling down at her, he waited until she realized what he was saying.

"His successor? Ye mean the next Laird?" She raised her eyebrows hopefully at him, and he nodded as she began to understand. "Weel, then, ye have that authority!"

"Aye. I most certainly do. And I declare yer marriage contract to Silas isnae binding. Ye will nay be marrying him," he declared.

Her excitement was short-lived, and she hung her head.

"But, if I dinnae marry, he will continue to fight it."

"Aye, ye are right about that. We will need to find ye someone suitable fer yer status." She cared for Liam, but he obviously did not return her affections if he was willing to give her to another man. Tilting her chin up to look at him, he wiped her tear-stained cheek.

"Ye must marry, Kenna. I'm sorry to tell ye, lass," he apologized.

"Liam." She swallowed the lump in her throat before continuing. "It must be ye."

"What?!" He started. "Nay, lass, ye cannae be serious. I cannae marry ye." He backed away from her quickly.

"Ye must!" she pleaded after him. "Ye are the only one. Anyone else I marry may do the same thing Silas McLindon wants to do. Don't ye see? It must be ye. Ye are already the Alpha. Ye will nay make me lay claim to my birthright."

He ran his hand through his hair, huffing in defeat.

"Ye are right, lass. I will never make ye claim yer birthright." Her heart leapt in her chest. She couldn't believe what he had said. He would really risk marrying her?

"Silas will seek his revenge. He willnae give up so easily." She wanted him to be certain of his decision.

"I ken, lass, and we will be ready for him. Ye have my word." Liam stroked her cheek. And she had all the reassurance she needed.

Chapter Thirteen

Liam found Hannah gathering her medical supplies to tend to the wounded. He knew she would be happy over the news of his plans to wed Kenna. He was still unsure, but if he were being honest with himself, he cared for her. The feelings he had as a boy seemed to have matured, even though he tried to deny those feelings. He wasn't sure if Kenna felt the same way but hoped she would grow to care for him as well.

Hannah shook her head, eyeing the state of his clothing. After stealing Kenna's bath, he had thrown on his battle-worn clothes, ripped and smeared with blood and soot.

"Tis nay as bad as it looks," he tried to reassure her, but she insisted on checking him over for any wounds. Once she was satisfied he wasn't dying or even truly injured, she went back to her work.

"Kenna has seen her ma?" She wasn't really asking, and he knew this was her way of getting information.

"Aye she has," he answered. "I let them speak privately," he added quickly to keep her from pushing for more details. He remained quiet for a few minutes before continuing.

"Hannah, did ye notice she was a wee bit off? She didnae seem to be in her right mind."

"Aye," Hannah agreed. "I dinnae think it will last.

141

If it doesnae seem to wean in a few days, I will make her a tea."

Of course she will, he thought. Hannah had a tea for every ailment, and he wasn't sure he wanted to know what she mixed in them.

"Thank ye, Hannah. I ken ye will look after her, and I want her to be present, in every sense," he stressed, "for the wedding." He waited for Hannah to catch on to what he was saying, and it didn't her take long. She turned from her table, gripping the dried lavender she had been stripping from its stalk.

"And whose wedding are ye be referring to?" she said, unable to hide the grin forming on her face.

"Dinnae get yerself excited," he said calmly, trying to convince her the wedding was only a formality and to protect Kenna.

"Kenna is a Cameron by blood and as Laird, I, nay her uncle nor any other, have the final say as to who she will and willnae marry. If I wed her, Silas McLindon will have nay right to object or pursue her. And nay any other will try to use her gift against her."

She clapped her hands in excitement, forgetting the lavender and causing the purple flowers to stain her hands as she crushed them.

"Och!" She threw the flowers down and wiped her hands on her apron. Standing on her tiptoes, she gripped him in a bear hug, laughing and crying from happiness. Pulling away from him, she placed her purple hand on his cheek.

"I ken yer fond of the lass. And dinnae fash, I ken she is fond of ye too." She winked at him.

"Ye ken a lot of things, Hannah," he teased.

"Aye, I do. I do ken a lot of things." Her tone

became serious as she moved across the room to an old cabinet, locked for as long as he remembered. He had never seen Hannah use anything she kept stored in the cabinet and had no idea what it held. She reached behind the cabinet, fiddling for a moment before she produced the key.

"This old cabinet has a lot of secrets. The herbs it holds are verra dangerous and can even kill a man. I dinnae use them often, but when the lass came with all of her wounds..." She paused, taking a deep breath. He could tell remembering the severity of Kenna's injuries had been hard for the old woman. It was hard for him as well, and anger built up inside him.

"Kenna needed more than my usual remedies could provide, something a wee bit stronger. Weel, the cabinet was in such disarray, I couldnae find anything I needed. When ye went fer her ma, I thought she may have suffered some of the same injuries as the lass and began arranging my herbs, I found this." Hannah reached into the cabinet and pulled out a piece of parchment, the wax seal had been broken.

"What's this?" He took the letter hesitantly, not certain he wanted to know what it said.

"Go on. I think ye will find it verra interesting." She pushed him toward a stool and moved an oil lamp closer for him to see in the dark room. His mouth formed a tight line, and his jaw clenched tight as he read the letter. After several moments, he looked up, his eyes narrow and his face pulled into a scowl.

"Where is she?" he asked coldly.

"Mayhaps in the kitchen, 'tis almost dawn. She should be preparing the morning meal with the other cooks. But I wouldnae be surprised if she wasnae." She shook her head in disapproval.

He stood to leave, holding the letter close.

"Dinnae mention this ta anyone. I want ye ta keep an eye on her. If this is true," he tapped the letter in his hand, "I dinnae think they are finished yet." She nodded in agreement.

"Aye, I suspect ye are right."

He opened the door to leave.

"WAIT!" she shouted at him before he left. "The wedding!? I have much to do afore ye can marry!" Laughing, he walked back over, placing a kiss on her head.

"I ken ye want to make it special, as Kenna deserves. However, ye must hurry. We need to wed as quickly as possible."

"Will ye allow three days? I am certain, with help from the other women in the village, it will be enough time to prepare something special fer the lass." She pleaded her case.

"Aye, three days," he agreed and hugged her goodbye. As he pulled the door shut behind him, she squealed with excitement.

The next morning, word spread quickly the Laird was to be married. Not everyone in the keep was happy with the announcement Kenna was to be the Laird's new wife. Disgruntled whispers from some still held the notion neither Kenna, nor her mother, should ever have been welcomed back into the clan. The whispers had reached his ear by the evening meal.

Rising from his seat in the center of the large table, he pulled Kenna up to stand beside him. The look on his face was not one of pleasure, and those in the hall murmured in nervousness. An uneasy quietness fell over the room. Hannah, who had been standing behind him, nudged his elbow. Nissa was standing in the corner of the room. Eyeing her, he hoped his announcement reached Judson's ears. Clearing his throat, he spoke loud enough for everyone in the hall to hear him perfectly.

"As ye all ken by now, Lady Kenna and I are to be wed. I ken there are some of ye who dinnae agree with our arrangement." Whispers began to circulate around the room.

"However," he shouted over the noise, "I am yer Laird, and on this ye will take my word. It has been discovered neither Lady Evelyn, nor Lady Kenna, played any role in Audric's death." Gasps of shock filled the room, and Kenna looked at him wide-eyed. He continued, announcing he believed the culprits, or one of them, were still living within the keep. Hoping to instigate someone to come forward with information, he let it be known anyone hiding information regarding the death of the former Laird was to be banished. However, if they came forward before the wedding, they may be punished for keeping information, but he may allow them to stay on Cameron land and under Cameron protection. His eye caught Nissa's as she ducked her head and slipped through the doors, escaping his scrutiny.

****

Following Liam's orders, Hannah worked side by side with Nissa in the days leading up to the wedding. Preparing food for the feast, she was able to keep a close eye on the woman. Hoping to get a confession, she tried small talk about the past, reminiscing over Evelyn and Kenna's time at the keep. She knew Nissa probably still felt affection for Judson, the only man she ever remembered showing the woman any attention, and tried to encourage her to speak about him. The woman was quiet, though, and this worried her. Nissa was usually the first to gossip, and her silence had her keeping an even more watchful eye on the woman.

Nissa had been rude and cross to Kenna ever since she'd arrived, and Hannah had words with her on more than one occasion. Now, though, she suspected the irritation was more than jealousy or just having another mouth to feed. She did not think Nissa was smart enough to have thought of poisoning the Laird herself. She was certain Judson had been behind the evil, and her gut instinct told her he was still controlling the woman.

Not even her distrust in Nissa hid the joy she felt over the thought of Liam and Kenna wed. She had known, even when they were children, they were meant to be mated. Right now, Kenna thought Liam was marrying her out of necessity. She knew it wouldn't take them long to figure out just how much they truly cared for each other. After all, she saw it written all over both their faces. They belonged together. The feeling of distrust she had when Kenna first arrived had disappeared quickly. She now knew the lass only wanted what was best for the ones she loved. In this, she was very much like Hannah, and she respected her for it.

The wedding was in two days, and there was still much to be done. Foods to prepare, cleaning to be done. The great hall must be swept clean. They were one of the few keeps who had a stone floor and did not depend on rushes to keep their floor clean, a privilege she was proud to boast of. And of course preparations must be made for the wedding night.

The chapel hadn't been used in some time, and it needed a good cleaning as well. She had assigned Agnes to help her with the task and set Elin upon overseeing preparations for the wedding night. Elin was excited to be able to assist her and took it upon herself to sew a beautiful chemise for Kenna to wear.

When Liam had told her of his plans to wed Kenna, she had an idea for a surprise for both Kenna and her mother and hoped she hadn't misplaced what she needed to make it happen. She had found Evelyn's wedding dress in an old trunk locked away in the turrets. All of their belongings left behind were stored away when they were banished. Using pieces of the worn fabric, she had requested the maids to make a special dress for Kenna and one for Evelyn. The maids worked quickly, and when she had presented the dresses to them, they were moved to tears.

When Evelyn had first arrived at the Cameron keep, she had examined her for any injuries Silas may have bestowed. Finding none physically, she was however concerned for Evelyn's mental state. Voicing her concerns to Liam, she felt Evelyn had been kept sedated for quite some time and she may never fully gain a clear mind again. She had been right, and even though it had not taken long for the drugs Silas had given Evelyn to wear off, oftentimes she found Evie staring blankly into space, and she had to be pulled from whatever memory or place her mind had escaped to.

Evelyn had been devastated when she discovered how Kenna had truly been treated and vowed to never forgive herself for allowing it to happen. Seeing her distress, she made her a soothing tea to help her sleep each night. Kenna insisted her mother be moved to a chamber near her own as she did not want to waste any more of the precious time they had together.

Although there was some hesitation at first, Evelyn reluctantly moved from the tiny servant's quarters into a room more fitting of her stature and even allowed her to assign a young servant to look after her needs.

As the days quickly passed, it seemed to her more and more of the clansmen were becoming accepting of Evelyn's presence. They smiled and greeted her as she moved about the keep. With her help, Evelyn had reconnected with several women she considered friends before her husband's death.

Unfortunately, she knew Evelyn planned to leave right after the wedding to return to the McLindon keep. She had confided in her that returning without Kenna she would surely be punished, but she needed to return and chase her own happiness. She confessed that she had grown to love a man named Sampson and hoped to return and find he felt the same. She felt that in order to find her own happiness she had to return and face Silas. Kenna, however, was happy with the Camerons, and Evelyn trusted by marrying Liam Kenna's future was going to be secure and peaceful.

Kenna and Evelyn had spent most of the days leading up to the wedding busy with preparations and surrounded by women from the village offering their help. She found them sitting on a small stone bench in the inner courtyard. They finally managed to find some quiet time alone, and she was happy to see them getting reacquainted. She knew Kenna was desperate to find out the truth of who killed her father and wanted to know everything her mother remembered. It seemed to her it was easier said than done. Evelyn still showed signs of being influenced by Silas' drugs.

She knew Liam wanted Kenna to question her mother about the events leading up to her father's death but also knew she struggled with how to go about it. Liam had no problem questioning Evelyn though, and any moment he could spare he sought her out with a new series of questions. She had tried to stay on top of him, intercepting his interrogations when possible, trying to allow Kenna as much time as possible with her mother.

He had found them once again in the garden. As Kenna and Evie sat on the bench, holding hands and heads bent in conversation, he paused before interrupting the quiet moment. Hannah appeared beside him, holding a tray of tea and biscuits for the pair. She eyed him reproachfully, hoping he got her hint to leave them alone.

"I promise, I am nay going to question her. It's time they saw the room. I think it will surely put a smile on both their faces." He smiled down at her, and she nodded her approval, a smile of her own brightening her face.

Clearing his throat, Liam waited until they looked up before approaching.

"I thought I may find you two out here," he said lightly.

"Hello, Liam." Kenna smiled sweetly up at him and Hannah. "What brings ye both out here?"

"We should ask ye the same thing, dearie." She placed the tray on the bench beside them. "'Tis near freezing out, and the sky looks like it will bring another fresh layer of snow soon. Wouldn't ye be more comfortable inside the walls?"

She responded with a shake of her head. "The fresh air is nice. Besides, there are too many prying eyes and ears inside." Evelyn nodded her head in agreement.

"Well, yes, that can be a little irritating." Liam looked down at them. "I wonder if ye both may like to join me. I have something fer ye. Hopefully it will help ye feel more at home here." He held out a hand to each woman.

Taking his offered hand, they rose and allowed him to lead them inside. Hannah shuffled behind them, clapping her hands in excitement. He led them down a narrow hall with a spiral staircase at the end. Heading up the stairs, he opened the door to a small turret chamber. The circular room had long, narrow windows along the walls, letting in just enough light.

Usually used for storage, the room was transformed and quite comfortable. A small table was set with breads, cheese, apples, and wine. Cushioned chairs covered in a soft fabric offered welcome seating. A woven rug covered the cold stone floor. Wall sconces lit the room with a soft glow. The room had been taken from a cold, militant guard post to an inviting lounge. Kenna didn't appear to believe Liam had done this for them.

"What's all this fer?" she asked.

"This was yer home." He looked at both of them. "And unjustly ye were removed from it. I ken ye havena been treated as though ye belong here." He looked specifically at Evelyn. "I had hoped this may help." Moving over to where several trunks were pushed against the wall, he continued.

"These are yer belongings. Everything left behind here when ye were..." He trailed off.

"Banished?" Evelyn raised her eyebrows at him.

"Aye," he sighed. "It was all packed and stored up here. I thought by making this room comfortable, it may be somewhere ye could reminisce about yer time here and," he added, "hopefully remember what ye loved about the Camerons."

Kenna's eyes filled with tears, and she looked around the room in shock.

"Ye did this all yerself?" she asked, and he laughed.

"Oh, nay! I dinnae have the eye for things like this." He stretched an arm over to Hannah. "Hannah arranged it all. She wanted to make sure we were comfortable." She blushed at the compliment.

"Ye kept it all?" Evelyn asked her, moving toward the trunks.

"Aye, all that was left. It's here, in these trunks. No one has been up here fer years. This is yer space now, thanks to Laird Cameron." She looked over to Liam.

Lifting the lid to one of the trunks, Evelyn sank down onto one of the cushions placed on the floor. Clothing lay in the trunk, and she ran her fingers along the fabric gently.

Kenna approached Liam and looked between him and Hannah. "I cannae tell ye how much this means to me. Ye didnae have to do this. Thank ye."

He reached out and stroked her cheek.

"He did this fer ye, lass," Hannah told her as she smiled at the couple.

"Consider it a wedding present." Pushing her

gently over toward her mother, Liam slipped out of the room, followed by Hannah.

****

Inside the room, Kenna sat with her mother in silence for a few minutes. She was still awestruck over the trunks. Liam had shown her what a caring and giving man she was marrying, and she no longer felt the strain of necessity pulling at her. She wanted to marry him, she realized, not just needed to.

She didn't want to read too much into his gift, however. Liam was marrying her only to protect her, she reminded herself. At most, she hoped he may become fond of her, but nothing more. Trying to block the sadness this thought caused her, she dove back into the memories the trunks held.

Chapter Fourteen

The snow fell softly as Kenna was escorted to the small chapel outside the keep walls. Primarily used for weddings, baptisms, and funerals, the chapel seemed forgotten until such an event took place. As she climbed the hill in her long dress, she thought the church never looked more beautiful. The night sky was covered in clouds, but the full moon shone through them illuminating her path. Candles had been lit in each window of the church, and beautiful wreaths made of moss and dried heather hung on each of the double doors.

As she neared the entrance, her mother was standing there to greet her. Evie had tears in her eyes.

"Oh, my love, ye are a sight to behold. Yer groom will surely be in awe of ye. If he doesnae already love ye, it willnae be long before he is head over heels fer ye."

She took her mother's outstretched hand and pulled herself up the last bit of the rocky hill. She blushed at her mother's words and dared to hope she was right. Accepting the flowers her mother offered, she was amazed at how fast everyone had pulled together such a beautiful and magical evening. And they had done it for her, which touched her heart even more.

Even if the wedding was only a plan to protect her,

Hannah and the other women had gone out of their way to make it a wedding fit for a princess. Her bouquet was fragrant, filled with wildflowers, purple thistle, moss, and vines and wrapped with a piece of Cameron plaid. Her hair had been pulled up on the sides and secured with silver combs adorned in rubies, ones her mother had worn on her own wedding day. Her curls hung down her back and caught snowflakes as they fell.

Hannah had escorted her to the chapel, and together with Evie they straightened her dress. The dress itself was simple but elegant, made of a natural linen from her mother's wedding gown. Cut low in a heart shaped neckline exposing her shoulders, the bodice fit snugly and accentuated her chest. She tried to take short breaths as the corset was tied tightly and she didn't want to cause unwanted attention to her bosom. The sleeves were long, coming to a point over her hand with a delicate trim of Cameron tartan.

She had noticed small pieces of the Cameron plaid had been used throughout the dress for trim and details, including the laces in the corset. The long skirt was very full and covered her shoes, picking up snow in the hem even though she tried to lift the heavy material when she walked.

A full Cameron plaid was folded into the bustle of the skirt. A sash of plaid hung around her hips and was pinned on her right side with a kilt pin decorated in the Cameron crest. There was no mistake in the intent for the details of the wedding dress. They wanted her to know she was one of them and they had accepted her back into the clan. Her loyalty would lie with them.

Two men opened the wooden doors, and she took a deep breath to steady her nerves. Looking up, she saw

Liam standing right inside the doors, ready to escort her to the altar. He was dressed in a black riding boots to his mid-calf. His kilt hung to his knees with a sash over his shoulder and pinned with a kilt pin identical to hers. His black coat covered a linen shirt and hugged his shoulders, showing his muscular frame beneath. He was a sight to behold and almost took her breath away. Holding out his arm for her to take, he gave her a comforting smile which soothed her nerves.

The walk up the short aisle felt never-ending, and once they finally approached the small wooden altar she was glad for the opportunity to kneel and make sure her legs were steady. Looking around, she noticed the heavy tapestries hanging on the stone walls to each side of the altar, the heavy iron sconces held candles giving the room a warm glow. Liam took her small hand in his as the ceremony began, guiding her through it. As their hands were wrapped in linen and vows were exchanged, it all seemed like a dream. Before she knew what was happening, she was being kissed lightly, and the clan was cheering loudly behind her. It had gone by in a blur, and all she remembered was how handsome her groom looked and how she had felt like royalty.

Liam led her from the chapel as they were surrounded by cheering and congratulations. Everyone was eager to get back to the main hall and celebrate. A prepared feast waited, and there was to be much drinking and dancing. She couldn't imagine being happier than she felt right then. She felt loved and protected and had her mother with her through it all.

When she and Liam walked through the doors of the great hall, she gasped at the beauty of it. White linen fabric draped the rafters, and balls made of moss and heather hung between them. Candles lined the walls and tables and their soft, flickering light gave the room a magical feel. Rich food and sweets lined the tables, and their aroma filled the air.

As they made their way to the head table, they were once again greeted by cheers of congratulations from the ladies and jeering from the men who hinted at the wedding night. Some of the comments made her blush and Liam gripped her hand, pulling her along toward the table to keep her from hearing too many of the lewd comments.

Once they were seated, the hall grew quiet. Fergus stood, raising his goblet in toast.

"Well, William," using Liam's formal name, "I'm nay sure how ye managed to snag such a bonnie wee lass, but ye better hold on ta her. There are plenty of braw men here who willnae hesitate to snatch her up!" A roar of cheering and laughter erupted from the hall, and she felt her face flush at his words.

"Lady Kenna," Fergus continued, "welcome home. Ye have our loyalty and our protection from whate're dangers ye face." He paused and then leaned toward her and said softer, but still loud enough for the crowd to hear, "Includin' yer husband!" and then gave her a sly wink and hoisted his cup higher. "May ye find every happiness together!" The hall erupted again, and she watched wide-eyed as both Fergus and Liam emptied their large goblets without spilling a drop.

Fergus' toast seemed to signal the beginning of the feast. Music began playing, and women in flowing skirts began dancing around the tables, teasing the men. A large plate was set in front of her, but she was too nervous to eat. Her stomach was in butterflies as she thought about what awaited her. Time seemed to fly by as she was ushered to her feet by Hannah and several young ladies. Once again, the jeering started from the men.

Suddenly, all the worries she'd pushed away came back to the surface, and the room started to spin. Liam gripped her elbow and smiling at her escorted her from the main hall. They were followed by Hannah and the young ladies who were to prepare her for the wedding night. Liam wanted to see her to his chambers and make sure she was settled before he rejoined the men in revelry as was customary for the groom before his wedding night.

She was shaking with nervousness. Her fear, however, was not for the wedding night. She knew Liam was going to be gentle and understanding with her. And she was not naive, even if she was innocent. She knew what he expected as well. She was more worried than ever for her mother and the clan's safety since the wedding had taken place. When word reached Silas, she knew he would seek vengeance.

Candles lit the small dressing room to the left of Liam's chambers. A large tub had been brought in, and the servants were preparing a bath. Liam pulled her aside in the darkness of the hallway, putting her back against the wall. Grabbing her shoulders, he turned her toward him, forcing her to look up to his face. His eyes were a pale blue, almost gray, and he was staring so intently on her she had no choice but to focus only on him.

He loosened his grip on her but didn't let go.

"You needn't worry anymore, lass. The bastard willnae risk coming here." He sounded confident, but she wasn't so sure. After all, Silas didn't think very rationally when it came to revenge.

"If he has gotten news we are wed, he will seek revenge. If he doesnae yet ken, then he thinks I still belong to him…" she said hesitantly.

Giving her a gentle shake, he gave her a stern look.

"Ye belong to *me* now," he stressed in a low, possessive tone, almost growling the words. His possessiveness of her did not scare her but made her feel safe, wanted. Although she didn't think he loved her, she knew he held at least some affection for her. She blinked away tears and prayed her voice didn't catch in her throat.

"I always have," she whispered to him. He reacted swiftly, crushing her to him.

Pulling her up, he kissed her urgently. It wasn't the soft, gentle kiss she had always imagined, and it took her by surprise. Her eyes widened, and her body tensed. Noticing her reaction, he relaxed his grip but did not remove his lips from hers. His hands still held her arms, and his thumbs made small circles along her biceps. She allowed herself to lean into him, feeling his body against hers, and her hands found their way to his waist. Grabbing his shirt, she gasped a little for air when he finally pulled away.

Her lips were swollen and pink from his kiss. He moved a hand to her hair, playing with the curls coming loose around her ears. Cupping her cheek, he traced her lips with his thumb, sending a shiver throughout her body. She had never been kissed, he realized.

"Can I ask ye something, Kenna? It may be a bit…personal."

"Ye can ask me anything." She blushed up at him.

"The bastard—has he ever touched ye? Like a husband touches a wife?"

She blushed again but was thankful for answer she was able to give.

"Nay. He believed I should remain pure for our wedding. He may have beaten me to the point of death, but he didnae want to marry someone who wasnae a virgin." Liam scoffed at her reply.

"I am sorry for the abuse he caused ye, lass, but I am pleased to ken he never touched ye in that way."

Still gripping his shirt, she looked up at him, ready for another kiss, which he eagerly obliged.

This kiss, however, was different. Holding her face in his hands, he kissed her softly. She smelled faintly of roses, and a soft moan escaped her as she felt her body respond instinctively. She pressed herself against him, and he pulled her even closer, deepening the kiss. His tongue teased her mouth open, and as she allowed him in he let out a low groan of his own.

After a few moments, he pulled away, leaving them both breathless. Resting his forehead against hers, he gave her a final light kiss on the nose and led her into the room.

"I believe they are ready for ye. I shall see ye soon." Smiling at her, he gave her a little shove in the direction of the servants and bowed out of the room.

She turned toward the young ladies in the room. There were four of them, and Hannah of course. They had prepared a hot bath, which admittedly looked very inviting after such a long day. Turning for them to undo the laces up the back of her dress, she touched her cheeks. They were warm, and she knew she was flushed from Liam's advances. She didn't need to wonder if the girls had witnessed them in the hall. She knew from their giggles they had seen and heard everything.

Stepping out of her dress, she allowed them to lift her chemise over her head, and she eased down into the steaming water. They had added lavender to fragrance the water and help her relax. She let her hair fall down into the tub. One of the girls began removing the flowers from her hair while another unbraided it. Pouring the warm water over her head, they began massaging her scalp, and she let her tension ease away. On each side, a young girl began to massage her arms and hands. After falling asleep easily, she woke to find the young girls had left and only Hannah remained in the room.

Helping her out of the tub, Hannah dried her and showed her into Liam's chambers and shut the door. She heard men come in to remove the tub while Hannah began to massage her body with a fragrant lotion.

"'Tis my own recipe," she explained as she massaged her legs and arms. "I use lavender and goats' milk. Helps the ache in my old hands."

Hannah laid out the new nightdress Elin had made for her to wear. This one was cut in a low V and laced loosely in the front, exposing more than was acceptable. It was embroidered in a gold thread around the neckline and down the front along the laces. The pattern was delicate and simple but added an elegance to the gown.

"Oh, Hannah! It's lovely!" she proclaimed as she ran her fingers over the delicate fabric.

"Aye, lass. It is lovely. Ye have yer maid, Elin, to thank fer it. She is the one who stitched it fer ye."

She gasped in surprise. "Elin did this?! I must

thank her right away!"

Hannah pulled her in front of the fire and began to comb out her curls. "I think ye will have time fer that tomorrow, lass." She laughed and then added, "Or the day after." When she was done, the old woman led her over to the bed, offering her a cup of tea.

In the tea, she noticed leaves floating to the surface. Looking at Hannah questioningly, she sipped it anyway. She trusted the older woman and knew she was only trying to make tonight easier for her.

"Dinnae fash, dearie, twill only help ye relax." Taking the cup from her, she winked and poked the fire to life before she slipped out of the room.

Chapter Fifteen

Kenna waited anxiously in Liam's chambers. The boisterous laughing and yelling that had spilled from the great room out into the courtyard traveled up the stairs to her ears. The feast ended long ago, but the drinking and revelry would last until dawn. She knew it was to be a long night but was ready for her groom and her wedding night. Her mother had been escorted back to her own room after she was taken to Liam's chamber. She had thought it strange her mother didn't accompany her to ready herself for her groom, but then she was probably tired as well.

She paced the room. The clan would be celebrating the Laird's wedding all night. At least until the wedding was consummated. The elders wanted to know they were "good and truly wed" as they had put it. She chuckled when she thought of Hannah telling her about her first marriage. Someone had to watch to ensure the deed had been done. At least she was being awarded a little privacy and dignity. The clan taking Liam's word for it, seeing as he was Chief and Alpha.

Wringing her hands, she alternated between pacing the room, staring out the window, sitting on the bed, and poking the fire. She brushed her hair over and over and finally collapsed on the bed. Staring at the wooden beams along the ceiling, she played scenarios over and over in her head. She suddenly realized the hallway had grown quiet and heavy footsteps approached the door.

Her heart began to race, and a light bead of sweat formed along her brow. The footsteps stopped in front of the door, and she sat upright, breathing heavily. The door, however, remained closed. She sat stiffly on the bed, suddenly nervous. After what seemed an eternity, the footsteps started again, this time pounding away from the door. Letting out an annoyed huff, she stomped to the door. She hesitated to open it but wanted this game to be over. He knew she was waiting on him! She heaved the door open slightly and risked a glance in the hall. No one! There was not one single soul in the hallway. And not a sound coming from anywhere else in the castle. The whole place had gone silent.

Pushing the door closed again, she was tempted to put the bar down and teaching him a lesson. She knew she couldn't do it though and hung her head at her predicament. At least Liam was kind, even if he didn't share her affection. He was attracted to her, she knew, but he didn't love her, and right now she would have to settle for that. She knew he was safe, protecting her and her mother. He was reliable and a good leader in her father's place. Sitting on the bed, she scooted against the pillows and pulled her shift over her knees, hugging them to her chest.

The tears welled up in her eyes, and she began to rock back and forth. She had been strong enough. Her nerves and her fears about the future had finally reached the surface. Rolling onto her side, she let the tears flow. Surprisingly, it wasn't the rush of tears she expected would come. A few trickled down her cheeks, and before she knew it she was on a ship sailing across the ocean. Running away from it all—Silas, the shifting, the need for a husband, and memories of a home stolen from her. She left them all behind as the ocean breeze blew through her hair, the warm sun on her face. She had only seen the ocean once before and never imagined the feeling of freedom it gave.

Dark clouds suddenly blocked the sun, and the waves picked up, causing the ship to sway. Rocking back and forth on the ship's deck, she gripped the railing as she felt her stomach begin to roll, and the nausea took over. Groaning, she rolled farther onto her side, and her eyes fluttered open to see the fire roaring to life. Gasping, she jerked up, fully awake and turned her head to see Liam sitting on the edge of the bed. Shirtless, his muscular back toward her, he was bending down to remove his boots. His movement on the bed must have caused the storm in her dream.

She sat silently, not making a move, even though she felt sure he knew she was awake. He turned his head slightly over his shoulder and allowing a quick smirk at her nervousness, he continued to undress. Without turning to look her in the eye, he apologized.

"I'm sorry for waking ye, lass. I ken ye must be exhausted from today's...adventures."

"Adventures?" she whispered sarcastically under her breath.

His back and shoulders rose in a silent chuckle. The heat from the large stone fireplace, along with the heat rising in her cheeks made the room feel stuffy. He must have felt it too. He rose from the bed, his trousers still on but the ties loosed, and walked over to the window. A rush of cold winter air blew into the room as he opened the shutters. He hesitated, turning back to face her.

"I hope you dinnae mind. It seemed a wee bit warm in here."

She stared at him, unable to find her voice. He was a sight to behold, and she couldn't seem to look away. He stood there, letting her eyes roam up and down his body. She took in his shape, noticing how perfectly his chiseled jaw flowed into his muscular neck and shoulders. His chest, strong and sculpted, was covered in a light layer of soft blond hair.

Her eyes trailed down to his stomach, noticing a thin scar along his right side. Mixed with his hardened muscles, it only added to his intimidating appearance. His trousers hung on his hips, exposing a trail of hair slightly darker, disappearing behind the lacing. A single knock sounded on the door, shaking her out of her trance, and she audibly gasped in surprise.

"I thought some wine would be nice," he explained as he picked up the tray left outside the door. A pitcher of wine, loaf of bread, and a small bowl of drippings from a roasted boar were placed on the table, and her mouth watered at the smell. He poured them both a cup of the wine and reached a hand out to her.

Taking his hand gently, she climbed off the bed and took a seat at the table. As she brought the wine to her mouth, her hand shook, splashing a little onto her fingertips. Liam noticed it as well and took the cup from her. He gently wiped the drops off her hand with a linen napkin and then placed the bread in front of her.

"It's probably been quite some time since you've eaten." He began slicing the bread and taking some for himself dipped it into the juices.

She hungrily dipped her own and began shoveling it into her mouth. He laughed quietly, and she covered her mouth with her hand in embarrassment. Shaking his head at her, he pulled her hand away. Not letting her hand go, he looked at her earnestly.

"Dinnae be embarrassed with me. I like to see your appetite." Locking eyes with him she felt he wasn't only talking about the food..

"I think I'll try some of the wine again," she whispered, and he set the wine back in front of her and reached for another piece of bread for himself.

She felt his eyes on her as she sipped the wine. Looking up, she met his gaze. He looked different to her, like he wanted to devour her. Rather than scaring her, it sent a thrill through her.

A drop of the wine trickled on her lip and she licked it off, biting on her lower lip in the process. He stood and walked over to her. Reaching for her hand, he pulled her to her feet. Holding her one hand in his, he placed his other along the curve of her bottom and instinctively pulled her closer.

"I think it's time for bed," he whispered gruffly into the top of her head. She nodded, allowing him to lead her across the room to the edge of the large bed. He lifted her chin, forcing her to look him in the eyes. There was no fear in her face. She was ready to follow his lead.

Slowly, he began to untie the laces around the neckline of her chemise. As it fell away from her shoulders, he followed its trail with light kisses along her collarbone. She inhaled deeply, causing her breasts to rise against him, and he swiftly let the garment fall to the floor. She stood naked in front of him, his eyes moving over her. Her small frame in clothing looked like a child. Naked, however, she was very much a grown woman, and his body reacted. He grew harder and pulled her closer, kissing her.

She returned his kiss, slightly timid at first. A quiet groan from him encouraged her, and feeling a little more confident she reached up to hold his arms, bringing herself even closer to his body. Feeling his manhood press against her belly, she gave a small gasp and tried to back away. He held her tightly in place, moaning as she squirmed against him. Seeing her effect on him, she moved her body against him even more, hoping to please him. Suddenly, he picked her up and she was lying across the bed with his large frame hovering over her.

Leaning down to kiss her, he urged her mouth open and began exploring her mouth with his tongue. She was unsure of how she should respond and mimicked his actions with her own. Lowering himself down to her, he broke the kiss, his lips moved along her jawline. Breathless from the kiss, she felt along his waist and around his back, instinctively scratching his back in a soothing rhythm. His hands matched that rhythm, massaging her breasts.

He nuzzled her neck, nibbling at her throat and moving his hands down her body. He took his time, kissing every inch, but she arched her back, pushing her breasts up to meet his lips. His hands moved over her body, massaging the muscles under her smooth skin. His kisses continued down over her ribs to her stomach. His hot breath on her skin sent goose bumps all over her body. He lifted her hips, spreading her legs for him, and he lowered his head between them.

"Oh!" Her surprise was followed by a pleasurable moan. She was hot and damp with arousal. The scruffiness of his day-old beard was rough against her tender flesh, exciting her even more. She gripped her hands in his hair, pulling her hips up to eagerly meet his mouth.

He used his tongue to trace along her folds, eventually coming to her core. She didn't know if her body could handle much more. The heat she felt in her stomach had moved throughout her body, and she felt like she would explode. Panting with desire, she pleaded with him.

"Please," she whispered, but didn't know if she wanted him to stop or keep going. Her body knew though and continued to buck against his mouth.

He raised himself up to look her in the eyes. Using one hand to gently push strands of hair, damp with sweat, away from her face, his other hand trailed across her thigh.

"Kenna, ye havenae a clue how sensual ye are." His thumb rubbed the inside of her thigh, and she opened willingly for him. She had never been like this, powerful and vulnerable at the same time. Teasing her open, he slid his fingers into her. A quiet moan from her urged him on, and she rocked with his hand. The heat began to build again, and this time she couldn't stop the explosion. Her body shook, and she called out his name.

As the shudders from her body began to cease, he didn't remove his hand right away. Lying beside her, both breathless, he slowly slid his fingers from her.

"Kenna." He rolled on his side to look at her, placing his hand across her stomach, and gave her a serious look.

"I wanted ye to ken how good this can be. I dinnae

want to hurt ye."

A look of fear crossed her face, and he quickly added, "Yer first time...it can be..." He trailed off.

"Painful", she finished his sentence for him. "I ken," she sighed. "I'm nay as naive as I seem. I've heard women talk."

Placing a hand on his cheek, she continued.

"But I've never heard them talk about it feeling like this." She moved her hand to play with the damp hair around his temples.

"Liam, I'm ready. I ken ye willnae hurt me."

"I'm nay sure I can go slowly." He moved over her to settle between her legs. His hardness pressed against her, and she reached up to his shoulders, pulling him down for a kiss.

He began to rock against her, still not entering her, but she was ready for him, needed him, and began to move her body with his, deepening their kisses. His hands moved down her leg and brought her knee up along his side. She lifted her other knee, cradling his hips. His fingers found her again, but this time, she was ready for all of him. Breaking their kiss, she held his face in her hands. His eyes locked on her, and she nodded, eager to feel him inside her. He needed no further invitation.

He entered her slowly, her body stretching to accommodate his size. He let out a huff of air, and she hoped she hadn't done something wrong.

"Are ye hurt?" she whispered to him.

"Nay, lass, quite the contrary. Ye are so hot and wet fer me. Ye feel amazing." Nuzzling her neck again, he began to thrust harder and harder. He could feel her barrier and gave one quick hard thrust to break through.

As he did, his teeth bit into her shoulder. She gave a small shriek and turned to examine the bite on her shoulder.

"I'm sorry," he said in a husky voice. "Now we are mated. Everyone will ken ye belong with me."

She pulled his face to hers and kissed him passionately. She began to move her hips, urging him on. Feeling the tingle rise in her stomach again, she reached around his hips to bring him closer. He thrust harder and harder, and she was on the verge of climaxing again when she felt herself being lifted. His hands slid under her, and he held her tightly, rolling with her and causing her to sit astride him.

Still joined, she was confused, but he guided her hips and she started riding him. They locked eyes as her body moved over him. He reached up, massaging her breasts and bringing her nipples to a hard peak. Leaning back, she bucked harder and faster. The tremors started slowly but hit fast, and she gripped his chest throwing all her weight onto him as her climax took over. He exploded with her and let out a guttural growl as he came.

Breathless and sweaty, she collapsed onto his broad chest. She heard his heart pounding, and she rose and fell as he breathed heavily. When she finally caught her breath, she rolled off him and onto her side.

"Is it always like that?" she asked innocently. In all the stories she had heard, none ever told of experiences like this.

"Only with ye, Kenna." He smiled at her. Biting her lip, she looked at him sheepishly.

"Can we do it again?" She ran her fingers along the trail of hair leading to his groin. He shot her a wide-eyed look and smirked.

"I'd love nay anything more than to bury myself in ye again, but ye must rest, lass. Ye may be sore tomorrow." Placing a small peck on her forehead, he moved her hand and began to get out of bed. Her pride was hurt until he returned with a rag and bowl of warm water.

Leaning over her, he soaked the rag and began to wipe the inside of her legs. She was surprised to see the blood even though she had known of the bleeding. The warm rag felt soothing, and she closed her eyes as he instructed. Drifting off to sleep, she felt him bring the blankets around her. When he finished, he climbed in beside her and pulled her close. She gave a soft purr of contentment, and he placed a kiss on the bite mark on her shoulder before he fell asleep as well.

Chapter Sixteen

Kenna stretched her arm out lazily, reaching for Liam to pull him closer to her. She had gotten used to waking up slowly, curled into him, since their wedding. Instead of the warmth of his body, her hands found the bed cold and empty. Letting out a soft whine, she sat up in bed, pulling the blankets around her nakedness.

She had grown accustomed to sleeping like this as well and didn't miss the heavy, wool gowns she had worn before. He had insisted she get rid of those right away! She had enjoyed getting to know her husband each night and waking in his arms each morning. He awakened sensations in her the mere thought of which made her feel a heat throughout her body. She leaned her head back against the large, ornate headboard and began to imagine Liam with her. Her hands moved over her body as she thought about their time together and how he touched her.

A disturbing knock sounded on the door, and groaning she raised her head groggily. Another knock, slightly quieter shook her out of her haze as the door began to open slowly. Elin's petite frame peeked around the door, and her mood lightened. The two had become fast friends once Elin and her new babe had moved into the keep. She enjoyed the maid's company and felt she had a confidante in Elin.

"Good morn, milady," Elin whispered to her, but

she was fully awake and greeted her excitedly in return.

"Elin! Good morn! Ye are a pleasant surprise this early!" The smile Elin gave her in return warmed her heart, and she felt like her life was finally following the path it was meant to be on.

"Aye, 'tis good to see ye as weel this morn. Although," Elin confessed, "I must admit I am nay here of my own accord."

"Oh?" She was puzzled and waited for her to continue.

"Aye, the Laird and yer mum have asked me to fetch ye and have ye join them to break yer fast." She had become accustomed to breaking her fast with Liam, in bed. She hoped their morning routine wasn't coming to an end and pouted to herself as Elin helped her get ready. What was so urgent he was pulled away from spending the morning with her?

Playing out different scenarios in her head, each one more absurd than the first, she made her way to the great hall. Much to her surprise, neither Liam nor her mother were there. Grabbing a roll from a basket on the long table, she delicately pinched off a small piece. Nibbling slowly, she thought to herself where they might be, a sense of worry descending over her like a cloud. She wasn't sure what made her anxious but knew she needed to find them quickly.

Racing out into the courtyard, she found one of them. Liam was preparing a horse, placing several wool blankets over its back, obviously concerned for the comfort of the rider. The animal carried a large leather pouch, and she spied a loaf of bread peeking through the flap. Provisions, she thought to herself. The rider must be going on a long journey. She eyed Liam questioningly, and he hung his head, looking at the saddle and stirrups, pretending to adjust them and avoiding eye contact.

"Liam," she started but had a sinking suspicion she already knew the answer to her question. "Why are ye readying the horse? Are ye going on a journey?"

"Nay." He shook his head as he walked around and placed his hands on her shoulders. "It isna fer me. It's fer yer mother." Her brows narrowed and her eyes darkened at him.

"How could ye?" Her voice was low, barely a whisper, but the icy tone sent a shiver down Liam's spine. Before he was able to answer, she had her finger in his chest and was marching him backward.

"Ye promised! Ye said she was welcome here! And now?! Ye are just throwing her out after ye wed me?!"

She was near hysterics, and he rushed to put a stop to her tirade before she had the whole Cameron clan turned against him.

"Nay, Kenna! Ye have it all wrong!" He professed his innocence, but she turned her back to him, crossing her arms.

"Kenna, love," his tone softening. "Please." He tried to turn her around to face him, but she stood firm. "I'm nay sending her away! She came ta me asking ta go! I swear to ye!"

Spinning around, dumbfounded, her mouth gaped open. How dare he think her so naive?!

"Dinnae lie to me, Liam Cameron! I am nay a wee lass ye can tell yer stories to! My mother wouldnae leave me! Nay after all we've been through to find each other again!" Her eyes filled with tears.

"Och, Kenna, it pains me ye think that. I wouldnae ever lie to ye. But…" He paused, running his hands through his blond hair.

"If ye dinnae believe me," Liam pointed behind her and she turned to see her mother heading toward them, followed by Fergus and Agnes and then Hannah, trailing slowly behind dabbing at her eyes with a handkerchief.

"Ask her yerself."

Evelyn walked slowly to her daughter. Looking back at him for reassurance, she met her mother halfway. She wanted a little privacy and didn't want everyone to know she had questioned Liam's intent. Her mother, gripping her shawl tighter around her shoulders, smiled a large, fake smile.

"Kenna! Ye look well this morn!" Although her tone was happy, she saw right through the facade her mother presented.

"Mother, have ye asked Liam to get the horse ready? Where are ye going? I'll go with ye!" She didn't want her mother riding away from the Cameron keep unprotected. Silas probably had men hidden all through the territory, and she would at least be able to protect her mother in wolf form.

Placing a hand gently on her arm, Evie smiled at her apologetically.

"Och, my dear sweet Kenna. I love ye so! But nay, this isna a journey ye can take with me." A sense of dread came over her, and she gripped her stomach as her mother continued.

"Ye have found a home here again, with Liam, with everyone. They love ye and are yer family now, and I am so happy!" Kenna wiped the tears starting to slide down her cheeks. Shaking her head, she pleaded with her mother.

"YE are my family! YE must stay with me."

"I'll never be far from ye. Nay as long as I'm in here." She touched Kenna's chest. A sob escaped her, and she threw her arms around her mother.

"Why?" she begged. "Why must ye go? Are ye nay happy here as weel?" She didn't understand what her mother wanted the Camerons didn't offer.

"Oh, lass, I am verra happy here! But—"she paused"—ye have a life here and ye will have a beautiful future with yer husband. It soothes my soul fer leaving ye here. 'Tis time I found my own happiness again, and it's waiting fer me back at the McLindon keep." Kenna let out a loud gasp.

"NAY!" She shook her head, unable to believe the words her mother had just told her. "Ye cannae go back!" She gripped her mother's shoulders, trying to shake some sense into her.

"Kenna, 'tis all right. I've found someone as weel."

She stopped shaking her, looking at Evelyn confused. "Found someone?" she asked.

"Aye." Evie smiled. "I've fallen in love. And I wasna sure it was possible, but I believe he loves me as weel."

Still trying to wrap her mind around what her mother had just confessed, she let go of Evie's shoulders and took a step back.

"In love? With whom?" she asked slowly and suspiciously.

"He's a good man, love. Kind and strong. He will look after me." Evie looked down at her hands, waiting on Kenna's response. She knew right away who her mother had fallen for, the only kind soul at the McLindon keep.

"Sampson." she said softly, answering her own question, and Evie's smile and nod confirmed it.

She liked Sampson. He was the only one who had ever shown any compassion to her during her years with Silas. If he truly loved her mother, she knew he would try to protect her. Silas was cruel though, and she knew he would punish Evelyn. How could she let her go, but how could she keep her mother from happiness now that she had found her own? Hugging Evie tightly, she begged her to stay.

"Please, please. Dinnae return to him. We will send word to Sampson and have him join ye here!"

"Och, lass, that is verra generous but if he will have me, we will leave Silas McLindon and begin our own life together. Perhaps we may return to his clan."

Unable to control her emotions, she sobbed into Evelyn's shoulder, and her mother gripped her tightly, letting her own tears flow. They both knew the danger she was in, returning to the McLindon keep without Kenna.

After several moments passed, Evelyn pulled away from her as she sobbed. Hannah moved behind her to hold her shoulders as her mother spoke to her.

"I'm so proud of ye, lass. Ye have grown into a fine woman. Now it is time fer ye to learn yer true heritage." Her eyes rose to Liam as he held the horse steady. Placing one last kiss on her daughter's head, she turned toward the horse. Holding out his hand to assist her, Liam gave Evelyn a tight hug and one last kiss before helping her up in the saddle. Looking up, he continued to hold her hand.

"Thank ye, Laird Cameron, fer all ye have done fer Kenna. And fer me." She smiled down at him, recognizing Kenna had given up her birthright for the man she loved. After saying her goodbyes to everyone, she turned to look at Kenna one last time. She could not hold back her tears as her mother blew her a kiss before leading the horse through the gates.

****

The journey to the McLindon keep would take Evie a couple of days. She had brought provisions for the journey and wasn't afraid of being alone in the woods. She knew Liam had sent a patrol of wolves to look over her while she was on Cameron land. Then she was on her own.

She took a deep breath to compose herself. Kenna's face, tears staining her young, rosy cheeks, was her last memory of her daughter. She knew Kenna was safe and loved, and she looked forward to a new life with Sampson. She hoped she had not misread his affection but was willing to take the chance. They must leave Silas and together find their own place in the world. She knew it was wishful thinking, but still, she let her mind wander, imagining their new life together.

She was pulled from her thoughts by the rumble of her stomach reminding her it was long past time for her to make camp. She was in the middle of the dense forest, and there was plenty of tree cover overhead. Liam had provided several thick blankets and a Cameron plaid to keep her safe from the elements.

Dismounting, she tied the horse to a low branch. She doubted the animal would go anywhere, but just in case she was wrong, she wasn't prepared to walk to the

McLindon keep. She built a small fire from the brush she collected and the flint Liam had put in her bag. She filled her belly and settled in for the night, knowing she was safe. Even though she couldn't see them, she knew the wolves were watching her, protecting her from any harm. A lone howl answered her thoughts, and she fell asleep quickly and soundly.

The next morning, she woke to icy trees and even more snow that had fallen through the night. She hadn't even noticed, wrapped in the warm blankets, and was reluctant to rise. Stretching her limbs, she grabbed a chunk of bread and shoved it in her mouth. It was not ladylike, but she was in a hurry and didn't have time for manners. Her horse was stomping at the snow, his breath coming out in frosted puffs. He was ready to move as well.

"Okay, fella. We will be on our way." She chuckled at his impatience as she picked frost from his mane and untied him from the tree. She didn't mount him but instead chose to walk and lead him for a while, warming herself as she moved. She needed to stretch her legs this morning, and it was best to walk where she knew she was safe. Once she entered McLindon territory, she wouldn't be safe until she found Sampson. Even then, she wasn't sure.

At the edge of the forest, she climbed onto her horse. She said a silent goodbye to the invisible wolves she knew were somewhere watching her and left the cover of the trees. The distance from the forest to the McLindon keep was only about half a mile or so, but there was nowhere to hide. Proceeding with caution, it would be a slow journey, with the thick snow and constantly looking over her shoulder for any dangers.

She gripped her dagger tightly to her waist. Liam had given it to her for protection when she first approached him about leaving, after he tried to convince her otherwise. It was not meant to do much, but she felt better knowing she had something to use to defend herself.

Trudging through the snow there was not a soul around. She had expected to see some of the clansmen around, but as she neared the keep she was surprised at how uneventful her journey had been. She saw several men along the walls and some guarding the gates. Armed with swords and crossbows, they did not take long to spot her. She was too far to hear what they were saying, but based on their actions they did not see her as a threat. A few of the men pointed their weapons, not at her, but rather around her, as if she was a cover for some secret attack.

As she got closer, one of the men recognized her.

"'Tis Lady Evelyn!" he yelled to others, and she let the blanket she had pulled around her head and shoulders fall to reveal her identity.

"Aye," she called. "'Tis only I." She stopped at the gates, waiting on them to be opened but was only met with suspicious eyes. "I've returned. Please open the gates," she said quietly, pleading to the men.

"How do we ken ye are alone? Nay, a lass wouldnae travel this land by herself." The lead guard did not believe her and had the others on alert.

"Aye, I did though!" she persisted. "I left the Camerons of my own will. It wasnae my home. I've come to rejoin my brother." She hoped by bringing Judson into the conversation their suspicions were satisfied and they would open the gates. After hearing what Liam and Kenna suspected of him though, she was not sure she wanted to see him at all. The guard still hesitated, but to her surprise and excitemen, Sampson had walked into the courtyard to see what the commotion was about and now approached the guard.

"Evelyn?" Sampson asked hesitantly. "Ye have returned?"

"Aye, I've come home." Her tone was full of affection, and he was certain it was not for the McLindon keep. Nodding to the guards, he ordered them to open the gates and allow her to pass. Once inside, she dismounted, and the horse was taken to the stable.

She hoped the beast was taken care of, but if she knew anything of Silas, she knew it would be killed. Her heart broke for the beast and for the one who would be given the task of slaughtering the poor animal.

"Evie, ye must be frozen! Come, we will get ye warm and fed." Taking her by the shoulders, he led her into the keep, using his large frame to hide her from prying eyes.

Her chamber was just as she had left it, and Sampson rushed to build a fire to warm the room. She sat on the bed, watching his masculine frame as he moved around the room. She wanted to tell him how she felt. She didn't want to waste another moment of her time with him, and the words started coming out of her mouth before she knew what she was saying.

"Sampson, I didnae come back to see my brother." He stood, turning toward her.

"Aye, I figured as much." He smiled at her, and she felt the flush go up her neck and into her cheeks. "When ye left," he continued, "I wasnae sure how I felt.

I was glad ye were escaping Silas' nature. Surely the Camerons didnae hurt ye."

"'Course they didnae!" She felt the need to interrupt and defend the Cameron clan, even though the last time he had seen them they appeared to be kidnapping her.

He sighed, relieved, and continued. "Aye, I ken being reunited with Kenna was what ye wanted."

"It wasnae *all* I wanted," she stressed, looking up at him, silently urging him to know how she felt. "I came back, Sampson—"she paused"—ta be with ye."

He fell to his knees in front of her, and she gently touched his cheek. Clamping her small hand in his, he kissed her palm.

"Evie, I thought I'd never see ye again when they took ye from us. I dinnae ken how this can work between us. At least nay here." His words stung, and she blinked back the tears filling her eyes. She took a deep breath to compose herself.

"Och, I want nothing more than to hold ye close. I love ye, Evie. I love ye so, and if need be we will leave this place." His last words rushed out.

He loved her too! She threw her arms around his neck, kissing him in desperation.

He returned her kiss, deepening it and twisting his hands in her hair. She didn't want this moment to end.

"Sampson." She pulled back gasping for air. Her breathing was heavy with desire. "I want ye. I want all of ye. To be with me now."

He didn't wait. They only had a short time before word got to Silas she had returned. Laying her back on the bed, he hovered over her, careful not to put his full weight on her. Sliding his hand up her leg and under her skirt, he could tell she was ready for him. He pulled his shirt over his head, exposing his massive chest while she tugged at the laces on her bodice.

Kissing her neck, he only allowed her to undo enough laces to loosen the bodice before he pulled it away from her, exposing her breasts. Hungrily, he suckled each breast in turn, bringing her nipples to their peak. She wanted him and needed him more than any other man she'd ever known. Tugging at his belt, she encouraged him to quickly free himself of their restrictions. As he pushed his pants lower, she stroked his hardened manhood. He entered her swiftly, and she gave a soft moan of pleasure.

He moved quickly in her, fueled by his arousal, and she moved against him, urging him to go faster and harder, her lust equally as powerful. His strong hands gripped her hips, pulling her up to meet each thrust. As she reached her climax, she screamed his name softly, and he found his own release. Collapsing onto the bed beside her, he caught his breath and rolled onto his side, smiling sweetly. Sweat covered both their bodies, and he brushed away the hair matted to her forehead.

"Ye are a verra beautiful woman, Evelyn." He kissed her shoulder as he spoke. "And now, I get to call ye mine."

"I am yers, Sampson. With all of my heart." He kissed her passionately.

"I have made my decision," he said matter of factly, pulling away from her. "After we see the McLindon, I will tell him we are leaving. We will return to my own clan."

"Aye, I'd like that verra much. With Kenna now wed…"

His eyes widened.

"She is wed? To whom?" he asked, hopeful this would end Silas' pursuit.

"She has wed the Cameron Laird. Now, Silas will have nay reason to come for her." She seemed satisfied, but he was not so sure.

He sighed and kissed her tenderly on the lips before rising to sit on the edge of the bed. He began to dress, and she let out a dissatisfied groan.

"Are ye done with me so fast?" she teased him. "Ye dinnae have to leave so soon."

"Och, woman, I will never tire of ye." Turning to her, he stroked her cheek. "But I ken Silas, and he will have heard word of yer arrival. He will be looking fer ye." Nodding, she understood and climbed out of the bed to dress herself. Once they were both presentable again, he escorted her to the main hall.

The hall was stifling warm as the fire had been stoked so the flames licked the bottom of the tall chimney opening. Standing in the doorway, she scanned the room for familiar faces. Judson stood near the fire, trying to keep out of sight as usual, she thought to herself. As she glanced his way, his eyes darted down to his feet, and he did not look her in the eye. What had he done, she wondered, realizing Liam's suspicions may be correct. She thought about when the Camerons had taken her away, her mind was in a haze, and when she first arrived at the Cameron keep she had tried to convince Kenna to return. Had he planned all along to sacrifice her to get to Kenna?

Sampson walked her slowly to the end of the hall where Silas sat, his thumb rubbing against her arm in a soothing, comforting way. When they finally reached

Silas, Sampson didn't let go of her arm. Instead, he began speaking for her.

"Lady Evelyn has returned to us with news of her daughter. Unfortunately, she was unable to convince Kenna to return home with her." Sampson's flat tone showed no emotion.

Silas stood, walking around the long table to face her. She pulled herself upright and stood tall and regal like the wife of a Laird should be, even if he was long dead. He stood in front of her and Sampson, strumming his fingers along the table. Taking a deep sigh, he pulled her hands into his own.

"She wouldnae come with ye?" he asked her sympathetically. Her shoulders relaxed at the kind tone in his voice. Looking down to her feet, she shook her head. "But ye left her. To return to us? To return to yer home?"

"Aye." She looked at Sampson for reassurance, but he looked straight at Silas. She knew he didn't want to show any affection toward her. Silas only sought to use it against them.

"Ye left her," Silas repeated. "Ye LEFT her." His voice had started to rise, and his tone had grown angrier with accusations. "YE LEFT HER to be treated like an outcast, tortured like a prisoner!" He was yelling now, and she looked at him in confusion.

"She wasnae being tortured at all!" she blurted out in defense. She realized she had spoken out loud against Silas, but it was too late. "She is being treated like the lady she was born ta be!" Her shoulders rose again, and she pulled her head high. Whatever the consequences, she resolved to face them proudly.

"What do ye mean?" Silas narrowed his eyes at

her.

"Kenna has wed Laird Cameron. They lead the clan together as equals," she said proudly. "Ye need nay worry about her welfare anymore."

Anger flashed in Silas' eyes, but he quickly regained his composure. Pulling her away from Sampson into an embrace, he gently caressed her hair along the back of her neck.

"Och my dear, ye dinnae understand. He wed her ta start a war. He stole her from me," Silas whispered into her ear, sending a cold chill throughout her body. "I will get her back," he hissed, squeezing her tighter and tighter in his arms. Sampson stared at Silas as he kept her in his embrace.

"Ye have failed me. Ye have failed yer daughter. And ye will both die for this betrayal." She began to struggle against him, but Silas had her immobile. His hand gripped her small, fragile neck tightly and with one quick jerk of his wrist, he snapped her neck instantly.

Her body went limp, and Sampson watched in horror as Silas let her body collapse on the floor. Staring at her body, he couldn't breathe. A haze of anger clouded his vision, and he swore to himself he would kill Silas McLindon.

Silas, however, seemed to have forgotten the woman already and was focused on her brother. Judson had been cowering near the fire and gasped audibly in horror as Silas had murdered Evelyn. Seeing Silas studying him, Judson quickly regained his composure.

"Ye'll miss her." He stalked toward Judson.

"She was useless." Judson's replied flatly, looking straight ahead. Pushing him further, Silas continued.

"Still, she was yer sister." Silas egged him on.

"Half-sister. And she was nay longer a help to us." Judson looked at Silas with dead eyes.

"We shall see. She may be of use to me yet." Silas turned toward Sampson, who had picked up Evelyn's body and was carrying it from the hall. He would not bury her with the others but would find a special place only he knew to visit.

"Send her body to the lass. It will be my wedding present to her. If she returns—"Silas paused to look at Judson"—her uncle willnae have to be next."

Stopping in his tracks, he did not turn around to face the bastard.

"Wait! I think a few other gentle reminders may be in order. Place her body in the stables. I'll be out in a little while," Silas called after him as he marched out of the hall.

He carried Evie's body away to say his own goodbyes, tears streaming down his face. He wanted to take her body and flee, but she was no longer there. He knew her body no longer held her sweet soul. As he left the hall, he heard Judson, obviously no longer able to hold back his nerves, retching on the fresh rushes scattered on the hall floors.

Chapter Seventeen

The riderless wagon approached the castle gates slowly. It was being pulled by what should have been a fine horse but had been starved so its skeleton was visible through the skin. The guards watched, unsure if the animal was going to make its destination. Opening the gates, the guards allowed the beast inside while the stable lads brought hay and water. It was too late though, and to no one's surprise the sad animal collapsed into the snow and mud. The horse had been not only starved, but as the men got a closer look it was obvious by the scars and open wounds the animal had lived an abused existence. This was clearly intended to be the last journey for the poor animal, no loss to the owner.

Liam and Kenna were headed to the stables for an evening ride and were distracted by the commotion. Joining the small crowd that had gathered around the beast, Liam looked around for a rider, paying no attention to the wagon the animal had been pulling.

Kenna, however, noticed the small mound of worn woolen blankets in the back of the wagon and began to timidly pull back one corner. Her hand shook, a sense of dread filling her body. It only took a second for her to realize what was under the blanket. Evelyn's body lay stiff, limbs bent in an unnatural position, her skin a pale, ashy gray.

She heard the scream, an excruciatingly mournful howl, and felt herself being pulled into strong arms, her face shielded from viewing her mother. She still saw though. Everything seemed to be unfolding below her, as if her mind had left her body and hovered over the grisly scene. She saw Liam hugging her to his chest, felt his arms around her. He was yelling at the guards to quickly shut the gates.

She watched as Fergus shook his head sadly and placed the blanket back over Evie's face. Just as quickly as she was above them, she was back in her body, sobbing and gasping for air. Hannah pulled her out of Liam's arms to rush her into the walls of the keep, but her body was trembling, and she could feel the shift coming on. Breaking free of Hannah's arms, she sprinted toward the outer walls, heading toward the forest.

"Scour the lands! The body didnae arrive here on its own. They may still be in Cameron territory." Chasing after her, Liam yelled over his shoulder as he rushed from the keep.

"If ye find them, bring them to me. I will punish the bastard who delivered her, and then I'm going after the one who sent him!" It was obvious Silas McLindon planned to stop at nothing to get control of Kenna, mind and body. He must put a stop to the maniac before more innocent people were killed and protect her if it was the last thing he did.

****

The last of the daylight barely penetrated the dense woods. Liam followed the sounds. He knew better than to sneak up on a wolf shifting, especially one not yet in control of their gift. He found her in a clearing, already on guard. The hair on her back stood on end, and when she heard him approach she spun on him, her lips curled back showing long, sharp canines. She eyed him nervously, pawing at the ground. He stood firm, hand out, a signal to her he meant no harm.

A few unsure moments passed, and as she began to recapture her surroundings the hair on her back began to lay down and her lips uncurled. He sighed, relaxing his shoulders but still on alert. She was learning to control her wolf instincts but was still new. She could lose control again in seconds.

She hesitantly stepped toward him, lowering her head submissively. He stayed put and allowed her to approach. Moving closer, she circled him, and with the moonlight the auburn tint of her fur reflected in the snow. She had made a full circle around him, and coming around to his front she nudged her forehead into his chest. He slowly raised his hands, caressing behind her ears and bowed his head to hers.

"I'm so sorry, love," he whispered into her fur, and her body quivered with unshed tears.

Pushing against him, she backed away into the clearing. She let loose another mournful howl. Her pain was palpable, and the weight of her sorrow almost made his knees buckle. The howling continued for several long moments. Anyone who heard the horrible sound would have been scared for their life. She was not a threat to anyone right now. Not intentionally anyway. Her grief was too great. She finally collapsed, exhausted, in the snow, and he moved quietly to sit beside her.

"We will avenge yer mother, Kenna. The bastard willnae get away with this. I'll rip his throat out myself!" He clenched his hands, rage evident in his voice. She looked up at him and nudging his arm slid her head underneath to lay in his lap.

He had no idea how long she would remain in wolf form. Her shifting was being controlled by her emotions, as they all were at first. He had told her his lasted from a few moments to several days. Once he learned to control his emotions, he controlled the shifting. Now, he shifted in an instant or he may not shift for months at a time. She was learning as well, but until then he would not risk her returning to the keep. Stroking her fur, he offered her an apology.

"Kenna, I'm so sorry, but I cannae allow ye to return this way. Nay until ye can control yer wolf. I hope ye understand, love." She looked up at him, her green eyes soft and gentle, and she licked his hand.

"O'course I willnae leave ye!" he rushed on to say. "I will show ye te a safe place. 'Tis where I stayed when I was learning what it meant to become the wolf." She rose up, her ears perking in interest.

"Come," he encouraged her. "'Tis nay verra far from here."

****

They walked side by side through the icy trees until they came to a rock cliff beside the frozen riverbed. A thin crack ran down the length of the rockface, but as they came closer, it was actually an opening into the rock wall. Ducking into the opening, Liam motioned for her to follow. She easily slipped through the opening, surprised since it appeared as only a crack from the outside.

Inside the rock, a cave opened into high ceilings. Stalactites hung threateningly, small drips of water coming from them to form pools in the cave floor. She was in awe of the beauty and secrecy of the cave. He smiled at her as she took it all in.

"Wolves have been using this cave for centuries, or longer. It is a safe space for us. Fergus brought me here when I first shifted. He helped me through it and taught me how to control it. I would have been lost without him."

She felt the same way about Liam, lost without him and the Cameron clan. Right now, he was the only thing keeping her from falling apart. She bowed her head at him and closed her eyes. She hoped he understood her feelings. When she returned to human form, she wanted to be sure to tell him.

He had started a fire in what was obviously a well-used fire circle. Stone circles surrounded the pile of wood, and years of ash lay in the bottom of the circle. Looking around, she imagined after centuries of use, some comforts of home had been stored here. She was right and smirked to herself as he led her to the back of the cave. Trunks had been placed back there and held blankets, iron pans for cooking, and a few dried herbs and ointments for healing.

Liam pulled several blankets and thick wool tartans from the trunks and laid them on the ground, forming a makeshift bed. Removing his boots and clothing, he folded them into a pile and placed them in the chest. He turned, naked, to face her, and her eyes widened in appreciation. He smirked and shook his head. Even in wolf form, she still appreciated his human body.

"Dinnae be afraid of me," he started explaining, and she tilted her head, looking at him questioningly. "I'm going to shift as weel. We will keep warmer," he continued, "should ye return to yer human form before sunrise."

Pausing, he added sheepishly, "And it may protect me from yer shifting since ye are still a little reckless as it happens." He winked at her teasingly.

She backed away, allowing him space to change. It happened swiftly and effortlessly. Within seconds, he had gone from a naked man to a large, beautiful wolf. The light color of his fur matched the dirty blond of his hair. She approached him, her head bowed, and nuzzled his neck. Lying out in front of him, she rolled onto her back. She wanted him to know whether in human or wolf form, he was her Alpha.

Licking her face, he stepped over her and went to lie down beside the fire. She followed and curled up beside him. She was exhausted and hoped sleep brought only dreams of running through the forest and she forgot the gruesome form of her mother's body. It did not take long for him to begin breathing soundly, and soon after she fell asleep beside him, feeling safe and protected.

****

An icy breeze covered Kenna's body, and instinctively she reached for the blanket to shield herself from the cold. Feeling around, not quite awake, she felt the hard ground beneath her body. She sat up quickly and took in her surroundings. Liam was still in wolf form, curled up beside her, sleeping soundly.

Groaning, she held her head in her hands as she remembered the events from the night before. Or was it still night? She had no idea of what time or day it was, how long she had let the wolf take over. Wrapping herself in the Cameron tartan Liam had pulled from the trunk, she walked to the entrance of the cave. Peering out, she saw a clear night sky. The stars were bright, and the moon was large and round, its light reflecting brightly off the snow-covered ground.

It seemed to her this day was never-ending. She wanted to stay in this cave forever, hidden away from the reality of her mother's death. It was hard for her to believe that her mother was gone. While they may not have had the relationship she wanted, she had grown closer to her mother in the past few weeks. She had hoped staying with the Camerons would allow them to rebuild all Silas McLindon had torn apart.

Any chance was gone forever now. Hiding away was impossible though, and she needed to learn how to get control of her shifting. She must be the one to avenge her mother, and the sooner she learned to master her shifting, the sooner *she* could kill Silas.

Liam would never let her, of course, which is why she had no intention of him knowing. Once she learned to control herself, she planned to convince him to go back and make sure all was right with the clan, leaving her to practice her shifting alone. With him away, she would go alone to the McLindon keep and end Silas' hold on her forever.

She sighed, pleased with the plan she had arranged but feeling a slight twinge of guilt for keeping it from Liam. She turned to look at him and was surprised to see him rise and stretch, still in wolf form. Pulling the tartan tighter around her, she could have sworn there was a smirk on his wolf face. He had seen her body many times, but she still felt shy around him when they were not being intimate.

Stretching, he lumbered off to the back of the cave.

She heard him relieving himself, and a few moments later he returned in human form, a tartan wrapped lazily around his hips. She watched him saunter back, wide-eyed at his typical masculine behavior. Liam, eyebrows raised, offered her a shrug of his shoulders in return. She shook her head at him, but as he settled back down on the pallet of blankets she admired him again.

The plaid hung low over his buttocks, and she could see the dimples at his lower back and the top curve of his muscular behind. A warm blush crept up her neck and face. He rolled onto his side and patted the area beside him. The plaid had come loose and draped over his hips as a blanket. She was eager to be back in his arms and didn't hesitate to curl into him, her head buried under his chin.

He pulled her close, wrapping his tartan around them both. She was breathing fast and shallow against his chest, and he stroked her back soothingly.

"The bastard willnae harm a single hair on yer head." He kissed into the top of her hair. Pushing away from him, she was surprised to realize he thought her breathlessness was fear of Silas.

"I will tear his throat out." Her tone was low and flat, void of emotion.

His eyebrows pulled together quizzically.

"Nay, love," he said, touching her cheek gently. "I willnae see your goodness and kindness be tainted by such evil. Ye willnae ever see the man again. Ye are mine to protect, and I will make him pay for all he has done against ye and the Cameron clan."

He pulled her head back to his chest and placed another kiss on top of her head. She knew Liam would protect her at all costs, and she felt safe and secure with him. She also knew this was her battle to fight, and she was strong enough handle Silas alone, at least in wolf form. She felt powerful now and wanted to be in control.

She would never use her Alpha gift against Liam. She had made a promise to him and to herself. But still, she wanted him to see how strong she was. She could feel his maleness beside her and brought herself even closer, stretching her body alongside the length of his. A small groan escaped his lips.

"Kenna," he whispered disapprovingly. "Ye dinnae have ta please me now. Ye have been through hell. Ye need ta rest. Yer mind *and* yer body," he told her in a scolding manner.

She was not a child to be reprimanded though, and she knew what she wanted. Right now, she wanted him. Circling his nipple slowly with her finger, she brought it to a hard peak, and his body responded. He grabbed her hand and held it tight against his chest to stop her.

"Kenna." His voice was husky with his desire. "I'm nay sure this is the right time. Ye may na be ready." She understood his concern and she loved him even more for it, but she had never been more ready and wanted to show him.

She placed small, light kisses along his chest. Her hand still held prisoner by his, she used her tongue to gently bring the already taut nipple to an even higher peak. A huff of air came from him as he tried to hold back, but she began to move against him, and his strength was lost.

Releasing her hand, he grabbed her head, pulling her face back with gentle force. Her hand, now free to roam, ran down the length of his body, reaching around to grab his firm backside. She pulled him against her, grinding into him, and he returned with a hard, deep kiss.

This was not to be the gentle lovemaking she was used to. She was looking for something, and he let her lead until she found it. Eagerly, she pushed him onto his back, rolling with him until she was lying atop him. Pushing herself up, she sat astride him and could see the desire clouding his eyes.

"Ride me, Kenna," he commanded, his arousal pressed against her. He gripped her hips and lifted her to allow himself inside. She was ready, and he entered her in a swift, smooth movement, filling her and sending a shock of excitement through her body. Without hesitation, she moved against him, allowing him to guide her hips. His calloused hands massaged her hips, and she began to ride harder and faster. Leaning back, she placed her hands on his muscular thighs, and her long auburn hair fell away, exposing her breasts.

His hands moved from her hips and ran up and down her thighs until he stopped at her center. Using his thumb, he massaged her bud, sending a warm sensation through her body. She bucked against him, moving her hips faster to meet his hands. She was panting with desire, and small moans of arousal slipped from her lips.

The trembling started in her legs as the heat spread through her body. She could feel her release coming, and leaning forward she gripped his large chest, digging her nails in with the force of her release. He gave one last thrust into her, and both let out soft screams as they reached their peak together.

Collapsing on his chest, she was breathing heavily and covered in a fine sheen of sweat. Stroking her back while they both caught their breath, he wasn't surprised when a loud sob shook her body. She had been through so much, and a physical release of that strength was sure to bring on an emotional release as well.

Liam didn't try to quiet her. Instead, he rocked her soothingly as she let out her grief.

"Let it out, lass. I will be here with ye. When ye are ready, we will return together. And when the time is right, I will see this threat to ye and our clan eliminated once and for all."

She clung to Liam, knowing Silas was not going to rest in his pursuit of her. Not until she was back under his control or dead by his hand.

Chapter Eighteen

Evelyn's body was taken to a small chamber in the back of the chapel. The horse had been dragged away from the keep, its body set afire, along with the wagon it had pulled. Everyone moved around the keep as if in a daze, unsure of what to do or how to act considering all that had transpired. Liam and Kenna had not yet returned to the keep, and Fergus had stepped in to guide the clan. It had only been a day since the body had arrived, but superstitions had already taken control, especially among the older clansmen. They wanted the body returned to McLindon, removed from the Cameron lands in fear of Evie's unsettled spirit haunting the keep.

While Fergus would never admit to fearing spirits himself, he was cautious not to say so in front of clan elders. They still believed in light and dark magic. And why shouldn't they, he thought to himself. After all, the clan's blood carried the shapeshifting trait. He had heard tales of others changing into different beasts than the wolf, but for centuries only the wolf gene had survived. While no magic was practiced in the clan, Fergus had seen wonders worked with healing herbs. Maybe what they considered magic he considered healing arts.

He had placed guards to stay with the body, to ensure these old fools Evie's spirit would not leave the chapel. Two men had been stationed outside the door to the small room where the body lay, another two at the doors to the chapel. He had not asked for volunteers, knowing many of the men would be too scared to refuse, but too scared to stay in the chapel as well.

However, to his surprise Niall, Liam's young cousin, had insisted on being one of the guards. The boy had formed a special bond with Evie when she first came from the McLindon keep. Niall had insisted he could never be afraid of Evelyn in life or in death, and he would be honored to guard her spirit. Impressed with the boy, he had agreed to let him stand the first guard. After all, what harm could it do?

Evie's body had lain in the chamber for several hours while Hannah and Agnes gathered women willing to help prepare the body for burial. The superstitions among the women were even stronger than among the men. They were afraid touching the body would tie Evie's spirit to them. Some even insisted she could use their bodies to house her soul. Hannah searched for one woman in particular who she knew should be especially scared of Evie's spirit.

Hannah had been keeping an eye on Nissa and was now certain that she, along with Judson, had played a role in Audric's death. Now the woman's absence made her wonder just what plans the crone had.

Nissa had disappeared from the keep soon after the body arrived. She had last seen her with the crowd gathered round the wagon. Once the blanket had been removed from Evie's face, everyone's concern had turned to Kenna. She, however, had watched Nissa closely.

The terror on the woman's face was evident, and

she had quickly run for the kitchens. Since then, there had been no sign of the woman. She knew Nissa believed in the old ways, and if she truly had something to do with her or Audric's death, Nissa believed Evie's spirit was coming for her.

Since she and Agnes were going to be occupied preparing Lady Evelyn's body, she needed someone else to be on the lookout for the woman should she return. Liam had told her not to disclose the information, but now she had no choice. She must let someone in on their suspicions, and she only thought of one other she trusted to do it. She had to find Elin.

The young maid was in Kenna's chamber as she thought, hanging the freshly laundered dresses. Elin's newborn babe lay beside her in the large basket she used as a bassinet. The tiny hands and feet were visible over the rim of the basket as the babe wiggled and cooed. Elin was weeping quietly, and she wondered what had happened to the lass.

"Elin, dear," she said softly as she entered the room, not wanting to frighten the poor young girl. The girl's gasp of surprise told her she had not succeeded.

"Oh! Hannah! Ye startled me." Elin wiped at her cheeks with the back of her hand.

"I didnae mean to, lass, but what has ye so upset?" She patted the young mother's hand as she pulled her along to sit in a chair by the fireplace.

"I'm so worried about Lady Kenna. Her grief must have been too much to bear. She ran off into the woods and hasna returned to us. What if something has happened to her?" Elin's voice rose, and she couldn't help but smile at the girl's panic. She was glad to see the bond Elin and Kenna had already formed.

"Nay, dear, dinnae fash about Kenna. Yer lady is goin' ta be just fine. Laird Cameron has gone ta be with her until she's ready to return." She tried to soothe the maid's nerves.

"But she will return?" Elin looked relieved, and Hannah squeezed her hands in her own.

"O'course she will! She is Lady Cameron now. This is her home." She smiled kindly at the young woman. She had thought Elin was worried to lose her friend but had not considered she was also worried over her position in the keep.

"Elin, dear, I told ye, dinnae fash about Kenna. Or yerself and yer bairn," she added. "Ye both are part of this family now and will always have a place at the Cameron keep." She looked over to the basket at the sweet sounds coming from it and smiled. She knew the babe needed to be around Fergus and the others if he carried his father's wolf blood.

"Thank ye, Hannah. It means a lot to me. And…I'll try nay ta think on it." Elin rose, giving her a tight hug, and went back to straightening the fabrics to dry.

"Elin," she continued. "Being part of this clan means loyalty and doing what is necessary to protect the clan."

"Aye," Elin said slowly, turning to look at her suspiciously.

"I ken ye are loyal to Lady Kenna and to all the Camerons, and right now we all need yer help." As she spoke, the girl's brows drew together in worry.

"This is ta be kept between ye and me fer the time being, understood?" She raised her eyebrows at Elin until the girl nodded quickly. Rising from her seat with a huff, she moved over to help Elin with the dresses while she explained.

"The old kitchen maid, Nissa, has disappeared." Elin shook her head, sighing, unsurprised by the information.

"Aye," she continued, understanding Elin's reaction. "I have known for some time she had something to do with Laird Audric's death. Now she is gone, and I'm worried she may be up to something."

Elin stared at her wide-eyed. "Where do ye think she has run off ta? She doesnae have family or friend I ken."

"Weel, I suspect she has run to the McLindons." Elin's eyes grew even bigger as she continued. "Ta warn them."

"Nay!" Elin exclaimed, shocked at what Hannah was saying. "She wouldna be that foolish, do ye think?"

"Aye. I do. I remember she had feelings at one time for Lady Evelyn's half-brother. He was banished with them but chose to stay with the McLindons when Lady Evelyn was brought home." The sneer in her tone showed her disgust toward Judson.

"The McLindon will kill her. If he doesnae, she will nay be welcome back here. She will be an outcast." The pity was evident in Elin's voice. "I will help ye keep an eye out for her. If she does return, I willnae let her out of my sight."

Confident of Elin's word, she patted the maid's shoulder gently as she left the room. Elin stopped her in the doorway.

"Hannah, thank ye. Thank ye for trusting in me. And fer nay asking me to help ye with Lady Evelyn's body!" Elin gave a shudder as she pulled the door shut behind her.

Heading down to her study, she gathered the oils and herbs she needed to anoint the body. She had no idea when Kenna might return but knew she would want to see her mother buried. These oils helped preserve the body. For a few days at least. Luckily, the winter weather also slowed the natural process.

Agnes was waiting for her outside the small chamber. Niall and Ian, another young lad, were keeping watch over the door but had drifted off to sleep. Agnes hadn't the heart to wake them and instead let them doze while she waited.

Hannah shook Niall gently, and placing a finger to her lips instructed him to keep quiet and go back to sleep while they slipped into the room. Closing the door behind them, she handed two small bunches of tightly wrapped linen to Agnes. Keeping two for herself, they crammed them into their nostrils quickly before the smell of death overpowered them in the small space.

Evie's body lay on a long table covered by the dirty woolen blanket she had been delivered in. Her limbs, twisted and bent unnaturally, were peeking out from underneath. A large basin of hot water had been brought to the room, and it sat steaming on a smaller side table. Laying out her oils and spices, she rolled up her sleeves to get started washing the body.

Slowly pulling the blanket away from the body, she closed her eyes at the sight before her, trying to pull herself together. Evie's beautiful hair was matted and covered with dirt and debris. Seeing it made her eyes fill with tears as she remembered how lustrous and soft the woman's hair had been.

Sighing heavily, she began to pull the twigs and leaves from Evie's hair as Agnes began to reset her limbs. It was a gruesome, heavy task, and they worked solemnly. The disturbing sound of the bones snapping as they forced them into a more natural position echoed through the small chamber.

Hannah had seen many battle injuries and even horrific deaths, but this was almost too much for her to bear. She wasn't sure what torture Evie had endured. Her neck had been broken and she knew it was what ultimately killed the woman but prayed the injuries happened after she was already dead.

Wiping the sweat from her brow, she heard a quiet knock on the door. On the other side, she heard Niall trying to speak through the heavy wood. Unable to make out what he was saying, she cracked open the door.

The boy caught a brief glimpse into the room followed by the pungent smell drafting out, and it was too much for him to handle. The young lad hit the floor hard and fast, waking Ian. The young man saw his friend unconscious on the floor and immediately looked around for his attacker. Hannah had to laugh at the scene but regained her composure to calm the boy down.

"Och, lad! There isnae anyone else in here! Calm yerself." She gripped his shoulders, turning him to look at her. Facing the door to the small chamber, Ian got a peek into the room as well and started swaying on his feet. She quickly ushered him into a pew in the chapel area, away from the sights and smells. Once Ian was settled with his head between his knees, she rushed back to tend to Niall, but Agnes already had the boy sitting up with some smelling salts under his nose.

She looked at him pitifully, her mouth in a thin

line. "Weel, Niall, I think that will abou' do it fer yer shift on guard duty."

He nodded and began to stand with Agnes' help when a cold breeze filled the room. The door to the chapel had been flung open, and Ian was gone. Sputtering, Niall gasped at Ian's absence.

"She's got him!" Niall's eyes were wide in fear, and he gripped onto Agnes who was still standing beside him. "She's taken him! Her spirit came fer him!" He shook her shoulders, convinced the cool blast was Evie's spirit, but Agnes paid him no attention. She took a deep breath in through her nostrils and nodded toward Hannah. The breeze they had felt was Ian trying to outrun his shifting.

Hannah shut the chapel door and came back to help Agnes calm the lad when they all heard a loud moan come from the small room where the body lay. All of the blood left Niall's face, and he began stammering, but no words came from his mouth.

"Niall." Hannah spoke sternly trying to get the boy's attention. His eyes darted around the room, looking crazed. "NIALL!" she yelled to shock him, gripping his cheeks, and bending his face to hers. "It's a natural thing for the dead to make noises. 'Tis only gas! It is nay a spirit!" A fine bead of sweat had formed on his forehead, and he looked like he was going to be ill. She called to the men keeping watch at the chapel door, but no one was there. They must have all run scared, she thought to herself.

Wrapping herself under Niall's other arm, she and Agnes carried the boy from the chapel back to the keep. By the time they arrived, Niall had pulled himself together enough to speak and walk on his own. Hannah was certain they would have to do a cleansing ritual before he would step foot in the small church again.

She and Agnes returned to the chapel to finish preparing the body. As they moved Evelyn's body into different positions to rub oils on her skin and change her clothing, several more moans escaped from her body. While Hannah knew it was perfectly normal for gases to escape the bodies of the dead, Agnes was taken off guard each time and was visibly shaken.

"O', Aggie! Dinnae ye start with that nonsense. Ye ken Lady Evelyn would ha ne'er hurt a fly!" She scolded her friend in a teasing manner.

"Aye, I ken. Still, I'm glad ta be done with it," Agnes replied matter-of-factly.

"Aye, me as weel," she admitted. "Now we must see to getting a box built. The men can handle in the morn."

The two women locked the door to the small chamber behind them and, huddling close together in the dark night, made their way back to the keep. When they entered the great room, the sudden silence was deafening. Niall sat in the center of the room, a large crowd gathered around him. He had obviously been telling them about the spirit of Lady Evelyn coming to him. Hannah shot him a look of disappointment. The boy surely left out the parts where he was rendered speechless and motionless, helped by two women from the church.

The silence lasted only a moment as Hannah and Agnes were rushed by the crowd wanting to know if Niall spoke the truth. Coming to protect his wife and Hannah, Fergus stood, arms crossed in front of the two women facing the people who had crowded around them.

"Yer all acting like a bunch of damned fools!" His loud, deep voice shook the room. "Ye should all be ashamed!" As Fergus chided the hall of people, Hannah looked around to see the fear and doubt on their faces. Placing her hand gently on Fergus' arm, she interrupted his lecture.

"Thank ye, Fergus, but let me speak to them. I believe I can set the record straight."

Speaking loud enough for the whole hall to hear, she began retelling the story. She explained how a dead body fills with gas, and movement pushes the gas through different orifices, causing sounds of moaning to leave the body. While some took her explanations to heart, others shouted questions, wanting more explanation. They wanted her to explain the door opening, the cold breeze. Which she did easily since the wind was blowing and snow was swirling outside. After all of their questions seemed to be answered, Niall stood up quietly.

"Hannah," he said quietly, still obviously shaken by what had happened that night. "Where is Ian?" Everyone began looking around, scanning the room.

"Has he nay returned?" she questioned Niall, who shook his head sadly. Looking at Fergus, she knew what had happened to the boy. Fergus understood her look and nodded quickly.

"I'll go find the lad." He placed a kiss on Agnes' forehead before he ducked through the doorway. Once he had left, she dismissed everyone back to their activities. She had tired of the superstitious talk and wanted to speak to Niall. Urging him up to help her put away her oils, she led the boy to her healer's study. He needed to get his wits about him again, and she needed to make him understand Evie's unsettled spirit had not whisked Ian away.

Settling the boy on a small wooden stool, she fixed the lad a tonic to drink. Sipping the bitter tea, Niall's color began to return, and he seemed to grow increasingly tired. He agreed with her it could not have possibly been the spirit of Lady Evelyn. Hannah and Agnes would have seen her spirit leave her body, which they did not. By the time she shooed Niall to bed, the boy was all but sleepwalking and repeated what she had told him word for word. The drink had worked, and the boy should sleep soundly. This night at least.

****

Fergus found Ian huddled near the edge of the woods against a weathered old shed. The shed had been an old healer's hut where herbs were hung to dry but was in such disrepair the roof had all but fallen into the floor. The young man's clothing was in shreds, and he shivered with the cold.

"Och, lad! Ye will catch yer death out here like this. Why did ye nay stay the wolf?" Fergus removed his coat, covering the boy's exposed chest and shoulders.

"I wasnae sure if Niall followed me. I havenae told him about my shifting yet. I ken how badly he wants to be able to change. I didnae want him to see it like this," Ian sputtered out, his teeth chattering with the cold.

He was still coming to grips with possessing the wolf gene and had come to Fergus when he first started developing the gift. He and Liam had helped Ian get through the first several shifts and had explained what being the wolf meant. Ian was glad to own the trait but was worried about how his friend might react.

"Yer a good friend ta Niall. And...I understand ye wanting to protect his feelings." He did understand but also knew Ian had a duty to the clan since he now possessed the gift.

"Ian, yer Laird will have need of ye now. Ye cannae hide away from this anymore." He spoke gently to the boy. He knew Ian was scared. Scared of losing his friend, scared of dangers he would be facing, and scared of disappointing his Laird.

"Aye." Ian rose to his feet, grabbing his boots that had been thrown off during his shift. He stood tall and straight, trying to appear more man than boy. "I wasnae sure but being able to leave the chapel and get away before I shifted, I ken I am ready."

"Aye, ye are." He clapped his hand on the young man's back and proudly led him back to the keep.

Chapter Nineteen

It was several days before Liam and Kenna returned to the keep. During that time, several more individuals had shifted. Fergus had been busy helping the men, while his wife, Agnes, helped the women through the transition. Altogether, there were now about twenty mature wolves in the clan. Fergus thought it was because of the recent threat to the clan from Silas, or because the true Alpha may have returned. With so many wolves, they were well prepared for battle with Silas.

Liam had stayed with her, even though she had tried to send him away. He, unfortunately, had seen right through her plan. He knew that left alone she would have run straight to Silas, her reasoning clouded by anger, and so he had waited with her.

She had learned quickly to control her shifting and was able to shift when and where she wanted. She was no longer controlled by her emotions. Liam had helped her understand how to recognize the signs a shift was coming and how to use her mind to push the animal instincts away and regain control.

She would never be able to thank him enough for being there to coach her but also for being with her as she grieved. She missed her mother terribly but knew she was no longer under the McLindon's power. She was ready to lay her mother to rest and was eager to avenge her death.

She had worked hard to learn to control her instincts, convincing him to allow her to join them in attacking the McLindons. While she hoped no innocent lives were lost during the upcoming battle, she had no intention of resting until Silas McLindon had paid for all that he had done, whatever the sacrifice.

The Cameron keep was a bustle of activity and excitement when they returned. Fergus had not let the clansmen rest, and Liam found everything in order. He greeted the man warmly. Kenna was engulfed in embraces by Hannah, Elin, and Agnes, all thankful to see her well. She smelt the familiar wolf scent on Agnes. It was strong, she thought. She must have shifted recently as the scent lingered when she hugged Elin as well. After several moments of tears, the women led her to the chapel to say her goodbyes before her mother's body was laid to rest.

The wooden box still lay in the small chamber in the back of the chapel. She nervously went inside, walking around the table, eyeing the box. It had been beautifully made, not just a simple coffin. The men had painstakingly carved the Cameron crest into the lid, and the edges had been delicately scalloped in an intricate design. It was fit for a woman of Evie's stature, and she was pleased her mother received the burial she deserved, even if she didn't get the life she did.

The next day, she was once again escorted to the small chapel. This time, however, it was not her groom waiting inside, but her mother. It seemed like everyone attended the burial for Lady Evelyn, wanting to say their goodbyes and make amends for believing her guilt in Audric's death. The service seemed to fly by, and as she went through the motions it seemed unreal to her.

Evie's body was buried alongside Audric's. Laying a bouquet of heather and thistles over both the stone markers, she was surprised no tears came to her eyes. She knew Evie's spirit was no longer there but hoped she heard her wherever it was. She had come to terms with the fact she would no longer see her mother on this earth, and in place of grief a new feeling of action had taken its place. She used the pain Silas had caused her to fuel her. She would never allow a man like him to win in this world, and his cruelty will never be forgotten or forgiven. She was ready to face him, ready to make him pay for his actions to her and those she loved.

She had sat alongside the fresh grave, spending some time alone with her thoughts and devising a plan for revenge. Standing, she brushed the dirt from her skirts and turning saw Liam waiting for her. He had been standing far enough away that a normal human could not have heard the words she whispered to her parents. She knew though he had heard every word and wondered if he might try to stop her plan. Together they made their way back to the keep. As they entered the great hall, many people came to hug and offer their condolences to her. She was moved by the sincerity of the clan and truly felt like she belonged with the Camerons. She must fight for their survival.

Hannah had seen to it a large meal had been prepared, not only to comfort the clan in the wake of Evie's death, but also to welcome her back and usher in a new chapter in the clan's history. After enjoying the delicious food and company, she was exhausted. She excused herself to go rest, and Elin followed behind to help her prepare for bed.

****

Liam and Fergus stood as the women left, and Liam nodded at Fergus to follow him, leading the man into his private office. He wanted to be filled in on what had happened during his absence but also wanted to discuss Kenna's plan he had overheard at the graves. While he was not happy she was to be involved in the battle, he was impressed with her plan of attack, and he knew she gave them an advantage, knowing the inside of the McLindon castle.

He poured them both a large cup of ale before beginning. "Kenna spent some time speaking to her mother and father."

Fergus looked confused, causing him to laugh out loud.

"I ken, 'tis strange to be sure. She sat at the graves for a long while speaking to them of her plans to defeat the McLindon."

"Nay! The lass cannae go with us! Ye willnae let her, Liam!" Fergus chastised him for allowing Kenna to return to Silas' keep.

"Aye, I dinnae have another option." He hung his head. "If I dinnae allow her to go with us, she will go alone. I cannae have her facing him without our protection."

"Nay, ye cannae allow it. And yer right. She does seem the type of lass to go off on her own. Weel, if she must go, then aye, 'tis better she goes with us. We can protect her."

He was glad Fergus agreed with him on the matter. They both knew Kenna refused to take no for an answer, and she did not care about the risk to her life to get her revenge on Silas.

"To be fair, though," Liam continued, "her strategy was actually verra good. She kens the ins and outs of the castle. And having the wolves on our side…"

Fergus held his hand up to stop him. "I've been meaning to speak to ye about the wolves."

His face fell, and his eyes widened in disappointment. Seeing his expression, Fergus laughed and quickly reassured him it was quite the opposite.

"Nay, lad! Since ye've been away, we've had several more join our ranks."

"What are ye saying, Fergus?" He questioned the man, unbelieving more men had shifted.

"Since ye left with Kenna, there have been no less than seven new transformations. Four of them lads of about sixteen and three of 'em young lasses. Agnes and me, we've been trying to train them and get them ready to be of use to ye."

"And are they? Can they fight alongside us?" The hopefulness clear in his voice.

"Aye, they're ready," Fergus announced proudly.

Unable to contain his excitement, Liam laughed out loud, clapping Fergus on the back, and raising his cup to toast a successful battle.

The next morning, with a plan in place, Liam felt confident in an easy defeat of Silas McLindon. And if Silas wanted wolves, wolves he would get. He planned to utilize every single one of those in the clan carrying the wolf trait. He wanted to take no chances in something happening to Kenna or one of his clan members. With their strength and power, the bastard had no idea what was coming for him. The only thing he had specified to Fergus was he wished to be the one to kill Silas. He knew Kenna wanted to make the final blow, but he did not want her to carry the guilt on her conscience.

He had spent the night in his study planning with Fergus. He hoped Kenna had not missed him too much and went looking for her to break their fast together. Wandering through the kitchen, he saw Hannah bent over the fires preparing the morning meal.

"Hannah? Aren't ye a pleasant surprise this morning. Where is Nissa? Is she nay supposed to be within yer sight at all times?" he asked suspiciously as he took the poker from her, bringing the fire to life. Hannah *tsked* disapprovingly in response, confirming what he had thought.

"Och, the old hag! She disappeared the night Lady Evelyn's body arrived and has nay been back since!"

"Oh aye? Where do ye think she has gone?" He already knew the answer. He was certain the woman's guilt drove her away. He suspected she had gone to Judson, to warn him. Or for protection. Either way, no warning could prepare them for what he intended to do when he found them. Nissa's absence, however, reminded him he must speak to Kenna about the letter Hannah had shown him. Time had slipped from him, and as Kenna had dealt with her grief he had pushed the task aside. Now, he could wait no longer. Kenna must know all of the threats to her before they attacked McLindon.

****

Nissa had been camping in the woods for a couple of days and still had seen no sign of Judson. Perhaps he hadn't gotten her message. After making love to her, she knew he must still care for her. He would not just

216

leave her unprotected in the woods. Besides, she had to warn him. She knew Liam planned to avenge Evelyn's death, especially if Kenna bid him to do so. She gathered up her measly belongings. She had taken everything she owned when she left the Camerons knowing she was not going back.

She knew they had discovered the role she and Judson had played in the death of Laird Audric. Whispers of Liam's suspicions were circulating before she left, but he had no idea how close he was to the truth, she knew she had to leave. While she did not come up with the murderous plan, she had helped Judson poison the Laird, slipping it into his food over time. Judson had promised her she was to be lady of the keep when Audric was gone and he took over as Laird. Perhaps it was still possible, she thought. If she warned Judson, he could surely get the McLindon chief to help them overtake Liam.

She trudged through the snow, arriving at the gates looking more haggard than her normal appearance. The guards cringed at the sight of the old crone and laughed at her when she announced she was there to see Judson.

"O'course ye are!" they teased her, but still they let her in, showing her into the main hall.

Judson was seated at the long table, a large plate of food before him, and her mouth watered as she watched him eat. It had been quite some time since her last meal. Looking up, Judson's expression turned to anger when he saw her. Was he not happy she was there? Smiling sweetly at him, she was saddened when his anger turned to disgust. He quickly stood, grabbing her elbow painfully and ushering her out of the room into a dark hallway.

"Wha' are ye doin' here, ye daft woman!? I told ye it isna safe here fer ye!" he hissed, scolding her like a child, but she relaxed and smiled again.

His anger was not at her, she thought. He was truly concerned for her welfare. He did share her affections. She leaned forward to kiss him, but he pushed her away.

"Explain yerself, woman!"

Huffing, she backed away. Now it was her turn to get angry. She had risked everything for him, and here he was acting like he was put out by her.

"Weel, ye sorry arse! I came to warn ye!" Her voice rose, and he tried to quiet her but was unsuccessful.

"To warn me?" he questioned, his tone softer but not enough to warrant any affection.

"Aye! The Camerons were nay pleased when Lady Evelyn's body arrived. Lady Kenna took off into the woods, and the Laird followed her. I think he kens it was us!" Her eyes were wide with worry.

"What de ye mean, he kens it was us?" he repeated.

"They ken! The Laird and Lady Kenna ken it was us who poisoned Audric!"

She was in a panic and rightly so.

"If they ken, if they truly ken, they will be coming for us all." He ran his hands through his thin, greasy hair. He must warn Silas. It was time the McLindon stood by his word to protect him.

She was crying loudly, and he pulled her farther into the dark hallway.

"Nissa, ye must tell me. How do ye ken the Laird is certain it was us? What proof does he have?"

She tried to catch her breath. The exertion of the

past few days was catching up to her. Taking a deep breath, she explained that she had overheard rumors of Kenna and her mother finding a letter Audric had written. He had suspected he was being poisoned but had already lost his ability to speak.

"He named us! He called us by name in the letter!" She pleaded with him to realize the gravity of the situation.

"Get ahold of yerself, woman!" He shook her shoulders but quickly dropped his hands when a light shown on them in the hallway. Holding a torch, Sampson lit the sconces mounted to the walls and shed light on the pair huddled close together. Silas stood with Sampson, a smirk on his face.

"Weel, what do we have hiding here? A lover's meeting?" Silas teased them.

She fell to her knees facing Silas.

"Och, my Lord," Her head was bent, too scared to look up at him. "I've come ta warn ye!" she pleaded.

Silas, softening his tone, placed his hand on her shoulder.

"My dear woman, rise. Ye dinnae need to be frightened." She looked up at him and gave him a toothless grin, and he shuddered. Placing his arm around her plump shoulders, he nodded to Judson to follow and led them into the great hall.

The hall was full of clanspeople mingling about, and when Silas entered the room a hush came over the crowd. Dismissing them with a wave of his hand, he made his way over to his seat at the head of the table, steering her as he went. The room slowly got louder as conversations went back to normal, and she relaxed slightly. The food smelled delicious, and her stomach growled loudly.

"My dear," Silas insisted, motioning for food to be brought over. "Let's get ye fed. We dinnae want our guest to go hungry." She thanked him and sat in the chair he had pulled out beside him.

"Now, lass, please tell me what is this warning ye've come to deliver?" Silas watched Judson cringe out of the corner of his eye. Judson squirmed, and it seemed the man was about to come out of his skin. It was obvious he was uncomfortable around her, and it encouraged Silas to engage her even more.

"The Camerons, my lord. They are coming to avenge Lady Evelyn's death," she whispered, not wanting to voice out loud it was Silas who had killed Evelyn.

"They will be coming after me as weel. And Judson." She pointed to the man who was hiding behind Sampson.

"They ken it was us. They ken we poisoned Laird Audric. He'll kill me. He'll put an end ta me fer sure. Please, my lord, please dinnae let them get to us!" she begged, grabbing Silas' arm in desperation.

"My dear. I'm verra thankful ye were brave enough to come here and deliver yer warning. Dinnae fash though, love, I willnae let the Cameron Laird touch a hair on yer bonnie head."

She swooned on his every word, and as the servant set a plate before her she relaxed enough to begin eating. They watched as she finished her plate of food and chugged a goblet of wine. She was a sloppy eater, leaving bits of food scattered over her clothing and smeared across her chin.

"Did it meet yer liking?" Silas asked her after she

had cleared two plates of food. She nodded up at him, grinning with food still in her sparse teeth.

"Oh aye, my lord! It was delicious!"

"I'm glad, my dear. I ken ye are exhausted. I'll let Judson show ye to his chamber. I'm sure he is eager for a reunion." He gave her a wink, and she blushed a deep pink. Standing, he helped her to her feet and escorted her to a side door, followed by Judson, hanging his head.

Pausing at the doorway, Silas turned back to look at her.

"Before ye head off, I do have one question. Ye see, I'm worried now that yer Laird kens ye have warned us."

She shook her head soundly.

"Nay, my lord. He doesna ken where I am!" she promised.

Nodding, Silas continued. "Aye, understood. But still, ye see, I cannae risk ye changing yer mind and going back to the Camerons."

"Och, nay, my lord. I willnae ever change my mind." She looked back at Judson and smiled.

"Nay." Silas smiled at an eerie grin at Judson. "I dinnae think ye will. Goodnight, Nissa."

"Goodnight, my lord." She curtsied awkwardly as Silas placed a kiss on her chubby hand and steered her toward the stairwell. Before she climbed the first step, Silas reached around and slid a sharp dagger smoothly across her throat. Her blood splattered on the stairs in front of her, and her head fell back.

The whites of her eyes were visible as they rolled back in her head as she collapsed on the stairs. Judson stood motionless, staring at her body. The blood rushed from his face, and Nissa's blood seeped toward his shoes. Silas knelt beside her body. He wiped the dagger he had taken from Evelyn on her dirty clothes and held it up admiringly.

"Looks like yer sister was good fer something after all," Silas sneered, giving Judson a cruel smile. Judson's stomach churned, and he fought to hold down the vomit rising in his throat. Looking over his shoulder as he walked away, Silas paused.

"Yer welcome," he said coldly as he left Judson staring at her body crumpled on the stairs.

Chapter Twenty

Kenna packed a small leather satchel with clothes and a thick plaid for warmth. Everyone was doing the same as they prepared to leave for McLindon territory. Each wolf was packing a bag of clothing to be hidden in the woods for the return trip home in case injuries prevented them from being able to shift. Liam insisted they travel in wolf form so their senses would be on alert and they would not be ambushed.

The time she had been preparing for had come, and she was a mix of emotions. She had dreamed of one day making Silas pay for his years of abuse. Now, it was really going to happen. It felt surreal, and she would be glad when it was all behind her. A knock on her door brought her out of her thoughts.

"Kenna, love, are ye ready?" Liam stepped inside, closing the door behind him.

"Aye, I believe so." Her nerves were creeping up on her, and her palms were sweating. Seeing her wipe them on her dress nervously, he took them in his own, holding them tightly to reassure her.

"Good. Before we join the others, I have something I need ta tell ye." She didn't like the tone in his voice and knew he was going to tell her she would not be joining them. Jerking her hands away, she turned to grab her bag off the bed. Liam gripped her shoulders and spun her to look at him.

"I willnae stay behind!" she said forcefully with tears threatening to spill from her eyes.

"Nay, love." He tried to soothe her misunderstanding. "I willnae leave ye behind. I do need ta tell ye, before we leave for the McLindon land of something Hannah has found."

He pulled the letter from his waistcoat. She took it hesitantly and began reading it. As she read, she began to cry and fell back onto the bed as the sobs consumed her. He sat beside her, stroking her back, trying to comfort her.

"I dinnae understand," she sobbed. "Why would he kill my father? My father took care of everything for him! He never loved me or my ma." She turned into Liam's shoulders as he hugged her.

"Och, love, I fear his jealousy would never let him love anyone. He wanted yer father's title, land, and power. Jealousy is a verra vicious animal. I hope ye harden yer heart toward the man. Any sympathy ye may show him will only show as weakness. He has already used ye to his advantage long enough."

She gazed up at him, her eyes still filled with tears.

"I'm only sorry my mother didnae ken his true intentions before she died. She wouldnae have let him influence her so."

"Yer uncle has committed treason against his Laird, conspired murder, and offered his niece to the McLindon only to advance his position. Dinnae fash, love, I will make sure he kens what his position truly is."

Standing, she handed the letter back to Liam. "I dinnae want to see this again. I am ready to go face

Silas. And my uncle. I willnae stand for their cruelty and deception any longer."

He tucked the letter back into his coat and took her hand, leading her downstairs to join the others. The large group of about forty men and women had gathered in the courtyard. She was shocked to see the women, although she shouldn't have been, she thought. She, herself, was a female with the wolf gene. Why wouldn't others possess it as well. And Liam had mentioned that he intended to use every mature wolf to their full potential. He wanted Silas to feel the full impact of Cameron strength.

Kissing her gently on top of the head, Liam handed her over to Agnes and went to stand the center of the circle, ready to lead. She watched him, full of pride. He looked strong, like a true Laird, and she was happy to let him lead as Alpha. He would be much wiser in battle and had formed an unbreakable bond with his clan.

The scent of the wolf was so strong in the circle she was unable to tell who would be shifting and who wouldn't. It didn't take her long to figure it out, however, as those shifting carried their pack of clothes, like her, and nothing else. They would need no other weapons besides their teeth.

Niall stood near Liam, his sword in its sheath at his waist. He had matured in the time she had been at the Cameron keep, and he was ready to fight. She could tell Liam was no longer worried about the boy but had faith in the man he had become. Niall had accepted he did not carry the wolf gene and had focused on becoming a strong warrior. His best friend, Ian, stood beside him, holding his pack, ready to fight as a wolf.

Agnes leaned closer as she watched the friends and

whispered quietly, "Ye wouldnae ken now, but wee Niall was awful jealous when he first learned Ian had experienced the shift."

She was not surprised, seeing how much the boy looked up to Liam.

"I wouldnae imagine anyone would long fer this, although it does make ye feel powerful. I reckon I can see a man wanting to feel more powerful."

"Aye," Agnes continued. "It took a while fer the jealousy to pass. Fergus helped the lad see Ian didnae choose it but was born with it."

"Weel, it appears as though the two have learned to use their strengths together and will be a force to be reckoned with."

She felt pride in the boys as well and continued to study the group imagining what each person would bring to the fight. Some would offer patience and wisdom while others had brute strength. As she looked around her, she was overcome with emotion. She had grown to love these people, and try as she might she could not push aside her fear of something happening to any of them.

Hannah came to stand beside her and Agnes, followed by Elin, who was carrying her babe. Hannah offered them each a small hunk of bread from a basket she passed around. Accepting it, Kenna didn't have much appetite but pretended to nibble on it to appease the sweet woman. She, too, was worried about the clan, and Kenna could see it in the etched lines on the woman's face.

"Hannah, dinnae fash. Liam is a strong warrior and a good leader. We are ready." She urged the woman to believe as she did and hoped her words were enough to soothe both of their fears.

Liam sat on horseback for everyone to see him and raised his hand in the air to silence the crowd. Not only were the warriors gathered to hear him, but their families and other clansmen circled round to offer their support.

"Ye all ken what atrocities the bastard, Silas McLindon, has done," he started, and the group began to murmur. "He has nay only killed and tortured our loved ones. He has changed the course of our clan's history. It wasnae his right, and he must pay for his actions!"

Liam received a loud cheer from the crowd and held his hand up again to continue. Speaking her thoughts aloud, Liam made it known each warrior offered their own special talent and they would all be needed in this battle. The circle which had formed around him began patting each other on the back and agreeing with him, expressing what they thought each other's strengths would be.

Kenna listened intently, admiring her husband as he addressed the crowd while still making each person feel as though he was speaking directly to them. Even her. He truly was their Laird and Alpha. As he laid out the plan for attack, he welcomed anyone who had other ideas or opinions to voice it, but none did. They were all in agreement he and Fergus had developed a strategy bound to work.

They would travel to the border of the McLindon and Cameron territories, leaving unnecessary gear and their travel packs hidden in the Cameron woods. From there, the wolves would shift, and everyone would stay hidden in the forests lining the McLindon land, staying clear of the large, open spaces where there was no protection. Kenna would be able to offer her knowledge of the keep from there, and they would plan the attack.

The call was given for the men and women to mount the horses, and the gates were opened. There were many hugs, kisses, and tears as loved ones said goodbye, and the group moved out. Kenna turned to tell Hannah goodbye and was shocked when Elin kissed her babe and handed him to the older woman.

"Elin! What are ye doin'? Ye cannae go! Ye cannae fight! Ye have a bairn to care fer! Besides, what battle skills do ye offer?" She did not believe the woman would leave her babe to come fight beside her, but she would never have the strength to swing a sword. Truthfully, Elin would just be in the way, and she would be worried about losing her friend. Swinging a leather pack across her shoulders, Elin smiled at Kenna.

"Aye, I ken I dinnae look like much," embarrassed, she looked down at her petite frame, "but I am strong and fast. I willnae let ye down."

Her eyes were wide with the shock over Elin's admission. Liam had ridden over to bid Hannah goodbye and leaning down gripped Elin's hand.

"We are glad ta have ye, lass. I ken ye will be of much help to our cause."

Kenna looked at Liam like he had lost his mind. How could he let the young woman join them? She would be easily killed.

Giving Elin a little push, he encouraged her to walk ahead of him and Kenna, and she caught up to Ian and Niall, both of them fumbling over her.

"She cannae go!" Kenna pleaded as soon as Elin was out of earshot. "She'll get killed! And what of her bairn?" She had gotten worked up and was all but yelling at him.

"Shh. Ye dinnae want her to hear yer fears! I promise ye, love, Elin is goin' ta be just fine. She has been working with Agnes. And Ian." He nodded toward the pair walking closely together. "And several others to be certain. Ye will be surprised just how many new wolves we have."

He smiled at her as she realized what he was saying. Elin had shifted. She too possessed the trait. Breathing a sigh of relief, she laughed as she hugged Liam as he continued. "I'd say our numbers are about half and half now. I tell ye, Kenna, the monster willnae survive another night."

They walked together through the thick snow leading into the forest. She was quiet in her thoughts. Finally, after several long moments, he voiced his concern.

"Kenna, dear, do ye want ta turn back? Ye dinnae have ta join us." She looked at him incredulously. She would never send them into danger without being right beside them.

"Nay!" Sighing, she shook her head. "I cannae figure it out. When Elin was giving birth, I smelled the wolf, but it was definitely the bairn. Nay her. Collin carried the wolf and Elin ken. Did she nay suspect herself ta be as weel?"

Liam laughed at her questions.

"Nay, Kenna. She didnae ken. She is the first in her family to shift. It was a shock to her, and Hannah too, when it happened!"

She could only imagine. She knew how scared and unsure she had been when she first felt the tingle down her spine and saw the fur start to spread on her torso.

"Aye, I can imagine it was!" She laughed at the memory now. Liam squeezed his arm around her in a hug and grabbing her hand led her the rest of the way through the forest.

****

As they neared the edge of the Cameron territory, Liam moved to the front of the group. Gathering within the edge of the dark forest, he again held his hand to speak to the group. The distance to the McLindon keep was not far, but they were to be traveling through the woods, and the night had begun to set in. He planned to attack at night as the wolves were able to see well but the McLindons had a disadvantage.

He gave instructions as to where to leave their belongings—in a small cave near where they were gathered, their things protected and hidden, in the event any McLindons broke through and tried to attack the Cameron keep.

After everything was in place, all of the wolves, with the exception of him and Fergus, went into the woods to shift. Those not shifting stood in a tight circle while waiting on the wolves to return. Gasps of shock and awe erupted from the group as the large wolves emerged from the forest.

It was a sight to see, intimidating and encouraging, as they were fighting on the same side. There were close to twenty wolves, nearly half of their number. They looked large and strong, and Silas would never expect so many of them!

He looked around at the different wolves. Kenna stood out immediately. Her auburn fur shone in the reflection of the snow. Beside her, Elin's wolf, a smaller brownish-blonde animal, stood. Ian's form was a few feet behind Elin, not letting the young woman far from his sight. The wolves circled the humans, and all were waiting on his instructions.

Dividing the group, they planned to attack from each side of the keep, Fergus again leading one group and Liam leading the other. Elin and Ian would go with Fergus, while she and Niall would join Liam.

The woods branched around a large open span of land. It was hard now for her to imagine crossing that expanse while wounded. While it was the shortest route to the McLindon keep, they were not in a rush and used the cover of the woods as long as they could.

Liam's plan was for each group to travel the woods, arriving at the McLindon keep, he and Fergus staying in human form until it was absolutely necessary to shift. She would help communicate with the wolves in Liam's group, and Ian the same for Fergus. Liam's only instructions were to protect each other, try not to hurt those innocent, and if they found Silas, to deliver him to Liam. The wolves were pawing at the ground to go. It was time.

Chapter Twenty-One

Kenna walked silently beside Liam through the dense forest. The landscape had changed as they crossed into McLindon territory. It was no longer the rocky terrain that led up the mountainside to the Cameron keep but instead was flat, and the ground was soft. This made traveling easier as the snow had not penetrated the thick trees, and they reached the woods near the McLindon castle in record time.

Her nose was to the ground, as were the rest of the wolves. The scents were so different than those from the Cameron woods. She smelled blood and death. Some scents had all but disappeared with time, others were as fresh as if it had just happened. She wondered how many bodies had been carried through these woods.

Before they had left the Cameron keep, she had drawn Liam and Fergus a map of the inside of the keep. Their plan was for Fergus and his group of men and wolves to stay on the first level. Liam and their group expected to use an entrance leading into the bowels of the castle. Liam and Fergus bid each other well, and the groups split. As each group made their way to the intended area, they heard loud voices and raucous laughter. It seemed unbridled revelry was a nightly occurrence at the McLindon keep. They all hoped the men were too intoxicated to notice they were slipping in to kill the Laird. Each one knew, though, after their last visit, not to trust Silas' seemingly drunken clan.

Kenna led Liam and the others around the keep, hidden in the dark tree line to a gate which had long been forgotten. It had vines growing through it and was partially unhinged. No guard stood near it, and Liam crept forward quietly to check it. It was a rounded gate, and cutting the vines with his sword he lifted it easily off the rusted hinges. Behind the gate, a stone stairwell led down into a dark cavern underneath the castle. They moved quietly down the stairs. At the bottom, a shallow underground lake met the stairs. The water was undisturbed and lay still along the last couple of steps. The group made their way silently through the water and onto the wide bank across the cavern.

Taking in the landscape, Liam spotted several tunnels surrounding the lake, and a set of wide, rough, stone stairs had been carved into the cavern wall to allow access to the keep. At the top of the stairs, a table sat with one lone guard asleep in a chair. Surprised to see him, Liam expected he didn't see much action in the bowels of the castle.

Waving the others to stay low, hidden by the large stone staircase, he made his way up the stairs. His leather boots not making a sound, he was able to come from behind the guard without waking the man. A quick blow to the back of his head was all it took, and he slumped from his chair onto the cold stone floor. He removed the torch mounted in the wall behind the table and motioned for the rest of the group to follow him up the stairs.

Carved into the stone wall at the top of the stairs a

rounded entrance led the way into a dimly lit, damp hall. Torches were placed along the wall, spaced out in intervals to allow just enough light. Water dripped down the sides of the wall, keeping the area damp and cold. Moss and algae had grown along the floor, causing it to be slippery and treacherous. The tunnel was narrow and cramped and took several sharp turns.

He wasn't sure they were not just going in a circle, but the muscles in his legs told him they were moving upward. Kenna seemed confident of where she was going, and he had let her take lead and they moved slow and cautiously. She led them with her ears perked and her nose exploring the scents around them. He was glad her senses seemed heightened, knowing Silas would surely be expecting them.

They came to the end, and the tunnel opened into a large circular space. Several hallways branched off, lit by more torches. There was still a damp feeling in the air, and he suspected they were still underground but in an area more often used by those who occupied the keep.

Kenna nodded toward two of the hallways. He decided to split up, but before he could give his orders, they heard shouting and stammering coming from one of the hallways. Quickly ducking back into the tunnel, they watched from the darkness to see who was coming.

The shadows of two men were cast on the wall by the light from the torches. They were heading toward the center space, one much larger than the other. The large shadow was dragging the other man by his coat, all but lifting him off the ground. When they reached the tunnels core, the large man tossed the older man roughly onto his behind. He hit the stone with a hard thud and groaned in pain.

Liam recognized the man right away. It was Kenna's uncle, Judson. A low, quiet growl came from her throat. She recognized him as well, and Liam placed his hand on her back to calm her. He wanted to see the encounter play out. What had Judson done to upset the giant?

"Ye cowardly bastard! Ye think ye willnae face the Camerons fer all the pain ye have caused them?" The large man was red-faced in anger and spitting at Judson.

"Ye willnae run this time, ye slimy arse." He kicked Judson in the rear as the man tried to stand, sending him back down face first on the stone. When he rolled over, blood oozed from his nose.

"Weel, they've come fer ye. Hopefully ta make ye pay fer what ye did to Evie. And yer niece as weel. If I let them have ye and dinnae kill ye first." The man towered over Judson frighteningly.

So, Liam thought, they had seen the other group. All must be well with them if the man thought Judson in danger.

"What do ye care about Evie and Kenna? They are nay matter to ye!" Judson spat. The man roared and hit Judson square in the jaw with his massive fist. Judson lay on the ground, unmoving while the giant stood over him, bending close to his unconscious face.

"I loved her," the man hissed. A small gasp escaped from Kenna, and the man spun toward the hall. There was no hiding any longer, it was time to make their presence known.

Pulling his sword from its sheath at his side, Liam entered the circle slowly, followed by Kenna and the rest of the mixture of men and wolves. The man's eyes narrowed, and he stood even taller, facing them, his hand on the sword at his waist.

"I am William, Chief of the Camerons," Liam announced proudly. "We have come to avenge the death of Lady Evelyn Cameron."

Kenna moved forward, and the man eyed her auburn fur and green eyes. Recognition flashed in his eyes.

"Lady Kenna?" he asked uncertainly, and she bowed her head in acknowledgement. His shoulders relaxed slightly, and he removed his hand from his sword and held them, palms up, for Liam to see.

"I willnae stand in yer way," he told Liam. "I am truly sorry fer the actions of my master." He looked at Kenna, speaking directly to her. "I cared very deeply for yer mother. Please ken I feel her loss as weel, and I will help ye as I can."

Kenna approached him cautiously, and he seemed taken aback by such a large wolf being so near. She lowered her head, placing it under his hand. His hand was rough and calloused against her soft fur, and he petted her gently.

"Is he dead?" Liam interrupted the reunion.

"Nay." The disappointment was evident in the man's voice.

"But he willnae be moving anytime soon." Liam stepped over Judson's limp body and stuck out his arm. The two men gripped each other's forearms tightly in friendship.

"Ye must be Sampson? Lady Evelyn and Lady Kenna have spoken highly of ye. I am honored to meet ye and thank ye. Thank ye fer being the one kind soul

Kenna had here. We appreciate any assistance ye can offer." He was sincere in his thanks to Sampson. He imagined in another life they would have easily been friends. "Ye have seen the others?" he inquired, referring to Fergus and his crew.

"Aye, they are doing weel. The men in the keep didna offer much of a fight fer yer men. But Silas has called fer others from the village. They will be more difficult to fight as I trained them myself." Sampson still seemed to be hesitant of the wolves. The mixture of men and large wolves crammed in the circle were an intimidating sight.

"Where is yer chief? Where is Silas McLindon?" He didn't want to waste any time. He was ready to face the man and deal him the final blow. Kenna gave another low, menacing growl. She wanted to be the one to kill him. And she wanted him to know it was her.

"Follow me." Sampson grabbed the torch on the wall and led them through one of the dark halls on the other side of the circular space. Gingerly, they all stepped over Judson's form. Niall was the last one to cross over him, and looking back at the man gave him one last kick in his ribs, and the man rolled, groaning onto his back.

Creeping quietly through the hall, they knew they were nearing the main part of the keep as the noise grew louder. The sound of clanging metal joined with snapping and growling of the wolves reached their ears. Rushing toward the sound, they found the chaos had erupted in the great hall and spilled into the yard.

In the courtyard, it was dark and smoky. Fires had been lit for light and warmth and had now spread around the yard. Bales of rotten hay burned in wagons sitting on broken wheels and axles. They burned bright and hot and filled the courtyard in a smoky haze and sickening smell. Through the smoke, Liam made out the forms of several wolves as they fought off attackers. It seemed they were holding their own, and those in his own group were eager to join them. Giving them the go ahead, he grabbed Niall's arm as he hurried past him with the rest of the group.

"Niall." Liam's heart broke to watch the lad run into the fighting.

"T'will be alright! I promise," Niall reassured him and he grabbed the back of the boy's neck, bringing his forehead to his own.

"I ken ye will." Pushing him away, he didn't blame the boy for the smile on his face as he ran into the battle, his sword raised high. He knew the exhilaration of battle and prayed the boy fared well. He turned to Sampson.

"We need to find the McLindon."

Sampson gave a quick nod and led them along the inside wall of the courtyard. A thatch overhang lined the wall and provided cover for the trio as they moved through the darkness. Watching for sparks threatening to catch the grass, he moved the group quickly through the dark. He led them not into the great hall, but into a narrow corridor which ran the length of the hall and wrapped around to the back of the large room. The hall continued down the other side, forming a box around the great hall. Silas' study sat on the back wall, behind the great hall in the center corridor. When they reached the study, the door was open, and the room was empty.

Shaking his head, Sampson looked at Liam. "I was certain he'd be here. I dinnae ken where he may be hiding now."

Kenna, however, seemed to pick up Silas' scent, and taking the lead she moved cautiously down the hallway. The torches lining the walls had been doused, and those in human form fumbled in the dark. Liam knew Kenna's vision was perfect however, and as they turned the corner, he saw her stop short. At the end of the hall, there he stood, waiting on them. A low whimper escaped her, and her hair stood on end before she regained her composure, and Silas didn't miss it.

"Ah Kenna, dear. It's so good to have ye back home. And ye do make a fine wolf." The sneer in his tone made Liam growl low under his breath. Kenna glanced at him as she heard his reaction to Silas' words.

Dismissing her, Silas turned his attention to Sampson, giving him a wicked grin. "Thank ye, Sampson, fer bringing Kenna back to me. I'll be sure to treat her with the same respect I gave her mother."

Sampson's face gave away his feelings, and Silas's grin widened.

"Aye, I ken ye had feelings for Evelyn. Ye didnae hide them well, and neither did the daft woman. I did ye a favor by getting rid of her."

"Ye belong in hell!" Sampson's voice was low, and his words came through gritted teeth. He slowly pulled his sword from his sheath at his side and raised it over his head. Silas' eyes narrowed at Sampson.

"Aye, tis probably true." Silas' eyes darted behind Sampson, and he smiled slyly at the man. "But ye will be going first."

Sampson suddenly let out a loud roar of pain and collapsed onto the floor. A large pool of blood quickly surrounded his body, and standing behind him Judson leaned against the wall, gripping the bloody dagger he had plunged into the man's side.

Liam reacted instinctively and in seconds had taken on his own wolf form. Judson's eyes grew large as he watched the transformation. Before the man could raise the dagger again, Liam had pounced on him, his large mouth covering Judson's face and sinking his teeth into the man's skull.

As he attacked the man, Silas fled the corridor. Racing after Silas, Kenna caught up to him easily, cornering him. His back was pressed against the cold, stone wall, and he glared at her. Liam followed behind her leaving the others to finish off Judson, and when he found her she was a fearsome sight. Her lips were pulled back into a snarl, revealing her impressive canines. Sharp, long, and dripping with saliva, she crouched low, stalking toward Silas. He stayed back, realizing she needed to be the one to end him.

"Ye'll never do it!" he hissed at her. "Ye dinnae have it in ye. Ye dinnae ken what it is like to kill." He spoke in a low, slow tone. His words seemed to affect her, and she hesitated. Taking advantage of her pause, Silas grabbed a candle sconce from the wall and threw the hot wax into her face. She jumped back, yelping in pain, wax covering her eyes. Taking advantage of her weakness, Silas was gone again down the hallway. She shook the wax off and went after him again, Liam on her tail. He knew she would not hesitate again.

Without a torch, the hallway was pitch black, but they didn't need light. She sprinted down the hallway, again, catching Silas quickly. He turned to face her, and she leapt at him, her large form bringing him down easily.

She was snarling over him, and as Liam watched he could see the fear etched on the man's face. Silas knew this was the end. She licked her lips, a terrifying grin on her wolf face and her hot saliva dripping onto Silas' cheek. As she lunged for his throat, a light shone on her face, stopping her short.

Niall stood at the end of the hall, holding a torch, his eyes wide with terror as he stared at her. Before she could act, Silas regained his strength and forcefully threw her off his body and into the wall. Her head hit the wall, a loud crack resounding through the hallway. The impact had caused her body to shift into human form, and she lay naked, crumpled on the floor. Silas jumped up and ran toward Niall, pushing him into the wall as he sprinted past.

Liam easily ran down Silas. The man had no time to scream before his throat was torn from his body. Liam was in a rage and continued to tear Silas' flesh from his bones.

"STOP! STOP!"

Liam looked up to see Niall screaming at him. "He's dead." The boy looked at Liam calmly although tears filled his eyes.

"Ye can stop. The bastard is dead."

Liam read the exhaustion in the boy's face and knew that the sight of him tearing the man apart was not helping. Calming himself, he stepped away from the body. Lowering his head, he wanted to let Niall know he was in no danger. His emotions were too high to shift back into his human form, but Niall seemed to understand. Turning back, Liam ran to check on Kenna with Niall right on his heels, tearing apart his clothing to help cover her body and bind her wounds.

Chapter Twenty-Two

Kenna lay on the floor, unconscious but breathing evenly. Her head had a large knot on the back where it had hit the wall. Trying to wake her, Liam licked at her face, and her eyes fluttered. Groaning, she gripped the back of her head and tried to sit up.

Niall had ripped his plaid, using it to wrap her naked body and also forming a pillow behind her head. Silas was dead, and Liam left Niall to care for Kenna while he went to check on the other group. As he walked away, he noticed Niall's calm demeanor and thought what a good healer he might be. He must make a point to have Hannah teach him the art. At least then he may be involved in battle without actually fighting, and he needn't be so worried about the young man's welfare.

Making his way back through the corridors surrounding the great hall, he came upon Sampson and Judson's bodies. He paused, looking at Sampson's large form. Lowering his head to honor the man, it was a shame, he thought. The man was a good and loyal warrior.

As his head was bowed, he heard a loud, painful moan. Jerking his head up, his senses were on high alert. There was no way Judson could have made the noise. He had made sure of it. The man was truly dead and no longer a threat. The noise had to have come from Sampson, and nosing the body he was very happy when another moan escaped him. The man was still alive! Running toward the main hall, he needed to find help and fast.

When he reached the hall, his men were still engaged in battle with the McLindons, although it seemed they had things well under control. The fires had died down, but the smoke still covered the area. It stung his eyes as he looked for Agnes' wolf form in the haze. Spotting her not far from Fergus, who had not yet shifted, he swiftly made his way over to her, helping take down a few McLindon men as he went.

Fergus nodded at him but took a second glance, looking around him. A swift blow with the butt of his broadsword to the temple of his opponent quickly ended Fergus' fight, and he turned to question him.

"Kenna is nay wit' ye?" he growled out worriedly. Shaking his head, he pulled at Agnes' ear with his teeth. She followed him back through the halls with Fergus right on their tails. Seeing Judson's mutilated body, Fergus looked at him appreciatively.

"Ye've been busy!" he joked.

Liam went over to Sampson's body and nudged him, causing the man to moan out loud again, and a gasp escaped Fergus.

"Nay! He cannae be alive?!" Fergus stared at the body and the large pool of blood surrounding him.

Nosing Agnes again, Liam hoped she would be able to shift. Realizing what he needed, Fergus removed his own plaid, placing it in the shadows, and Agnes slipped away to shift back into her human form. A few moments later, she reemerged, wrapped in a toga of Fergus' tartan. Her hair hung down to the middle of her back in long salt and pepper waves, making her look younger and carefree. Agnes quickly had Fergus roll Sampson's large frame, allowing her better access to the deep wound in his side.

It was a jagged, ugly opening, not done by someone with a steady hand. Judson's cowardly hand had shaken, and while the wound bled and was painful the man had not dealt Sampson a mortal wound.

"Aye, he'll live. 'Twill be an unsightly scar, but it doesna appear to have gone too deep." Agnes' calm voice helped soothe his fear. Wrapping the wound with a strip of cloth, they left Sampson in the hall, and he led them to Kenna.

Niall had not left her side and was squatting beside her. She had come to and was more than happy to see them. Coming to sit on her other side, Liam licked her cheek, and she leaned against him, groaning with the effort.

"Och, lass, ye have had it rough again, aye?" Agnes eyed her sympathetically. Kenna's movements were slow as she placed her hand on the back of her head, indicating where the pain was. Feeling the large goose egg on the back of her head, Agnes sighed unhappily.

"Weel, I'm glad ta see it swelling. Means 'tis not bleeding on the inside," she said toward Liam to ease his fears.

"Niall." She turned her attention to the young man. "I'd like ye to run outside and get me a large ball of icy snow." The confusion showed on his face.

"Agnes, I dinnae think this is the time for games."

"Nay fer a snowball fight, ye daft boy!" She lightheartedly pushed him over. It was good to see him joking and lightening the mood now that he knew they were all ok.

"Pack it hard with as much icy snow as ye can find."

Turning to Kenna, Agnes pushed aside the hair falling over Kenna's eyes.

"'Twill help the swelling and the ache in yer head." Niall returned moments later with a large ball of snow wrapped in a thin piece of fabric. Agnes placed it gingerly against Kenna's head.

Liam knew it was time for him to shift back into his human form. He needed to address the McLindon clan and take control now that their Laird was dead. They would also need to see to the injured and dead. He licked Kenna lovingly on the cheek and she reached up, stroking his bloodstained muzzle. Her eyes remained closed but the smile on her face told him she would be ok.

He ducked into the shadows of the hallway, making his way back to where they had left Silas' body. He would need clothing when he shifted, and the man had seemed about the same size. When he arrived at the body, he was glad to see he had left the man's legs intact. It pained him to think Niall had witnessed that side of him, but looking around at the dismembered arms and mangled throat and torso he did not regret what he had done.

He felt the tingle move down his spine as his body shifted back into his human form. His shifts happened quickly, and within a few seconds the fur previously covering his body was gone and in its place was smooth skin, muscles visible as he moved. He quickly removed the boots and britches Silas had been wearing and used them to cover his own nakedness. A shirt he could do without. As a last thought, he grabbed the sword that lay beside the man and left the body naked and disfigured in the hall.

The fighting in the courtyard had slowed. Not many men were left standing, and some of the wolves were standing around in the smoky air looking for something to do. Their hair still stood on end, not wanting to let their guards down. Silas' men, having seen no sign of their Laird, had all but given up.

Looking around, he spotted a doorway to one of the turrets and ran up the stairs and onto the top of the outer wall of the courtyard. He stood tall above the courtyard and summoned his most commanding voice.

"I am William, Chief of the Camerons." His voice boomed over the noise.

"By my hand, Silas McLindon is dead. Ye will now answer to me. Lay down yer weapons."

The McLindon men did as he commanded and to his surprise looked happy to do so. The Cameron men walked around making sure they all disarmed, and after they had done so gathered all the weapons into the center of the courtyard. The McLindons looked up toward Liam for more instructions.

"Gather yer injured into the great hall. We will tend to their wounds. Yer dead, we will bury." He made his way down the turret stairs and as he entered the courtyard was greeted with handshakes and cheers from not only his own men but the McLindon's as well. They were as glad as he was to be rid of the monster.

The great hall was filled with men tending injuries, some of them his own. As he walked around, meeting and talking with the men, he knew they fought not out of loyalty to Silas but out of fear. Their healer had been summoned to the hall and had brought several of the village women with her. They were making their way around, stitching, bandaging, and offering food and drink to those who needed it.

Fergus and Niall had helped move Sampson and Kenna back into the main hall as well, and one of the maids had found suitable clothing for Kenna and Agnes.

Agnes had taken it upon herself to stitch Sampson's wound and had given strict instructions for the man to be kept as still as possible until it closed.

He looked around at the McLindon people. He knew they needed a leader and exactly who he wanted their leader to be.

As dawn broke, the smoky haze of the fires had burned off and the full destruction of the night before was evident. The day was filled with working to restore order to the keep. Those men who were able helped to bury the dead. Fresh bales of hay were brought into the great hall, transforming it into a makeshift hospital. Many of the Camerons had returned home carrying word of their victory. He and the others planned to return in a few days when he was certain the McLindons were no longer a danger to his clan.

Days passed, and injuries healed as fewer and fewer people remained in the great hall. Liam had insisted Kenna take it easy, but she was moving about the keep helping as much as she had the energy to. She was getting to know the McLindon people. He knew she felt a kinship to them as they had all suffered Silas' evil ways.

Sampson had been moved to his chamber, and

Agnes was overseeing his care. His wound was healing very well, and Agnes had finally allowed the man to start moving carefully about the castle. Things at the McLindon keep seemed to be in order.

He was no longer reluctant to leave but instead was eager to get home to his own clan and begin his life with his new bride. Summoning Sampson to Silas' study, he had been reviewing Silas' accounting. It appeared the man did not spend any wealth on his own clan, and he had an arrangement he wanted to present to Sampson.

Sampson's large frame filled the doorway as he entered the small study. Looking up, he was pleased to see him healing so well.

"Ye look weel, Sampson! Tis good to see ye moving about."

"Aye, 'tis good to be moving. I wasnae so sure I'd have the chance again." He laughed softly, holding his wound to guard the stitches.

Motioning for Sampson to sit, he poured them both a cup of ale. This time, Sampson had no hesitations in drinking what was offered. The two had developed a sense of trust between them and had become good friends in the short time since Silas' death. They sat together for a while, discussing the clan business—past, present, and future and after some time came to an arrangement.

While the McLindons now fell under the control of the Cameron clan, Sampson was named the new clan Chief. He would care for the day-to-day business of the McLindon clan, paying a respective rent to the Camerons. They, in return, offered the McLindons protection and help in times of trouble. Only if needed,

Liam was there to step in to take control of the McLindon territory.

The people of the McLindon keep were pleased with this contract. They easily pledged their loyalty to not only Sampson but also to Liam and the Camerons as well. No longer did they fear the wolves in the woods but instead respected them and felt protected by their presence.

The journey back to the Cameron keep was a peaceful and joyous one. They had taken the horses Sampson had offered, along with sacks full of food. Fergus and Agnes rode ahead of Kenna and Liam. Reaching the Cameron line, Liam breathed a sigh of relief.

"'Tis nothing like being in yer own woods."

Kenna smiled at him and reached her hand out to take his.

"Aye, tis nice to be home."

He was glad to hear her refer to the Camerons as her home. It always had been. He wished her mother were there to experience it with her, but she was starting to put her grief behind her. Now when she spoke of Evie instead of tears a smile came to her face first, and he knew she had reached a place of healing.

They reached the keep not long after Fergus and Agnes and could hear Hannah's excitement before they entered the gate. As they approached, Liam and Kenna both dismounted and led the horses in on foot. He knew too well Hannah was waiting to pull them down, squeezing them in one of her tight hugs, and he was not disappointed when she finally saw them. She showered them both with kisses and hugs as she ushered them into the hall.

As they entered the room, shouts of cheers erupted, and large amounts of food were being brought into the hall. He watched Kenna look around the room at everyone who had fought for her and her mother. She smiled up at him, contentment brightening her face.

Fergus was laughing heartily with a group of men, and Agnes was doting over Elin and Ian. Ian held Elin's babe gently in his arms, and it was evident he had already claimed the baby as his own. Everyone enjoyed the evening, spending time with friends and family and knowing there was no longer a threat looming over them.

Eager to be alone with his bride, Liam stood, pulling her along with him. He excused them from the hall, feigning exhaustion. As they left, Hannah smiled, giving them a knowing wink.

****

Kenna stood in front of the fire, combing her wet curls. The fire warmed the deer skin rug she stood on, and she wiggled her toes in the warm fur. Her long gown clung to her body, still wet from her bath. The snow had turned to rain in the past month, and spring was in the air. This meant new growth, new life, she thought as she protectively rubbed her belly.

She had not yet told Liam she was expecting but wondered if he somehow knew. He was becoming more protective of her, especially during their shifted runs through the woods. She was still learning about her gift, and Liam was having fun teaching her everything he knew. She knew she had to tell him soon though as her body was already starting to give away her secret.

They had been married only a few short months, but it seemed she had lived a lifetime in the span. There had been many changes within the keep. Niall had taken on learning the healing arts with Hannah. When Liam had approached him about learning her ways, Niall had been discouraged, thinking it only a woman's work. It wasn't until Liam mentioned he had need of those skills during skirmishes and battles Niall had agreed and had been eager to learn ever since.

Elin had married Ian and was expecting another babe as well. Ian had taken her son as his own and was a wonderful father. She was glad the two had found each other, but she did not want to lose Elin, especially since she was expecting also. She had mentioned her concerns to Liam, and he quickly moved the small family into the castle giving them a spacious chamber near their own and assigned Ian a job training some of the men.

A new cook had been hired by Hannah, who was more than happy to replace Nissa. Hazel, an older woman whose husband had passed, was a wonderful cook with a sweet disposition. Kenna loved that Liam and Hannah truly looked out for those in the clan. Knowing the woman unable to care for any household repairs or upkeep, they had quickly moved her into the keep as well.

Lost in her thoughts, she pondered all of the changes taking place in her life and was startled by a knock on the door. Liam entered the room, his eyes sweeping over her.

The gown clung to her curves, and the subtle changes in her body were becoming more noticeable. Her breasts had grown, and her hips had rounded. Moving across the room, he wrapped his arms around her waist and pulled her in for a kiss, which she gladly returned. She welcomed the feeling of his arms around her. When he finally set her free, she smiled lovingly up at him, wrapping her arms around his neck.

He lifted her easily, wrapping her legs around his waist and carried her over, placing her gently on the bed. Hovering over her, he kissed softly down her torso. Pulling her gown up around her waist, he gently rubbed her stomach and placed a sweet, gentle kiss on her navel, looking up at her smiling.

"Ye ken?" she asked, unbelieving he had discovered her secret.

"Aye," he answered, placing more kisses on her stomach.

"And ye are pleased?" she asked again.

"Aye." He looked up. "Kenna, ye have made me the happiest man alive. This bairn will ken more love than any child has before." Her eyes filled with tears at his words.

"Are ye all right love?" he didn't understand her tears as she nodded. Moving up her body, he wiped her tears with his thumb.

"Ye're certain?" She nodded again, and he placed a kiss on her lips.

"Good," he whispered, "because I would like to make love to my wife." She laughed, pulling him down to her, happy to be in his arms where she was meant to be.

A word about the author...

Kate James is a paranormal romance author. She is married and the mother of two. In her free time, she enjoys spending time with her family and their beagles. Kate loves spending time outdoors, especially hiking and camping or spending time near the beach. Kate has always had a passion for history and has enjoyed discovering her own Highland ancestors.

Thank you for purchasing
this publication of The Wild Rose Press, Inc.

For questions or more information
contact us at
info@thewildrosepress.com.

The Wild Rose Press, Inc.
www.thewildrosepress.com

www.ingramcontent.com/pod-product-compliance
Lightning Source LLC
Chambersburg PA
CBHW060540260626
47161CB00003B/979